Praise for the spectacular Playful Brides series by
VALERIE BOWMAN

THE LEGENDARY LORD

"A sweet and fulfilling romance."—*Publishers Weekly*

"Graceful writing enlivened with plenty of dry wit, a charming cast of secondary characters, and a breathtakingly sexy romance between a perfectly matched couple make Bowman's latest addition to her Regency-set Playful Brides series another winner." —*Booklist*

"The words funny, smart, sensual, and joyous come to mind when readers pick up Bowman's romance."
—*RT Book Reviews*

THE UNTAMED EARL

"Bowman delights with a humorous tale that could come straight out of a Shakespearean play. The charming characters are well developed, their cock-eyed motivations are clear, and the plot moves quickly, wrapping readers in an enchanting romance." —*RT Book Reviews*

"Valerie Bowman's stories sparkle with humor and her characters are absolutely adorable. *The Untamed Earl* is an engaging and romantic love story."
—*Fresh Fiction*

THE IRRESISTIBLE ROGUE

"Bowman's novel is the complete package, filled with fascinating characters, sparkling romance, and a touch of espionage." —*Publishers Weekly*

"With its lively plot, heated sexual tension, surprising twists, engaging characters, and laugh-out-loud humor, Bowman's latest is another winner."

—*RT Book Reviews* (4½ stars, Top Pick!)

"You will find no greater romantic escapade."

—*Night Owl Reviews* (Top Pick)

"The story is filled with humor, a twisting plot, and vibrant characters that have become Bowman's hallmark. The chemistry is near-perfect, and the will-they-won't-they back-and-forth is exactly what romance readers want; the simultaneous tale of deceit, revenge, and espionage makes it all the more rewarding."

—Sarah MacLean, *The Washington Post*

THE UNLIKELY LADY

"Bowman keeps her prose and characters fresh and interesting; her book is an entertaining renewal of a classic plotline and well worth reading." —*Kirkus Reviews*

"Rich with fully developed characters and a plethora of witty banter." —*Publishers Weekly*

"A definite must-read!" —*San Francisco Book Review*

THE ACCIDENTAL COUNTESS

"Bowman is one to watch."

—*Kirkus Reviews* (starred review)

"Readers will take the well-drawn, likable characters into their hearts, enjoying every moment of their charming love story as it unfolds in unexpected ways. Simply enjoy the humor and tenderness."

—*RT Book Reviews* (4½ stars)

"Merry, intelligent, and wholly satisfying. The plot is elaborate, and Bowman handles it with grace to spare."

—*USA Today*

THE UNEXPECTED DUCHESS

"Smart, witty, sassy, and utterly delightful!"

—*RT Book Reviews* (4½ stars, Top Pick!)

"Engaging characters, snappy banter, and the judicious infusion of smoldering sensuality will have readers clamoring for the next installment in this smart and sexy series."

—*Booklist* (starred review)

"A fun, smart comedy of errors and a sexy, satisfying romance."

—*Kirkus Reviews* (starred review)

ALSO BY VALERIE BOWMAN

Never Trust a Pirate

VALERIE BOWMAN

St. Martin's Paperbacks

This is a work of fiction. All of the characters, organizations, and events portrayed in this novel are either products of the author's imagination or are used fictitiously.

NEVER TRUST A PIRATE

For information address St. Martin's Press, 175 Fifth Avenue, New York, NY 10010.

ISBN: 978-1-250-12169-1

Our books may be purchased in bulk for promotional, educational, or business use. Please contact your local bookseller or the Macmillan Corporate and Premium Sales Department at 1-800-221-7945, ext. 5442, or by e-mail at MacmillanSpecialMarkets@macmillan.com.

Printed in the United States of America

St. Martin's Paperbacks edition / May 2017

St. Martin's Paperbacks are published by St. Martin's Press, 175 Fifth Avenue, New York, NY 10010.

10 9 8 7 6 5 4 3 2 1

For my sister, Laura Litchfield

"Each has his past shut in him like the leaves of a book known to him by his heart, and his friends can only read the title." —VIRGINIA WOOLF

ACKNOWLEDGMENTS

I can hardly believe it, but this is my tenth full-length published novel and it would not have been possible if not for the excellent guidance of my editor, Holly Ingraham, and the terrific assistance of Jennie Conway at St. Martin's Press. Also, to my friends, Virginia Boylan and Mary Behre, thank you for all you did to help make this book the best it could be.

I began writing this book shortly after beginning a new job. I want to thank my friends and coworkers at BKFS PowerCell®. Special thanks to Dan Cummings, Jeff Gibson, Shawn Mailey, Sherri McKinney, John Bergeron, Shekhar Adake, Lynette Rubio, David Smith, Christie Guppenberger, Logan James, Jimmy Avery, Geof Davies, and Regina Terrell for welcoming a romance novelist into your midst and being such great people to work with. Here's your pirate book!

CHAPTER ONE
London Harbor, July 1817

Only three steps. Only *three steps* separated him from the map. It was there, lying on the rickety wooden table in the captain's stateroom aboard a ship aptly named *Le Secret Francais.* The only sound in the cramped space was his own breathing. Sweat beaded on his brow. He'd come this far. Braved the murky, cold water, swum out to the ship moored at the London docks. Climbed aboard, silent as a wraith, dressed all in black. Wrung out his clothing to keep it from dripping so there wouldn't be a trail. Managed to steal into the captain's quarters as the man slept, and now, now only *three steps* remained between him and the priceless map.

One water droplet fell to the wooden plank floor like a hammer against steel. The sound of his breath echoed to a crescendo. The blood pounding in his head became a distracting whirring noise.

One step forward. The ball of his foot ground onto

the plank. Stealth and silence. Always. The calling cards of the best thief in London.

The captain stirred slightly in his bunk and began to snore.

He froze. One leather-clad foot arrested on the wooden plank. A pistol rested on two nails directly above the captain's bunk. If the man awoke, he might shoot first at any noise. The captain well knew the value of the treasure he carried.

He counted to ten. Once. Twice. He had long since mastered the art of keeping footing on a ship. He waited until his heartbeats became steady again before taking the next step. A slight creak in the wood floor. A hint of movement from the captain. Another endless wait. Impatience was a roiling knot inside his belly.

Out of the shadows now, he stood only one step away from the table bolted to the floor. The moon shone through the window above the captain's bed, shedding light on the man's balding head. The map lay spread out, anchored by pins in the four corners. He would have to remove those pins. Ripping the paper would make too much noise.

Another interminable wait as the captain turned away from him in his sleep. His snores subsided.

He glanced over at the bunk. The pistol shone in the moonlight. One hard swallow. He never carried a pistol. Too loud. Pistols brought the crew, the wharf police, and anyone else interested in such activity. The only weapon he carried was a knife, tucked in the back of his breeches. A weapon of stealth.

Another count to ten before taking the final step. There was no time for an in-depth study of the map now, but a quick glance revealed the destination. The island of St. Helena, off the western coast of Africa, circled in bold scrawl. The map of the route planned for a dangerous man's next escape. That bastard in the bed had been planning it.

All ten fingers itched to snatch the paper and run, but he forced himself to take a deep, silent breath. Carefully, he dislodged the first pin at the top right corner. It popped out easily. The top of the map rolled toward the center, making a slight flapping sound. Breath held, he glanced toward the captain again. No movement.

He stuck the pin back into the table to keep it from rolling, then his hand darted to the next pin at the bottom right corner. It also popped out easily. He quickly stuck it back into the wood. With two sides free, he carefully rolled the map toward the center. Reaching up to the top, he grasped the third pin. No movement. It was lodged deeply into the wood. *Must pull harder.* With one black-gloved hand, he clasped the pin between a thumb and two fingers, pulling upward with as much strength as he dared. His own breath in his ear was the only sound . . . that and the water lapping at the sides of the ship.

The pin finally gave way. He pressed a hand to the top of the map, to keep the freed top left corner from curling and making a noise. His chest and torso flattened against the map and the table, he pressed the third pin back into the wood.

Click. An unmistakable sound. One he had heard too often before. Another hard swallow. Damn it. He'd been so preoccupied with keeping quiet, he hadn't realized the captain's snores had subsided.

Half-splayed across the table, he contemplated his options. The door was ten paces to the left, the open window five paces to the right. Would he fit through the window? It'd be a hell of a time to learn the answer was no.

"Step away from zee map, if you don't want a bullet through your back." The captain's voice was harsh and angry.

He slowly rose from his position hunched over the map, arms braced upright at right angles near his head to show the captain he had no weapon. "Ye wouldn't shoot an unarmed man, now would ye, Cap'n?"

"I'd shoot a thief without thinking twice," the captain replied with a sneer, nearly spitting the word *thief*.

He glanced down at the map. Studying it in case he was forced to leave without it. He had been in worse situations, more times than he could count. He considered the knife in the back of his breeches hidden beneath his shirt. It would be simple and quick to snake it out and whip it into the bastard's throat. But a voice in his head reminded him . . . justice must be served in proper course.

"Turn around," the captain ordered. "Slowly."

"Why?" he asked, trying to garner some precious time.

"Because I want to see zee face of zee man who would steal my secrets."

He began his turn. Slowly. So slowly and so quietly that he could have sworn he heard a drop of sweat from his forehead hit the wooden plank of the floor. He finally stood facing the older man.

"*Êtes-vous le Renard Noir?*" the captain asked.

"*Pourquoi veux tu savoir?*"

Visible in the light of the moon, the captain narrowed his eyes. "Ah, perfect French? Why do I find zat difficult to believe from an obvious Englishman?"

"Obvious?"

"Who else would want zis map?"

His fingers ached to choke the bastard. He might not be able to kill him, but he could wound the scoundrel. Nothing wrong with a wound. He whipped his hand behind his back, grabbed the knife, and hurled it at the captain. It hit the arm that held the pistol. The captain howled. The pistol fired. Smoke filled the cabin with its acrid stench. He ripped the map and fourth pin from the table and ran to the door.

Steps sounded on the planks above the captain's cabin. In the pitch black belowdecks, he forced himself to wait in the shadows under the stairs until the first group of rescuers filed down the steps into the captain's cabin. He flattened the map's scroll and folded it into a six-inch square.

"He's escaped, you idiots! Find him before he jumps from the ship!" the captain yelled in French.

The group dutifully filed back up to spread across the decks. The captain came running out, clutching his injured arm, blood seeping between his fingers, crimson dripping down his nightshirt. He made his way up the stairs and ran off across the deck.

Springing from the shadows, the thief raced back into the empty cabin. He flew over to the window, said a brief prayer to fit through the tight space, hoisted up to the ledge, and pushed his upper body through. He ripped off his black tricorn, stuck the folded map to his head, and pulled down the hat as firmly as possible.

A rope swung outside the captain's window two feet to the right. Thank God for small favors. He lunged at it and grabbed it. Noiselessly, he lowered himself down the rope, bracing both feet against the hull to rappel toward the water. Lowering quietly, he winked back at the figure-head of a saucy French woman carved beneath the captain's cabin. As soon as he made it into the water, he let go of the rope and swam like a mackerel fleeing a shark toward the shore, careful to keep his head out of the foul-smelling drink. He counted on the black of night and the murky Thames to hide him from the searchers on the ship.

As he covered the distance between the French ship and the shore, the Frenchmen's shouts filled the night air. He dared a glance back. Every lantern on the ship appeared to have been lit and the crew was scurrying about like a bevy of ants on an infiltrated hill.

He swam to the darkest spot on the far end of the docks, around the bend from sight of the French ship, and pulled himself ashore beneath a creaky dock using only his forearms. Exhausted, he rolled onto his back and lay breathing heavily in the pitch-black night. One hand went up to clap the top of his tricorn and a wide smile spread across his face.

He'd done it. He'd escaped from a French ship with the map detailing the planned route to rescue Napoleon from St. Helena. Of course he had. He was the Black Fox.

CHAPTER TWO

The Black Fox Strikes Again!

Cade Cavendish glanced surreptitiously at the headline on the copy of *The Times* that sat at an angle on the table next to him. His twin brother, Rafe, reclined just across said table at Brooks's, the famous gentlemen's club in the heart of St. James. Cade wanted to crush the headline in his fist. He glanced at Rafe. Had he noticed?

"Did you hear me?"

Cade's blond head snapped around to face his brother. "No. Pardon?" Damn it. He shouldn't have allowed the headline to distract him so much.

"I asked if you were planning to attend the theater with Daphne and myself tonight," Rafe repeated.

The theater? Ah, yes, the pastime of aristocrats like the one his brother had become. Rafe, the white sheep of the family, had been a spy for the War Office during the wars. He'd been made a viscount by the Prince Regent and married the sister of an earl. Meanwhile, Cade had spent the last ten years doing something . . . much different.

Cade cleared his throat and steadfastly refused to glance at the paper again. "I suppose the theater wouldn't be the *worst* idea."

Rafe blinked his crystal-blue eyes slowly. "Don't make me twist your arm. I wouldn't want to *bore* you."

"Brother o' mine, in our twenty-eight years, you've done many things, but never bored me. Besides, I'm always happy to spend time with my gorgeous new sister-in-law." Cade waggled his eyebrows.

Rafe narrowed his gaze. "Careful there."

"Where is the fair Lady Daphne this afternoon?"

Rafe leaned back in his chair and crossed his booted feet at the ankles. "She's meeting with potential new lady's maids. Hers gave her notice. The woman's moved north to take a position closer to her sister in the country."

"A shame," Cade drawled. Another tedious problem for the poor aristocracy. Finding proper servants.

"It's not so bad, you know," Rafe said.

"What's that?"

"Having servants. Money. Power."

"I've no doubt," Cade said. He'd been staying at his brother's new Mayfair town house. Filled with fine furnishings and proper servants, it was a far cry from their childhood home in Seven Dials. "I'm quite enjoying being the recipient of such luxuries."

"While you're here?" Rafe asked, his eyes still fixed on the paper. "How long's it been now?"

Cade hid his smile. "I'd say close to nine months," he replied smoothly. Of course his brother didn't know why he'd come. The man had been shocked when Cade had appeared at the Earl of Swifdon's town house last year, introducing himself as Mr. Daffin Oakleaf, one of his many aliases. Rafe had thought he was dead. Hell, everyone had thought he was dead. That was how Cade liked it. But he'd come back for a specific purpose. One that he had no intention of revealing to his brother.

This also wasn't the first time his brother had hinted at wanting to know how long Cade intended upon staying. It suited his purposes not to tell him. It was downright enjoyable, actually, along with goading Rafe at every turn about his beautiful new wife. Cade might have been known in the past for his seductions and dalliances with women, but he would never attempt to seduce his brother's wife. Luckily, Rafe didn't know that, which meant Cade could continue to goad him.

"Yes, while I'm here," Cade replied with all the nonchalance he could muster.

"And how long will that be?"

"You know me. I tend to stay as long as I have a fancy."

"That's fine. As long as you keep your *mistresses* out of my house . . . and away from my wife," Rafe replied with a smirk.

Cade tugged at his cuff and sighed. "If you're referring to that unfortunate incident with Miss Jones, I've apologized a half dozen times already. How was I to know she would climb into your bed at that inn? Amanda had no idea I was a twin."

"Yes, well, perhaps if you conducted yourself with a bit more, ahem, decorum, neither of us would be subjected to such unfortunate incidents."

"Decorum?" Rafe shook his head. "*Such* a boring word."

Rafe muttered something unintelligible under his breath and rubbed his nose with the back of his hand. Cade grinned from ear to ear. His brother had been grumbling and rubbing his nose at him since they were lads. It was a sure sign Cade had got under his skin.

" 'The Black Fox Strikes Again'?" Rafe's voice was a mixture of suspicion and curiosity.

Cade winced. He should have tossed the paper aside when he'd had the chance.

Rafe's gaze captured Cade's over the top of the page. "Have you heard of him?"

"Who?" Cade asked, picking a nonexistent bit of lint from his coat sleeve. Bloody aristocrats and their bloody fancy clothing. It had nearly become a full-time occupation tending to his wardrobe since he'd taken up residence in Mayfair.

"The Black Fox," Rafe drawled.

Cade sighed. "Seems I might have heard a mention a time or two." He readjusted his cravat and cleared his throat.

Rafe's brows lifted. "Says here he's a pirate, an Englishman. He stole some valuable cargo from a French ship docked in the harbor last night."

"Is that so?" Cade made a show of looking about for a footman to place another order of brandy. He declined to meet his brother's eyes.

Rafe shook out the paper to see more of the story. "It also says he's a master of disguise."

Having located a footman and placed his order, Cade settled back in his chair and shrugged. He scratched at his eyebrow. "Does it? How interesting. Someone you're looking for?"

"You know I cannot discuss my assignments," Rafe said, still studying the paper.

"Ah yes, the Viscount Spy. Isn't that your new sobriquet? It's all quite clandestine, isn't it?"

"I suppose so." Rafe nodded toward the paper again. "Know anyone who's a master of disguise, *Mr. Oakleaf*?"

CHAPTER THREE

Danielle LaCrosse smoothed the skirts of her simple white gown as she waited in the viscountess's fancy drawing room. Gowns were highly overrated. Managing the skirts alone was a chore. She'd nearly tripped half a score of times today. She studied the gilt portraits, the sterling silver candlesticks, and the wallpaper that no doubt cost more than the entire little cottage near the shore she'd been saving for for so long.

She'd never seen anything so fine as the contents of this room. Tiny porcelain figures of birds that seemed to have no purpose other than to be pretty. An ornate gilded box resting on a nearby table that Danielle had been unable to keep herself from peeking into (it contained dried rose petals of all things). And carpet so rich and thick she'd momentarily indulged in the ridiculous desire to slip off her shoe and plunge her stocking-covered toes into the deep weave. And yes, it was every bit as soft as she'd imagined. She was exceedingly grateful no one had witnessed that particular behavior, however. No doubt it was conduct unbecoming of a proper English lady's maid, but for a French girl who had spent far too long in uncomfortable accommodations, the viscountess's house was luxurious indeed.

Danielle wasn't usually nervous, but she desperately needed this position. Being the maid to a fine lady like Lady Daphne Cavendish would not only provide her with more money in a week than a regular maid saw in a month's time, it would allow her to stay in London. At the moment, *that* was priceless.

The drawing room door opened and a diminutive woman with shining honey-blond hair and watchful gray eyes came gliding into the room. She couldn't have been more than twenty years of age. "Please forgive my tardiness," she said, her dark pink skirts sweeping across the top of the rug as she made her way over to where Danielle sat.

Danielle hopped from her seat and executed her best curtsy, the one she'd been practicing for days. "My lady."

"Oh, please," the slightly shorter woman said in a friendly, happy tone. "Do take a seat."

"Thank you," Danielle replied, already worrying that her French accent would be looked upon with distaste by her very English potential employer. The wars had been over for two years now, but Danielle knew well there was still a great deal of animosity between the English and the French.

The blond woman smiled at her with kind eyes. "I am

Lady Daphne Cavendish," she announced. Her English accent reminded Danielle of her mother. A sharp pain throbbed in Danielle's chest.

"Pleased to make your acquaintance, my lady," Danielle replied, biting her lip and watching the lady for any signs of disapproval.

"The agency tells me you come with excellent references," Lady Daphne said.

"*Oui.* I mean, y-yes." Danielle hated the stutter in her speech but she found that now that she was confronted with Lady Daphne, she was quite full of nerves. If she didn't secure this position, everything would be ruined.

Lady Daphne pulled a bell cord and a finely dressed butler soon appeared in the doorway. The lady prettily requested a tea tray. Tea served for a meeting about a maid position? Obviously, the viscountess treated her servants kindly. Danielle liked that a lot. She expelled a bit of her pent-up breath. Working in a fine London town house wouldn't be the *worst* thing she'd ever had to do, by far. Perhaps it might even be . . . enjoyable.

"You've previously worked for Lady Birmingham in Brighton?" Lady Daphne asked, studying her closely.

Is that what they'd said? "Er, yes, my lady," Danielle forced herself to reply. She squirmed in her chair. She wasn't used to being watched so carefully. Normally, members of the aristocracy tended to barely look at servants. They certainly didn't stare at them with an intensity that made Danielle believe Lady Daphne truly cared about her. It was unnerving.

"And you had to resign your position there . . . why?" Lady Daphne leaned toward her, waiting for her answer as if on tenterhooks.

Danielle plucked at the folds of her skirt. "I need to be in London, my lady. My mother . . . is ill." No doubt this fine lady didn't care a whit about her mother's illness but it was the truth and Danielle had learned long ago that the more she could follow the truth, the better.

"You have the loveliest French accent."

Danielle blinked three times before she could conjure up an appropriate reply to that surprising compliment. "Thank you, my lady. Not everyone in London is as charmed by it as you are."

"Nonsense. The wars are long since over and everyone knows the French are famous for their good taste in hair design and clothing. French lady's maids are all the rage in Mayfair these days."

Danielle blinked again. She should have guessed as much when Grimaldi had asked her to play up her Frenchness. "I'm terribly glad to hear that, my lady," she said before cursing herself for saying something so common. But the viscountess's twinkling laughter indicated the lady didn't disapprove in the least.

"You lived in Paris, did you not?" Lady Daphne asked.

"*Oui, madame.* I was born there."

"Why did you decide to come to England?"

Danielle was spared from answering *that* question by the arrival of the tea tray. The butler marched over, his back completely straight, his white gloves pristine. He set the tray on the gleaming rosewood table in front of them.

"Thank you, Henry, that will be all." Lady Daphne nodded at the man and he retreated from the room. The smile that rested in the crinkles of his eyes as he left, however, informed Danielle that he liked his employer a great deal. She stared after his straight-backed perfection as he left the room. Was Henry his first name or his last?

Lady Daphne poured the tea in the most dainty, ladylike manner imaginable, and Danielle lapsed into a momentary daydream where she pictured herself dumping over the entire pot and shattering the teacups. She was skilled at a great many things, but being dainty and ladylike were not among them. It would be a miracle if she were to be actually offered this position. Not to mention she would doubtless be sacked within the sennight, but first things first. She must be *offered* the position before she could be terminated from it.

She took the porcelain teacup Lady Daphne offered, fingering the little roses painted along the rim. The cup and saucer alone were probably worth more than she'd earned in a month's time in her previous life.

"Tell me," she said, trying to stop the shaking of her hand on the cup. It would not do to spill tea onto the immaculate carpet. "What exactly are you looking for in a lady's maid?"

Lady Daphne's teacup stopped, arrested halfway to her mouth, and she laughed again. "Why, I'm not certain I've ever had anyone ask me so directly."

Danielle silently cursed herself. *Maudit.* She should not have asked that question. Lady Daphne would think her too forward.

"I've heard the French are quite direct. I like that," Lady Daphne continued.

Danielle blinked again, her teacup arrested halfway to *her* mouth. "You do?"

"Yes, quite a lot. We English are often too polite for our own good. I admire someone who can say what they mean. For instance, what do you think of my hair?"

Warning bells sounded in the back of Danielle's mind. She brought the teacup to her lips and took a long sip while she considered exactly how to answer such a delicate question. Lady Daphne's hair was certainly a lovely color and the lady herself was a beauty, but her hair was a bit on the frumpish side, coiled around her head in a knot that did little to show off her fine features.

"I so admire your chignon," Lady Daphne said, pronouncing the French word perfectly. "I can never seem to get my hair to do that. And Miss Anderson, well, she was quite sweet, but not the most adept at arranging hair, I'm afraid."

"Miss Anderson?" More time bought.

"My former maid."

Danielle set down her teacup and rubbed her hands together. The best answer to Lady Daphne's question, she'd decided, was no answer. Danielle was not one to spend time on her hair or wear fine clothing, but she supposed having grown up in France, she did have a certain *je ne sais quoi* when it came to style, as many French women did. She had her aunt Madeline to thank for teaching her such things. "Would you like me to show you my favorite upsweep?" she asked, smiling conspiratorially at Lady Daphne.

"By all means." Lady Daphne returned her smile.

Danielle stood and hurried around to the back of Lady Daphne's chair. Finally, something she was good at. She plucked the pins from her blond locks, concentrating on not tugging her hair. She pulled them out efficiently, letting the viscountess's curls fall past her shoulders. Then she used her fingers to part the hair down the middle, sweeping it over her shoulders in two wide swaths before rolling first one side and then the other. She pulled the two rolls together to meet in the center and wrapped the pieces around each other, making a loose bun on the back of Lady Daphne's head. She replaced the pins and waved her hand in the air. "Voilà!"

Danielle bit her lip. A moment of panic set in. Would Lady Daphne be horrified by the fact that she'd just dressed her hair in broad daylight in the middle of the drawing room? How in the world would she ever make this work?

Daphne stood, patting the back of her head to feel the new hairstyle. "Well, that was quickly done." She stood and moved to the sideboard where a looking glass hung. She studied her hair from first one side, then the other. "It's positively charming, and what I like best is that I didn't have to sit still for an hour while you poke and prod. I cannot stand such things."

Dieu merci. She wasn't angry. Danielle glanced down at the carpet to hide her proud little smile. "A lady such as you has more important things to attend to than waiting half the day for her hair to be arranged."

"Indeed." Lady Daphne turned back to face her, smiling and still patting the bun on the back of her head.

The door to the drawing room opened and a tall, fit, *tres* handsome blond man with crystal-blue eyes and a dimple in his chin strode in. Danielle had done her research on this family. Not only had she learned that Lady Daphne did not enjoy spending long amounts of time having her hair and clothing fussed over, she'd also learned that the lady's husband was a famous war-hero spy known as the Viscount Spy. She hadn't been aware of how breathtakingly handsome he was, however. Lady Daphne was a lucky woman, indeed.

Danielle watched every movement he made. He had the tiniest hint, nearly unrecognizable, of a limp in his left leg, a faint set of lines around his mouth that indicated he'd been in pain in the past, perhaps a lot of it, and he moved with an easy, quiet style that made her think he was probably a proficient spy, indeed. She sat up straight. Would he approve of his wife's potential new maid? Was he the sort of man who would make the decision for her?

"Ah, Daphne. I didn't mean to interrupt. I'm looking for my—"

"Rafe, there you are. May I present Mademoiselle LaCrosse? Mademoiselle, this is my husband, Lord Rafferty Cavendish."

The man had the grace to stop what he was doing and acknowledge her. Danielle turned and curtsied. Then he promptly returned to his task of searching for whatever it was he came for.

"What do you think of what she's done to my hair?" Daphne smiled and spun around to allow her husband to see the chignon.

Her husband smiled back at her and a fetching dimple appeared in his cheek. "Daphne, my love, your hair could be a rat's nest and I would still think you were gorgeous." The couple shared a look that clearly indicated they were devoted to one another. Such a good-looking, happy couple. Danielle inwardly sighed. Those were few and far between. She stood and made her way over to a small table near the door.

"Mademoiselle LaCrosse comes with excellent references," Lady Daphne added.

"I'm glad to hear it." Lord Cavendish patted his pockets, preoccupied with searching the sideboard.

"She arranged my hair in no time at all. It was quite amazing."

"Sounds good." Lord Cavendish turned his attention to the table in front of the seating area.

Danielle slipped her hand under the newspaper that sat atop the table near the door. THE BLACK FOX STRIKES AGAIN! read the headline. She quickly grabbed the object she'd spotted from across the room and turned away from the paper.

"Is this what you're looking for, my lord?" She moved toward Lord Cavendish and presented him with a gold pocket watch.

The viscount stopped and looked up. His eyes widened. "Yes, actually. Where was it?"

"Here. Under the paper."

"My goodness, Danielle, I didn't even hear you get up. You move like a cat." Lady Daphne smiled. "And you saw that from all the way across the room?" the viscountess asked in awe.

"Just a guess," Danielle replied, hoping Lady Daphne wouldn't make too much over her knack for spotting things. "I noticed you patting your pockets so I assumed the item you were looking for must be small and something you carried upon you."

Lord Cavendish's eyes narrowed on her briefly, but

he inclined his head and smiled, too. "And so it is. Thank you, Danielle."

Lady Daphne put her hands to her hips. "I daresay you've done *two* impressive things during your interview. I suppose my next question for you is simply . . . when can you begin?"

CHAPTER FOUR

The theater was not the sort of amusement Cade looked forward to. He preferred a crowded, smoky gaming hell, or drinking far too much at a tavern filled with the type of women who might be up for a good tumble afterward.

Tonight he'd made an exception. His brother had asked him to attend. Daphne had nearly begged him. They'd spent the better part of the last year—ever since he'd arrived unceremoniously on their doorstep— attempting to make him respectable. They'd even ignored the Amanda Jones debacle. It was more of a family jest than a to-do. Regardless, make Cade respectable? Not bloody likely, but he admired their zeal. Upon occasion, like tonight, he indulged them.

Cade was in town for his own reasons, of course, reasons just now beginning to pay off. Earlier at the club, when Rafe had eyed the paper and mentioned the name Daffin Oakleaf, Cade's stomach had clenched.

Just how much did his brother know about him? Rafe was a respectable member of Society, an employee of the War Office. His livelihood, his life could be affected by Cade's choices. Cade regretted that he couldn't share his secrets with his brother, but it was best this way. To keep Rafe safe. The less he knew, the better.

If it was the last thing Cade did, he would avenge his brother's treatment at the hands of the French. But he'd die before admitting that purpose to Rafe. Cade's role as the black sheep of the family was important to him. Mustn't disrupt the natural order of things. At any rate, his brother had kindly allowed him to stay with him. He might as well at least *attempt* to do things the brother of a viscount was expected to do. Even if they were bloody boring. Like attending the theater.

The three of them entered Rafe's private box together. Cade still hadn't got used to the large number of people who called his brother "my lord" and looked at him twice since they were mirror images of one another. One good thing about having been gone for so many years was the fact that no one outside of London had confused him for his brother. Well, except once. In London, it happened daily. Sometimes hourly. At least when they were together, they might get stares, but no one asked *that* annoying question.

"What do you think of Danielle?" Daphne asked her husband as she settled into her seat in the box's front row.

"Was I supposed to think something of her?" Rafe asked. "She was deuced helpful with the pocket watch. I'll give her that. The woman's got a good eye."

"Who is Danielle?" Cade asked to be polite. The

entire time, he searched the rows of seats filled with other theatergoers. Was the man he was to meet later here? Watching him? Making sure he'd come? Knowing him, he bloody well was.

"She's my new lady's maid. I hired her just this afternoon." Daphne gave Cade her brightest smile. Like Rafe, Daphne was bright, pleasant, full of hope and heart. Nothing like Cade. Cade had seen too much of the world's underbelly. Hope and heart were best left to people who'd experienced more joy than pain. He was nothing but pleased his brother had found happiness, but Cade *knew* that it would never happen for him. Love wasn't for men like him. His brother was actually capable of making a commitment, being faithful, returning love, giving a damn.

Cade was imminently capable of returning love for say, the span of one extremely pleasurable evening, but any more of a commitment than that was asking far too much of him. No, he would never be meant for a proper little aristocrat like Daphne. He was more of a connoisseur of the type of women who liked to give pleasure and receive it with no questions asked or expectations to be met in the morning. And that's exactly how he liked it. Leave the commitments, titles, and London town houses to his brother, the white sheep.

This black sheep was only in town long enough to get the information he needed. It had already taken far longer than he'd anticipated, and dressing in fine clothing and pretending to be a Mayfair gentleman were wearing on his nerves. Things were finally falling into place. The newspapers were tracking the Black Fox and Cade had made appointments with the men he needed to speak to. Things would soon be resolved. Then he would be on his way, back to where he belonged, which was everywhere, or anywhere, except here.

"She's French," Rafe offered.

"Who's French?" Cade asked, his gaze still searching the enormous crowd piled into the theater.

"My new lady's maid," Daphne replied. "You aren't even listening to me, are you?" Daphne huffed, settling her pink skirts around her. "I like that she's French, Rafe. Just look at the darling way she arranged my hair tonight." She turned her head so both men could see.

"You know I'm not the biggest admirer of the French," Rafe replied, bitterness making his voice sharp.

Cade clenched his fist. He knew where that bitterness came from. During the war, one of Rafe's many missions to France was with Daphne's brother, Donald, the then Earl of Swifdon. The two had been captured and tortured. Donald had been murdered. Cade knew it was his brother's biggest regret that he hadn't been able to save the brother of the woman he loved.

Daphne, along with the rest of their friends, knew the details and didn't blame Rafe. Not after what he'd been through. It had been a miracle Rafe escaped with his life. Last year, he'd returned to find the men who'd tortured him and killed Donald. He'd brought the lot of them to justice, with Daphne's help, no less. Cade, or rather Daffin Oakleaf, knew even more than his brother did about who was behind Rafe's capture and torture. The French would pay. And soon.

"She lived in Paris and knows all of the latest hairstyles and fashions," Daphne added.

"Ah, yes, hairstyles and fashions are more important than the *wars,*" Rafe drawled.

"Danielle didn't have anything to do with the wars," Daphne pointed out. "Honestly, Rafe."

"I agree with your wife," Cade said. "An unsuspecting lady's maid hardly seems like someone against whom to hold a grudge." But Cade already didn't trust the woman, either.

"How do we know she can be trusted?" Rafe asked, though he had a smile on his face.

Daphne rolled her eyes. "I've no reason to believe she's a subversive agent for the French, for goodness' sake. She's a lady's maid and came with excellent references."

"French references?"

"No. Nice, solid, *English* references. You must be the most suspicious person I've ever met." Daphne grinned up at her husband.

"Darling, must I remind you, I am a spy." Rafe returned her smile, a sparkle in his eyes.

"On the contrary," Cade interjected. "I am actually the most suspicious person you've ever met. You just don't know me well enough to know it yet."

"Now *that* I'll agree with, *Mr. Oakleaf,*" Rafe replied.

"Yes, you never did tell us," Daphne said. "Why were you going by the name Daffin Oakleaf when you first came to town last year, Cade?"

"Because my brother has more aliases than a spy," Rafe replied.

"Nonsense." Cade straightened his cravat.

"You deny you have aliases?" Rafe asked.

"No. I deny I have more aliases than a spy has. I suspect we're even."

"But *why* do you have aliases?" Daphne asked.

"Don't ask, Daphne. I'd rather not know myself. I fear I'd have to drag him to Newgate if I knew the extent of what he's been up to." Rafe settled himself in his seat and faced forward.

The newspaper's headline flashed through Cade's mind and his stomach clenched again, but he remained steadfastly silent while Daphne peered back at him. "Very well," she finally said. "I probably don't want to know."

"You don't," Cade agreed, more than ready to change the subject. "But how did this conversation get turned around to be about me? Weren't we talking about your new French lady's maid? How old is she?"

"I'd say she's perhaps five and twenty."

"Is she pretty?" French or not, Cade always appreciated a fine-looking woman.

Both Daphne's and Rafe's heads snapped to face him. Daphne looked worried. Rafe glowered.

"Don't even think about trying to seduce the poor young woman. I'll toss you out on your ear if you so much as glance in her direction," Rafe warned.

Cade smirked and tugged at his cuff. "So touchy, dear brother. I'll take that as a yes, she is pretty."

Daphne crossed her arms over her chest. "Please, Cade, don't use your legendary charm on Danielle. The last thing I want is a scandal under my roof."

"I merely asked if she was pretty." Cade settled back into his chair, but he couldn't keep the grin off his face.

He'd really riled them this time. Mademoiselle must be quite pretty indeed. He was looking forward to meeting her.

Rafe's eyes narrowed on his brother. "Don't think I don't know what you were doing at the Monroes' estate with one of the maids in the middle of the night during our wedding party last month."

Cade winced. "You heard about that?"

Rafe scowled. "Deuced embarrassing. Had to apologize to Monroe."

Cade shrugged. "I don't see why. What happens between consenting adults in the middle of the night is none of your concern."

Daphne turned to him. "Danielle seems like a nice young woman. Please don't cause any scandal, Cade."

"I wouldn't dream of it," Cade said in the most innocent voice he could muster.

"Yes, you would," Daphne replied. "Your eyes are twinkling."

"Can I help it if my eyes twinkle?" He blinked at his sister-in-law.

"When Rafe's eyes twinkle, he's up to no good."

The brothers exchanged a surprised look.

Cade rubbed his chin. "Be that as it may, the only thing I did with the maid at the Monroes' estate was—"

Rafe put up a hand. "Please, spare us."

Another shrug from Cade. "Very well. I'll leave it to your imagination."

The music began and the theatergoers became silent. Soon, an enormous curtain was pulled open from each side of the stage and the performance began. Cade watched for the better part of a quarter hour before getting restless. He'd never been able to sit still for long. He would just go out and have a cheroot. He slipped out of Rafe and Daphne's box and strode down the carpeted corridor toward the lobby. He pushed through the large double doors and out into the courtyard in front of the theater. He lit a cheroot and had taken only one puff when an urchin ran by, knocking him off balance. "Oy, there. Watch where you're . . ."

The child kept running and soon disappeared behind the side of the large building.

Cade glanced down, brushing ashes from the front of his impeccably tailored black evening attire. A spot of white next to his foot caught his attention. A small folded piece of paper. He stooped to grab it and unfolded it. In scrawling handwriting it read, *Meet me in the alley behind the theater. Now.*

Cade glanced around. No one seemed to be watching. There were only a smattering of couples. A few other men smoking. A handful of waiting carriages and their grooms. He tossed the cheroot to the gravel and ground it under his shoe, strode to the side of the theater, glanced back and forth into the shadows, and strode toward the back of the building.

He'd made it nearly halfway when a man jumped from the shadows and punched Cade dead in the face.

CHAPTER FIVE

Was that . . . singing? A *man* . . . singing? Danielle glanced up from her work in Lady Daphne's wardrobe. She'd been organizing the delicate, expensive undergarments, lovely lace handkerchiefs, and gorgeous buttersoft gloves all evening.

It was calming work, placing things in order. It made her feel in control. Not a feeling she was familiar with. Her mistress and her husband had been gone for the last few hours. The theater, Lady Daphne had said, and she'd seemed extremely pleased by the way in which Danielle had arranged her hair before she'd left.

Another artful style done in record time. Just what milady wanted. Lady Daphne had thanked her prettily and asked her to make herself at home. She'd introduced her to the other servants including a *tres* friendly housemaid named Mary, two extremely helpful and energetic footmen named Trevor and Nigel, and the housekeeper, Mrs. Huckleberry. That lady had shown her to her room on the fourth floor with the other female servants. Everyone seemed pleasant and no one had been rude to her for being French. *Such* a relief.

After dinner of tomato bisque and cheese and bread with the rest of the servants belowstairs, Danielle had come back upstairs to survey Lady Daphne's things. It was Danielle's duty to ensure everything was clean and mended and in the right place. Apparently Miss Anderson had done a poor job because most of Lady Daphne's lovely items were squashed together in drawers, items mismatched and not folded properly. The horror. Danielle eagerly set about fixing it.

She'd been at her work for the better part of an hour when the singing caught her attention. Certain that she must be mistaken, she cupped her hand behind her ear. It was getting louder. Whoever was singing was climbing the stairs. Was one of the footmen foxed? She tiptoed to the bedchamber door and peeked out.

His shadow preceded him. Tall and broad-shouldered. She saw the top of his blond head before she saw the rest of him. His voice was deep and strong and he sounded quite happy for all that he was clearly three sheets to the wind. She smothered a smile behind her hand.

When the man emerged from the shadows and stood at the top of the staircase, she gasped. It was none other than Lord Cavendish himself.

Where was Lady Daphne?

Danielle watched in fascination as he continued through the corridor, passing by the room where she peeped out without noticing her (*dieu merci*). There was an awful bruise on his eye and his fist was—*mon dieu*—

dripping blood! She covered her mouth with her hand again, this time to keep him from hearing her gasp. He continued past her door, and to her further surprise, past his door.

She'd already explored, taking the liberty of opening the adjoining door from Lady Daphne's bedchamber and realized that her husband's room was adjacent. Why wasn't the man going to his room? He continued past both rooms to the end of the hall and entered a door on the opposite side of the corridor. Was he too inebriated to remember where he slept? This could be quite embarrassing for him when he woke up and discovered he was somewhere else. Would Lady Daphne be mortified? Would she even know where her husband was?

Danielle bit her lip. Should she run and tell Mrs. Huckleberry? Perhaps inform one of the housemaids and let her handle it? Or should she quietly steal over and tell the lord of the manor he was in the wrong room?

She'd never been one to pass up an interesting opportunity. She might learn a bit more about her employers while she was at it. She tiptoed out of Lady Daphne's room and scurried down the corridor to peer into the room Lord Cavendish had entered. He'd left the door wide open. Candles on the mantelpiece and the bedside tables lit the space.

"My lord?" she called in a hushed whisper.

At first he didn't hear. He was sitting on the side of the bed, tugging at his boots in an attempt to remove them. Where in heaven's name was the man's valet?

"My lord," she called again, a bit louder this time.

His blond head snapped up and he narrowed his eyes toward the door. "Who is it?"

She stepped into the door frame. "It's me, my lord."

"For God's sake, don't call me that. I cannot abide it." With that, he went back to grappling with his boots.

"My lord, I do not think that you . . . That is to say, you perhaps are not aware that . . . I mean, you are currently—"

"Are you a maid?" he finally bellowed.

"Yes." Was it possible the man had forgotten her since this afternoon? Given the state he was in, she decided it was more than possible.

"If you're a maid, then please make yourself useful and help me with my boots."

Maudit. The man was imperious. At least when he was intoxicated. "Perhaps you should take off your boots in your own room," she offered.

"I am in my own room." He'd managed to rip one boot from his foot and toss it onto the floor next to the bed.

She had experience arguing with drunken men. Quite a lot of it. "I beg to differ, my lord," she called out.

"Shh, woman." He clapped his hands over his ears. "Has anyone ever told you you're loud?"

Mon dieu. That did it. Employer or no, she wasn't going to allow herself to be insulted. Poor Lady Daphne. Had Danielle really thought earlier that the woman was lucky to have this man? He might have the face of a Greek god but he had the personality of a horse's ass. "Has anyone ever told you you're rude?"

That remark was met with a grin. "Countless times."

"And?"

"I chose not to believe them." His grin was unrepentant. "Now, either help or leave."

She clenched her hands into fists and plunked them on her hips. She wanted to slap some sense into her new employer, but reason fought emotion. She couldn't get sacked on her first day. Especially not for something so easily avoided like slapping the lord of the manor.

That would be exceedingly bad form, as the English liked to say. No, she'd get sacked tomorrow or the next day for not knowing white kid gloves didn't go with a fur-trimmed gown or yellow hair ribbons were never worn on Wednesdays. Something ridiculous. She *needed* this job. Needed it badly. Very well, she would help the lout with his boot. Perhaps after that, he would listen to reason when she told him he was in the wrong room.

She crossed over to stand in front of his booted foot. She knelt next to him and held the thing on both sides while he attempted to tug his foot free. He grunted and pulled. Nothing happened.

"Perhaps if you try from this side?" he suggested, gesturing to the front of his boot.

Her face flaming (and her face never flamed), Danielle stood and straddled his leg with both hands holding down the boot. At this point, she wanted the boot off, the man put to bed in the correct room, and to be done with this entire, unpleasant business. "Pull," she commanded.

He did so and his foot came free. He toppled back upon the bed, upending her, and she flew backward with him, onto his lap.

"Thank you," he said, his hands on her hips. Her backside cradled intimately against him. "You might be loud and more than a bit overbearing, but I can't say I mind this particular side of you."

"*Vous pouvez etre tres beau, mais vous etes un ane complet,*" she muttered.

"You think I'm handsome?" came his overly confident voice. "Why, mademoiselle, I am flattered."

She turned her head to glare at him. "If you understood the first part, you must have understood the second, *monsieur*." This was it. She was sacked.

"*Oui,*" he replied. "But I was purposefully choosing to ignore the part where you called me an ass."

She blinked at him and pushed herself up on her elbows. *Mon dieu!* This was a nightmare. One she was certain to wake from at any moment. She was literally lying in bed with her drunken employer. She had to get out of here immediately. What would Lady Daphne do when she discovered her husband had made an inappropriate advance on her maid? She'd be sacked for certain. She also couldn't stay in a house where her employer was so exceedingly inappropriate. She could handle herself, of course, but she doubted very much that a swift jab to the ribs to the man who paid her salary would be met with anything other than a dismissal.

A loud gasp at the doorway drew her attention and Danielle was horrified to see Lady Daphne standing there in the bright pink silk gown that Danielle had helped her into earlier.

Danielle scrambled off the bed. "My lady, you must believe me. I didn't mean to—" Danielle stopped and gasped. Next to Lady Daphne in the doorway materialized none other than *Lord Cavendish*.

Danielle glanced back at the man whose lap she had recently vacated and then at the man standing in the doorway, her eyes huge. What in the world? How could they both be . . . ? Wait. Now that she studied him more closely, the man behind her had longer hair than Lord Cavendish, a deeper tan than Lord Cavendish, and a much more mischievous look in his eye than Lord Cavendish. She'd been distracted by the blood earlier or she certainly would have noticed the differences.

Lady Daphne managed to find her voice first. "I'm so terribly sorry, Danielle. Allow me to be the first to apologize for the behavior of my husband's twin brother."

CHAPTER SIX

Twin brother? Danielle couldn't help it. Her mouth remained open as she glanced back and forth between the two men.

Lady Daphne calmly walked into the room and tugged Danielle's hand, pulling her farther from the bed. The woman's pretty gray eyes glared daggers at her brother-in-law. "Cade!" Lady Daphne looked as if she might stamp her foot. "Do you have something to say to Danielle?"

Cade? That was his name? Cade?

Cade leered at her. "Of course I've got something to say to her."

Lady Daphne crossed her arms over her chest, still glaring. "Yes?"

Cade stood, pulled at his lapels to straighten his dusty, ripped coat, and bowed. "Mademoiselle Danielle, you have the most enticing backside I have ever encountered."

He fell backward onto the bed, snoring, his hand still bleeding.

Danielle couldn't help but press her lips together to hide her smile. The man was positively outrageous. Now that she knew he was Lord Cavendish's *brother,* the situation wasn't nearly as awful as she'd thought. He was still rude. And an ass. And inappropriate. But she could handle a rude houseguest.

Lady Daphne gasped and gave her husband a look that clearly implied that he best come deal with his kin before she murdered him with her bare hands.

"He's been hurt," Danielle said, gesturing to Monsieur Cade's hand, trying to diffuse the tension.

"In a tavern fight, no doubt," Lord Cavendish said, coming over to stand next to the bed and stare down at his drunken sibling. He shook his head. Then he turned to Danielle. "I cannot tell you how utterly sorry I am for his ill behavior."

"Please, Danielle, don't leave us over this," Lady Daphne said. "I promise to speak with him tomorrow. I'll secure his solemn promise that he will never address you in such an inappropriate manner again."

"I saw him bleeding in the hallway and came in to see to his hand. I thought he was you, my lord." Her face heated as she nodded toward Lord Cavendish.

Lady Daphne turned red. "Oh, of course you did. An honest mistake. Just so you know, my husband would never be so . . . inappropriate. His brother is staying with us while he's in London and let's just say the two are quite . . . different."

"That's an understatement," Lord Cavendish added.

Danielle glanced at the man snoring on the bed. "Is

he . . . married?" She hoped an angry wife wasn't about to stomp in and demand answers.

"No!" Lady Daphne looked aghast. "He has the manners of a dockworker. No decent woman would have him."

Danielle had to laugh at that. "I've encountered worse."

Lady Daphne searched her face. She gave a sympathetic smile. "I'd not thought of that. Is that why you left Lady Birmingham's employ? Was someone there inappropriate to you?"

"No. Not there, but there have been times . . . in the past. I'm not unaccustomed to having to fend off drunken louts."

"You shouldn't have to do that here," Lord Cavendish chimed in. "I give you my word, if you stay, my brother will conduct himself as nothing but a gentleman in your presence."

"It's quite all right, my lord." The three of them retreated toward the door. "It's as I said. I am capable of handling myself."

"No doubt." Lady Daphne nodded. "Nevertheless, I apologize again."

Before the door shut behind them, Danielle spared one last glance at the man sprawled across the bed. When she'd first met Lord Cavendish she had been taken aback at his good looks. Now there were *two* of him? She smoothed a hand over her hair. Perhaps a stint as a lady's maid in Mayfair might turn out to be an amusing position after all.

CHAPTER SEVEN

Cade groaned and sat up. The pulsing pain in his left hand reminded him that last night hadn't gone exactly the way he'd planned. He pushed himself into a sitting position and rested his head against the headboard. He was still in his evening attire. He glanced at his hand. It was wrapped in white linen. Who the hell had wrapped it? It wasn't something he'd been bloody likely to do. He'd had far worse injuries.

He tested his jaw. Damn. The bastard had really got a good blow in. The bloody pulp he'd left the man in attested to the fact that while his assailant may have landed a hit or two, Cade had won the fight. The only problem was, he'd beaten the man so severely, he'd lost consciousness and couldn't be questioned. Cade had ransacked his pockets and found nothing more than some snuff, a bit more of the paper the urchin had delivered, and a pocket watch. He'd kicked the bastard one last time for good measure, tossed the pocket watch on his chest, and went to meet the man he'd been originally scheduled to meet at a tavern not far from the theater district.

Cade searched his memory. He'd had a bottle of scotch to numb the pain in his hand and face, may have sung a few bawdy songs, and come home at a very decent hour, at least for him. So how did he get his hand wrapped? He searched his memory further. Absolutely nothing.

The door to his room cracked open and a pair of bright blue eyes framed by black lashes and black bangs blinked at him.

"You're awake?" the voice said in a decidedly French accent.

"You've been waiting?" he replied, equally amused and confused.

The door opened all the way, obviously pushed by the French woman's foot. She carried in a silver tray. "I told Mary I'd bring this up to you."

"Ah, Mary. . . . Wait. Who is Mary?" He tested his jaw again.

"She's the downstairs maid. Don't you know her?"

"I do not. And I hate to point it out but I also don't know *you*. I hope to God there's a pot of coffee on that thing."

She blinked at him and he looked up from inspecting his wrapped hand and really looked at her for the first time. Dear God. Who was this creature? Straight black hair fell past her shoulders. Bright cobalt eyes blinked at him from beneath a heavy fringe of bangs. Her mouth was too wide to be called beautiful, but it was bright pink and ever so alluring. Her cheeks were like apples, her figure slim though enticing, but it was her stare that arrested him. Like some sort of an inquisitive woodland creature that he might scare off if he moved too suddenly. He did not want to scare her off. Not at all.

"You don't remember?" she asked, looking a bit crestfallen.

It was not the first time a beautiful woman had said such a thing to him in his bedchamber after an evening of drinking. In fact, it wasn't the twentieth time, truth be told, but he hoped to God he hadn't done anything he'd be ashamed of this time, not in his *brother's* fancy house. "Should I?" he asked tentatively, studying her face.

"You were quite foxed last night." She moved over to the bed and slid the tray onto his lap. "And there is a pot of coffee here."

He felt chagrined for having said the thing about the coffee. She wasn't *his* servant after all. He glanced down at the contents of the tray. Two slices of dry toast, the pot of coffee, and a small glass of something that looked a bit greenish and that he didn't recognize.

"My father occasionally drank to excess."

"You and I have *that* in common," Cade drawled. "I don't remember my father being sober a day in his life."

"This is what *Père* liked to eat in the morning," she continued.

"What is this?" He lifted the green glass.

"*Le elixir vert,*" she replied with a smile. "At least that's what my father called it."

"And what is in it?" Cade asked.

"A mix of herbs and brandy."

He brought the glass to his nose. "It smells revolting."

"It will make you feel better."

He arched a brow. "How do you know I feel poorly?"

She blinked at him. "Because you don't remember who I am and we met last night."

Cade winced. "How did I behave? Poorly?"

"Exceedingly poorly." But her smile belied her words.

"Did I sing?"

"Yes. A lot."

"I apologize."

"No need. Your brother and Lady Daphne already did that for you."

He groaned and pinched the bridge of his nose. "Blast. That's all I need. More of Rafe's censure."

"He does not approve of you?"

"Does the white sheep ever approve of the black one?"

A frown marred her brow. "I do not know what you mean. *Le mouton noir?*"

"It's an English saying," he replied, eyeing the green elixir warily.

"What does it mean, this, black sheep?"

He blew air into his cheeks and they puffed out. "It's used to describe the most disreputable member of the family."

"And you are *le mouton noir?*"

"In my family, yes."

"Lord Rafe is *le mouton blanc?*"

"Yes. Quite *blanc.*"

She laughed at that and Cade was enchanted. He lifted the concoction to his lips and tipped it back. It burned a path down his throat. He choked. "What the devil are these herbs? Brandy never tasted so vile, even at this hour of the day."

"Give it a moment," she said, pressing her lips together. Cade suspected it was to keep from laughing at his discomfort.

Cade took a swig of coffee to kill the taste of the bitter liquid he'd just consumed. But even he had to admit that moments later the spinning in his head and the churning in his stomach stopped. By God, he did feel better.

"*D'accord?*" she asked in her adorable French accent. "All right?"

"Yes. I do believe it's cured me."

She pulled his injured hand from his lap. A spark unexpectedly shot up his arm. Dear God. When was the last time a mere touch from a young woman did that to him? Before he had a chance to protest, she'd efficiently unwrapped the bandage. "It looks good," she announced. The movement of her thumb, rubbing in little circles on his palm was making him sweat. He swiped the back of his hand across his brow. It had to be the elixir. God only knew what was in that drink. "No sign of infection," she finished.

"I suppose I have you to thank for that," he said as she gingerly wrapped his hand again. He reluctantly pulled his hand away from hers.

"I couldn't allow you to bleed on these fine bed-sheets."

Cade cleared his throat. "Hmm. I daresay we haven't even mentioned how inappropriate it is for you to be in my bedchamber. Alas, to my proper brother's everlasting regret, I refuse to hire a valet."

Her throaty laughter followed. "I don't see why it's inappropriate for me to be here. You're fully dressed and I wanted to ensure your hand was all right. You English are entirely too proper."

"I agree, my dear. Thank you for seeing to my hand," he said, chagrined again. He was never chagrined yet he'd been twice in the span of mere minutes with this woman. Chagrined and sweating. That, along with the oddest feeling in the pit of his stomach, as if something exciting were about to happen. That usually only happened right before he dressed up as someone else and did something dangerous.

"I'll leave you to your coffee and toast," she said, turning toward the door, affording Cade the picture of her alluring backside. The flicker of a memory shot through his brain. He narrowed his eyes on her backside.

She got to the door and paused. Her hand rested on the handle, but she didn't turn around.

"You're looking at my backside, aren't you, Mr. Cavendish?"

Cade nearly spat his coffee. In a thousand years he wouldn't have expected that question from the little slip of a maid, and he certainly wouldn't have expected her to be reading his bloody mind.

"If I told you that I wasn't would you believe me?" he asked instead.

"Not a bit." She pulled open the door, but he could hear the smile in her voice. Oh, he was going to have fun flirting with *this* one. He was no fan of the French but a beautiful woman was a beautiful woman. Besides, hadn't the girl just said herself the English were too proper? They could agree on that at least.

"You can't leave," he called after her. "You haven't yet told me your name. All I know is that it's not Mary."

"It's Danielle," she said, tossing her straight hair over her shoulder and glancing back at him with mischief in her sparkling blue eyes. "I'm Lady Daphne's new lady's maid and last night, I accidentally fell onto your lap while helping you remove your boots and you told me I have the most enticing backside you've ever seen."

CHAPTER EIGHT

Danielle hurried down Harley Street. It was in a busy, safe part of London, not too far from Mayfair where her new employer resided. She'd relocated her mother here months ago. Dr. Montgomery lived near here. He was reputed to be the finest doctor in the country when it came to treating consumption. That's why Danielle desperately wanted to remain in London and the position at Lady Daphne's house afforded her that for the time being.

Danielle hurried up the stairs and let herself into the small flat using a key she pulled from her reticule. The smell of medicine and illness hit her in the face as it always did when she came here.

"Is that you, Miss Cross?" The nurse called from the bedchamber of the small apartment.

"Yes, Mrs. Horton. It's me."

Danielle took a deep breath and pasted the fake smile

on her face. The same smile she used every time she came to visit her mother. The one that was designed to be calm and reassuring. She entered the room and addressed her mother's caretaker. "How is she today, Mrs. Horton?"

"Not worse than yesterday," Mrs. Horton said with an encouraging but weak smile. Danielle knew the woman didn't ever want to tell her the worst but her mother was not improving, despite all of Dr. Montgomery's medicines.

"Yes, well, I'll just read to her for a bit," Danielle said. "You may take a break."

"Of course, miss." Mrs. Horton excused herself and soon the door to the flat opened and shut. Danielle knew the woman preferred to eat her lunch near the park and take a walk outside. Even London's smoggy, coal-filled air was a welcome change after being cooped up in a sickroom most of the day.

Danielle settled into the chair next to her mother's bed as her mother smiled weakly up at her. Her thin body looked so frail and thin, her eyes sunken and shadowed. Danielle didn't let her smile waver once. She poured some water into a glass from a pitcher next to the bed and held the glass to her mother's dry, cracked lips.

"Where did we leave off yesterday?" she asked, opening the book that remained on the bedside table. "Ah, yes, we'd just discovered that Manfred is Father Jerome's son, hadn't we?" They'd been reading *The Castle of Otranto*. Her mother adored a mystery.

Nearly an hour later, Danielle glanced up to see her mother's eyes closed and her chest moving with the shallow breaths of sleep. The wheezing sound in her chest never went away, but at least Mama was getting some rest.

When Mrs. Horton returned soon after, Danielle left the bedchamber to speak to her about the plans for the rest of the week and her mother's medicines. The doctor's assistant usually delivered medicine throughout the week and left the bills with Mrs. Horton. Danielle opened her reticule and fished out the necessary bills to pay first Mrs. Horton herself, then the doctor, then for the medicine. It was all of her money just as it was every week. But at least she had it. Many young ladies in her situation wouldn't have anything like the kind of money it took to keep her mother in the finest care. Mrs. Horton tried to reach out and pat her hand, but Danielle took an instinctive step away. Any tenderness now and she might break. "Thank you for all of your help," she murmured instead. "I'll be back tomorrow night."

It wasn't until she left the house and walked down the stairs to the outside of the building that Danielle allowed the tears to slide down her cheeks. But just as quickly, she brushed them away with the backs of her gloved hands. She didn't have time to cry. She had to meet the general.

Danielle made her way through the tidy little town houses on Shepherd Street. To the outside eye, this was a pleasant neighborhood inhabited by solid London citizens. Clean, neat, nothing extravagant like the mansions of Mayfair. That was exactly why it housed one of the most secret offices in the kingdom. No one would ever suspect it was here.

This place did not exist on any paperwork, did not appear on any reports. It was a location the other spies in the Home Office didn't know about. This was the second office of General Mark Grimaldi. At the age of thirty-three, Grimaldi was the head of an elite unit of spies. So elite they didn't know one another's identities. Only Grimaldi knew them all.

She marched up the stairs to the door marked twelve and knocked once. A slot in the door opened.

"How is the weather today?" a pleasant male voice asked.

"A bit too windy for my taste," she answered.

The pass code uttered, the door opened. Danielle stepped inside a spartan room that contained a silver sideboard, a desk, two chairs, and a wall full of bookshelves.

Mr. Groggs, the secretary who'd opened the door, stepped back. "The general will see you."

She stepped to the next door. It was made of sturdy wood and boasted a knocker in the shape of a lion's head. She knocked once there, too.

"Come in," a deep, authoritative voice answered.

She squared her shoulders and swallowed, then stepped inside.

She shut the door behind her.

The dark-haired man sat facing the opposite direction, staring out the window across the mews behind the building. His large chair swiveled. He was a giant of a man, tall, broad, dark. General Mark Grimaldi. This man had secrets. Secrets she didn't want to contemplate. She'd known him since she was a lass of fifteen. He hadn't been much older at the age of twenty-three. She'd been dressed as a lad, having joined a gang of smugglers in France at the ripe age of thirteen. Smugglers made money. Smugglers had connections. A smuggler could get her to England to save her mother who had been taken there as a prisoner, unjustly accused of her father's murder. It had left Danielle a virtual orphan. The smugglers had been her only choice, but smugglers weren't about to take a *girl* into their ranks. She'd done what she had to do. She'd dressed as a lad, cut her hair short, and took her first foray into doing what she must to make money.

Grimaldi, who hadn't been a general at the time, had dragged her kicking and screaming off a French smuggler's ship and asked her a stream of questions in fluent French. When she'd answered in similarly fluent English with an angry, narrowed gaze and not a hint of an accent, his eyebrows had risen in admiration.

He'd taken her to a small room outside a warehouse and privately questioned her. He'd ensured she was comfortable, given her tea—the English loved their tea—and biscuits and made certain the cut on her cheek was seen to by a real doctor. Then he'd asked her a series of questions, this time in English. She'd answered in French. She hadn't given much away and felt pleased with herself, smug. She certainly hadn't admitted to any crime. After two hours of interrogation, she stood to leave, hoping against hope the Englishman wouldn't stop her and arrest her for smuggling.

"I'll just be leaving now, Captain," she'd said.

She'd got as far as the door when his voice, smooth as cream but dangerous as a coiled snake, stopped her. "I'm impressed, Mr. Cross."

"Impressed by what, Captain?" Her hand shook against the door handle. She was so close to freedom.

"Impressed by your eloquence. Your lack of an accent when speaking either English or French. Your intelligence in one so young."

"Thank you, Captain." She'd pulled open the door and took one step outside.

"Don't you want to hear what I'm *most* impressed with, Mr. Cross?"

She gulped, but forced herself to face him, pinning a fake, bored expression on her face. "What's that, Captain?" She crossed her arms over her chest and waited.

"I'm most impressed that you've been able to convince a boatload of French smugglers that you're a *lad* for God knows how long."

And that had been that. She'd gasped, shut the door, and resumed her seat in front of him. In the two years since her mother's arrest, she'd never had one person guess her secret. Not one. This man had sussed it out in less than two hours.

"I don't know what you're talking about, Captain. Perhaps the sea air has made you *fou*."

"I'm not insane. Spare us both, Mr. Cross. Or should I say, mademoiselle? Don't make me rip open your shirt to prove I'm right."

Her eyes flashed fire at him. "You wouldn't dare."

"It's not my first choice, but I'll do what I must. Try me."

"What do you want?" she shot at him.

"It's quite simple. I want your help."

An unlikely allegiance had been born that day, between a French girl and an English spy. She would do anything to save her mother. Ten years later, Danielle was still visiting the general. He was still her employer. Her mother was safe, but the man who had murdered her father was still at large and Danielle intended to bring him to justice.

"Good to see you, Cross." Grimaldi turned in his seat to face her.

"You rang," she intoned with a smirk. They both knew he only asked her to see him in person if it was important. *Quite* important. They never risked such meetings otherwise.

"I did."

"May I ask why?"

"Isn't it obvious? It's time to tell you your mission. I received the information from your last mission, by the by."

"I'm glad to hear it. But I thought my new mission was to watch the Viscount Spy. Ensure he remains loyal to the Crown."

"That's not the mission. I trust Rafe Cavendish with my life. He's as loyal a subject to the Crown as you'll ever meet."

"Then why in the *nom de dieu* do you have me trussed up in gowns, traipsing around a town house in Mayfair, pretending to be a lady's maid of all things? *Maudit!*"

"Such language." He tsked. "It's unbecoming of a lady."

She eyed him carefully. "You know I'm no lady."

"Yes, it's particularly amusing to me that this latest mission of yours involves being a lady's maid. I'd pay a pretty penny to see you plaiting braids and sticking pins in a coiffure."

"I've learned my trade well. You've nothing to worry about."

Grimaldi knew she'd spent the last fortnight being trained by one of London's best lady's maids, one paid well enough to keep her mouth shut and ask no questions.

"I've no doubt. I've never seen you not fully committed to any task you've undertaken," Grimaldi replied.

"No more delays, General. What's the mission? I need to get back. My lady is attending a ball tonight and she'll miss me before long."

He sighed and the smile dissipated from his face. "Very well. Point taken."

There was no file. No words. Nothing written. It was the way this branch of the Home Office worked. They weren't even having this conversation. She'd be tortured and killed before she admitted she so much as knew Mark Grimaldi's name, let alone his identity as chancellor of this nonexistent office.

"The subject isn't Rafe Cavendish at all," Grimaldi said.

Danielle's brow furrowed. "Don't tell me it's Lady Daphne?"

"No. The Swift family has been nothing but loyal to the Crown."

"Then who?" Danielle furrowed her brow.

"It's the brother. Mr. Cavendish."

"Cade," she breathed.

"You've met him?"

"Last night."

"And?"

"He seems like a rogue and a charmer but not dangerous. Except . . ." She tapped her cheek.

Grimaldi raised a brow. "Except what?"

"Except he did get into a fight with someone."

"Who?"

"I don't know. He came home foxed with a bloody fist."

"Hmm. See if you can find out more about that."

"His brother seemed to think the man has a penchant for getting into drunken fights."

"He has a penchant for more than that. He's been out of the country for years. The fact that he's returned means he's up to something. We've been watching him for a while now but haven't been able to learn anything. Having you in the house so close to him may finally help us find something."

"What?"

Grimaldi grinned at her. "*That* is precisely what we need *you* to discover, Mademoiselle LaCrosse."

CHAPTER NINE

Blast and damnation. Cade had spent the better part of an hour this morning going about his morning ablutions while trying to remember what the hell had happened last night with Mademoiselle LaCrosse in his bedchamber. Obviously nothing *too* untoward. He'd been completely dressed when he awoke. And Daphne had been there with Rafe, according to Danielle.

Cade was annoyed with himself for doing exactly what his brother and sister-in-law had warned him against only hours before. Apparently he didn't have it in him to act appropriately even for the span of one evening. He sighed. On the other hand, his misstep with the mademoiselle last night just might prove useful in furthering his guise as a drunken lout. The more useless Rafe assumed he was, the better.

However, getting so foxed that he didn't remember everything that had happened was poorly done of him.

Losing control was a dangerous mistake in his position. People like him who lost control ended up dead. He needed to buckle down and focus on his plan. The sooner he could find the answers he needed, the sooner he could leave. Leaving here was preferable for many reasons, including distancing himself from a deucedly tempting and distracting lady's maid.

She'd surprised him. People *never* surprised him. She'd attracted him. He preferred tall, curvy blondes, but something about this small, dark-haired, willowy woman was alluring. Perhaps it was her confidence. She'd been at ease trading words with him and had marched into his room this morning, bold as you please, demanding he drink a glass of green elixir and examining his hand without so much as a how do you do.

The French were bold, but something about this woman was especially intriguing. She certainly was beautiful. Breathtaking even. More beautiful than he'd guessed, even after Rafe had warned him so strictly away from her. Perhaps Cade would do the right thing and apologize to her for his behavior last night. Perhaps he'd ask her to have a drink with him. One drink couldn't hurt.

He scrubbed his face and winced when he touched the bruise on his cheek. People said they couldn't tell the difference between him and Rafe. He had longer hair. Now he had a shiner to boot. It would be damn easy for anyone to tell the difference.

He shook his head and wiped a towel over his face. Despite being warned away by his brother and sister-in-law, he'd already decided a flirtation with Mademoiselle LaCrosse wouldn't hurt anyone. It wouldn't be the first time he'd taken a tumble with a maid, but pretty maids were a shilling a dozen, and he had more important things to worry about. Like how the hell he was going to explain his black eye to Tomlinson.

Cade dressed himself. He'd never understood how Rafe got used to a bloody valet. He couldn't imagine himself living with a picky little man hovering about, worrying about every wrinkle or (God forbid) bloodstain he got on his clothing. Though a valet would not be an affectation Cade ever acquired, he certainly admired his sister-in-law's lady's maid. Blast. There he went again, his mind drifting to Mademoiselle LaCrosse.

He'd been too damn long without a woman. That was all. He needed to get laid and he needed to get laid tonight. He'd stop by Madame Turlington's this evening after he met Rafe at the club.

He took the stairs two at a time, left the house, and walked halfway across Mayfair before hiring a hack to take him to a less respectable part of town. It had become his habit with Tomlinson to meet at the Curious Goat Inn. The tavern was out of the way enough that they weren't likely to see anyone they knew, but respectable enough to explain what they were doing there if they did come across a stray acquaintance.

The tavern never changed. In all the years Cade had been coming here (and he hadn't been here in more than ten), it remained the same dingy gray and brown interior, with the same worn wooden tables and chairs that had once been painted the reds and blues of the English flag but were now just faint, aging flecks on the nondescript wood. The patronage was usually more tired than rowdy and today was not unlike any other.

A buxom middle-aged waitress served him ale in a giant wooden mug. She leered at him and smiled a crooked smile. He wasn't that desperate. Not yet. A younger, slim barmaid walked past. He actually considered taking her up on her obvious offer, but decided Madame Turlington's would be less complicated. Barmaids tended to do things like remember you. And expect you to return. The last thing he needed on this particular trip to London was a complication. He'd made no promises to anyone and he fully intended to keep it that way.

He didn't have long to wait for Tomlinson. The man always hurried off the street as if he had a score of errands to run. He pushed open the door to the tavern, shut it behind him, and carefully doffed his hat. The man was shorter and older than Cade, with a wreath of graying hair and a cane he carried merely for affectation. The minute he looked up and recognized Cade sitting at a table near the back, he nodded and headed toward him.

"Eversby," he said in his upper-crust accent, nodding at Cade.

Like nearly everyone Cade associated with outside of Mayfair, Tomlinson didn't know Cade's real name. Tomlinson also didn't run in the same circles as his twin and therefore didn't know the Viscount Spy. Of course Cade suspected Tomlinson wasn't the real name of the man across from him, either. They were even.

"Tomlinson," Cade replied, nodding at the man, who quickly took a seat and was offered his own mug of ale by the slim barmaid. He ogled the woman for a moment before she flounced off.

Tomlinson spent a few moments propping his cane

against the wall, then he turned to face Cade. "I was going to punch you myself but it seems someone already got to it. What happened to your eye?"

"I was paid a visit by someone who is obviously not an admirer of mine." Cade grinned and the bruise ached. He touched it gingerly and winced.

"I see that," Tomlinson replied.

"Why were you going to punch me?" Cade ventured.

"Oh, I don't know. Perhaps because I thought you were *dead* for the last several years and you never lifted a finger to disabuse me of that notion until sending a letter yesterday asking me to meet you here."

Cade winced again but this time for an entirely different reason. "A lot of people thought I was dead."

"That doesn't make it right." Tomlinson thanked the barmaid who'd returned with his ale.

Cade tapped his foot against the dirty floor. "Look, I don't have much time."

Tomlinson pursed his lips. "Of course not. You never do. What are you looking for now?"

That's what Cade liked about Tomlinson, the man was always direct. Cade settled back into his chair and took a deep breath. "What do you know about the Black Fox?"

Tomlinson cracked a smile. "Isn't that a kick in the arse? I was about to ask you the same question."

Cade narrowed his eyes. "You don't know anything?"

"Not much." Tomlinson shrugged.

"You must know something," Cade prodded, his foot tapping again.

"The papers have the right of it. He has struck again," Tomlinson said, shaking his head.

"What else have you learned about him?" Cade asked.

"All too little, I'm afraid. The rumors are everywhere. He is French. He is English. He is Russian. He's a pirate. No one knows."

"He robbed *The French Secret* two nights ago," Cade prodded.

"Yes. Among other crimes."

"Why is *The French Secret* in London?"

Tomlinson took a swig of ale. "We don't know."

"But what are the rumors, Tomlinson? Come now, you *always* know the rumors." Nine times out of ten the rumors were exactly right.

Tomlinson sighed. "Very well. Rumor has it there's a group of English turncoats working with the French. They're in port to finalize their plans."

Cade's grin was wide. "And the Black Fox isn't making it easy for them?"

Tomlinson's eyes narrowed to dark slits. "Why are you so interested in the Black Fox?"

"That's my business." Cade sat back and took a long draught from his mug.

"Be that as it may, if you want to know what I know about the chap, you'd best tell me."

Cade rolled his eyes. "I'm trying to discern how much British Intelligence knows about him."

"And why would you want to know that?" Tomlinson's eyes were barely visible through the suspicious slits.

This time Cade shrugged. "Let's just say I have a vested interest in the matter."

"*You* wouldn't happen to be the Black Fox, would you?" Tomlinson met his gaze.

Cade was prepared for this question. He had perfected his card-playing face over many, many hands of cards with men who were a sight better at spotting lies than Ernest Tomlinson ever would be. Cade cleared his throat. "If I were, you couldn't possibly believe I'd tell you."

Tomlinson grinned, exposing crooked teeth. "Aye, that's a certain bet, there."

"What else have you heard?" Cade asked, his patience wearing thin.

Tomlinson took another long drink. "He's being hunted. But they can't find him."

Cade leaned forward. "They know nothing?"

"Not much. They're certain there was something he was after on the French ship but definitely not jewels as the papers would have you believe."

Cade nodded grimly. "They know nothing else?"

"Nothing I've been able to discern."

Cade stood, tossed some coins on the table, and turned for the door.

Tomlinson's voice stopped him. "Who do you think busted your eye, Eversby?"

"No way to tell, but if I don't mistake my guess, it was someone else who is looking for the Black Fox."

CHAPTER TEN

Danielle's skirts skimmed over the back staircase that led down to the kitchens. It was dinnertime for the servants. They ate early, before the rest of the house. She thought about Mr. Cavendish. *Cade*. He hadn't given her permission to call him Cade despite the fact that she'd ended up in his lap last night.

She considered what she knew about him. He was a twin. His brother was a viscount. Both his brother and sister-in-law seemed to expect the worst of him. Why? What had he done? Why was he living with them? For General Grimaldi to be keeping an eye on him, Cade must be up to something important. But what?

Grimaldi had asked her to leave a note under the flowerpot at the side of the mews each night letting him know if she'd learned of any appointments Mr. Cavendish kept. They were to be written in code, of course. The problem was, she had nothing to write so far. She hadn't learned much about him. She'd asked Trevor, the footman, a few innocuous questions and was only able to verify the man didn't have a valet, a fact she already knew. If she wanted to know more about him, the only alternative would be to ask the man himself.

She was sitting in the kitchens mending one of Lady Daphne's handkerchiefs. *Dieu merci* Aunt Madeline had taught her to sew.

She stuck the needle through the fine, soft cloth. What else did she know about Cade Cavendish? He thought nothing of getting foxed and bleeding on expensive rugs and bedding. He was a man who came home with a wound almost certainly caused by a blow to another person's face. Not that she was judging. She herself had had to participate in hand-to-hand combat upon occasion. Perhaps it was the nonchalant bleeding that seemed off. The man had surprised her. People rarely surprised her. Especially men.

She smiled to herself, remembering him saying she had the most enticing backside he'd ever seen. She wasn't about to tell him he had a fine-looking backside himself. The man was arrogant enough without her adding to his enormous opinion of himself. It had been foolish of her to assume he didn't understand French.

"Are you truly from France?" a small voice asked.

Danielle turned to see the housemaid, Mary, peeking at her from a corridor in the kitchens.

She turned toward the younger girl and smiled. "I used to live there. *Oui.*"

"How did ye get here? Ta London?" Mary asked, her hazel eyes inquisitive.

Danielle had learned not to answer too many personal questions. "How did you come to work here?" she asked instead.

The girl took a tentative step toward Danielle's seat. "Me mum's worked for the Earl of Swifdon for years and when Lady Daphne made her own household, why, she said she'd be sure ta hold a position for me."

Danielle smiled at that. "That was kind of Lady Daphne."

"Oh, yes. Me lady is one of the kindest, most generous people I've ever met."

"How long have you been in service to Lady Daphne?" Danielle studied her face. The girl couldn't be more than seventeen or eighteen.

"I only just began last month. Right after the wedding."

"The wedding?" Danielle blinked at her.

"Yes. My lord and my lady only just married last month." The maid dropped her voice to a whisper. "I ought not to say it but there's a rumor wot they were actually married last autumn."

"Last autumn?" Danielle blinked more. "If they were already married, why would they marry again?"

The maid glanced over her shoulder. Then she gestured for Danielle to follow her. Danielle stood and set the mending on the chair. They made their way down the corridor to a small antechamber just off the housekeeper's office. Wine bottles and kegs of beer sat stacked on tables in the corners. An assortment of spices and bags of sugar and salt sat propped upon shelves. Otherwise, the room was empty save for two wooden chairs and a small table. Mary sat on one of the chairs and motioned to Danielle to sit on the other. They were alone, even in the busy servants' wing.

"They ran off together, so the story goes," Mary said as soon as they were both seated.

Danielle leaned forward, fascinated.

"Lady Daphne was missing for near a week and on account of Lord Rafe being a spy and wot not."

"He's a spy?" Of course Danielle already knew that, but she couldn't allow Mary to realize it. How unfortunate it was for Lord Cavendish to have such a loose-lipped maid in his employ. But Danielle couldn't help but like Mary. She seemed like the friendly, helpful sort.

"Ah, I should not say any more." Mary blushed. "If Mrs. Huckleberry catches me gossiping . . ."

"She'll be angry?" Danielle prompted.

"Oh no, knowing Mrs. Huckleberry, she'd probably join right in on the conversation. I just would hate ta make her feel as if she should hafta scold me. On account of her being so very unhappy about havin' ta deliver scoldings."

Danielle pressed her lips together to keep from laughing. This was a strange group of servants indeed. Not that she'd been around a great many servants, but she expected the staff of a proper English lord to be refined and appropriate. Mary and Mrs. Huckleberry seemed anything but. However, the girl might prove valuable. "Tell me, what do you know about Mr. Cavendish, the viscount's brother?"

The girl's eyes widened. "Gor. He's a handsome one, ain't he? Why, I about fell off me seat when I saw him the first time and realized there were two of them."

Danielle nearly snorted at that. "I had nearly the same reaction myself. Tell me, Mary, has he ever . . . made any untoward advances on you?" She assumed the man had tried to charm every female servant in the house down to the scullery maid.

Mary shook her head. "Sadly, no. And it's a shame, fer if that man were ta make an untoward advance upon me I can't say I'd refuse."

Danielle had barely stopped laughing when Mrs. Huckleberry came bustling in. Danielle winced. Had the housekeeper heard that last part?

Mrs. Huckleberry was middle-aged and plump, with kind brown eyes and a round face. She tsked at Mary as soon as she saw her. Danielle jumped up from her seat, guilty for having been caught gossiping.

"Madame," Danielle said, nodding respectfully to the housekeeper. This woman was as likely to send her packing as Lady Daphne was when she discovered Danielle wasn't a proper lady's maid. She didn't need to add gossiping about Mr. Cavendish to her list of offenses.

"Oh, no need to stand," Mrs. Huckleberry replied. "I'm only in here searching for the extra sugar for Cook."

Mary hopped up, opened a cabinet, and pulled out a fat sack of sugar that she quickly handed to the housekeeper.

"Thank you, Mary." Mrs. Huckleberry turned toward the door, but paused when she saw Danielle's face. "My dear. Why do ye look like ye've seen a ghostie?"

"I just. I thought perhaps you might be angry with—"

Mrs. Huckleberry's dark eyes sparkled. "Aye. I heard. And I can't blame ye for mentioning how handsome his lordship and his brother are. Fine-looking men, they are, and I'm not too old yet ta notice." The housekeeper fluttered her eyelashes.

Danielle widened her eyes. "You're not angry with me?"

"Why would I be?"

"I thought, perhaps, because I'm French."

"You're not responsible for the wars, are ye, dear?"

"Certainly not."

"Lord Cavendish may not be the most admiring of the French, but you'll find he's good ta all of us."

"What happened to Lord Cavendish? With the French, I mean?" Danielle asked.

Mrs. Huckleberry hugged the sack of sugar to her middle. "He was beaten by them, he was. Something awful. Nearly died. Lost Lady Daphne's brother on that trip."

Danielle bit her lip. "I'm sorry to hear that . . ."

Mrs. Huckleberry shook her head. "It weren't Lord Cavendish what lost Lady Daphne's brother the earl, may he rest in peace. The truth is, Lord Cavendish did all he could to save the earl. It were a tragedy and nothing less."

Tears filled Mary's eyes. She pulled up her apron to dab at them.

"I'm certainly glad Lord Cavendish made it back safely," Danielle said, trying to turn the mood back to joviality.

"Yes," Mrs. Huckleberry replied. "It were a miracle that he made it back in one piece."

"And his brother?" Danielle prodded. "He's been visiting ever since?"

"Oh no," Mary blurted. "Just for the last several months."

"Yes," Mrs. Huckleberry said. "He and Lord Cavendish lived as bachelors here until the wedding. Then Lady Daphne joined them. Oh, but he's a fine-looking man. They both are, aren't they? But only one of them remains a bachelor." Mrs. Huckleberry wiggled her shoulders up and down.

Danielle pressed her lips together to keep from smiling. Mary couldn't suppress her smile, though, and soon they were both grinning.

"Now then, mademoiselle." Mrs. Huckleberry shifted the sugar to balance on her right hip. "Can I get ye anything, ye dear? A glass o' wine? A bit o' port ta fortify ye? It must be hard on ye, coming ta a new house and not knowing one o' the lot."

Danielle blinked. She'd always worked with men before. None of them were solicitous about her well-being. Certainly they weren't prone to offer her wine.

"No, thank you, Mrs. Huckleberry. I'm quite all right. I'll just be getting back to work." She stood and smoothed her skirts.

A knock on the door made all three women turn. Mr. Cavendish stood in the doorway. His broad-shouldered form filled the space and cast a shadow in the small room. Danielle gulped and took a step back.

"My apologies for interrupting," he said smoothly, bowing toward all three of them, "but I'd like to have a word with Danielle."

CHAPTER ELEVEN

"Why o' course ye can, sir." Mrs. Huckleberry gave a wide smile, grabbed Mary's hand, and hustled the girl from the room.

Danielle was alone with Cade Cavendish in the cellar room. She continued to smooth her skirts in an effort to feign nervousness. She glanced down at them. Her skirts were quite appallingly unwrinkled, but if he believed he was making her nervous, she would have the upper hand. "Can I help you, Mr. Cavendish?"

Cade's grin was roguish. "Apparently, you've sat on my lap. I was hoping you'd call me Cade."

Danielle hurried over to the door, pulled him inside all the way, and shut it so the others wouldn't overhear.

"I'm sorry," he said. "Did I say that too loudly?"

"Yes. You did." She stared at him.

"Does that mean you won't call me Cade?" The grin never left his face.

She crossed her arms over her chest and walked around him in a circle. "On the contrary. I'll call you Cade."

He arched a brow. "Not worried about your reputation?"

"Not particularly." How would she learn more about this man if she kept walls like names between them? Using his first name was nothing but a good idea. And he'd suggested it. Even better.

"Why did you come here?" she asked next, glancing down at her slippers to continue the ruse of nervousness.

"I live here. Well, I'm staying here at any rate." He swiped an errant piece of dust from the front of his light blue waistcoat.

"No." She couldn't help her smile. "Why did you come down *here*? To see me?"

"Because." Cade stepped past her and pulled a bottle of wine out of one of the crates stacked in the corner. "Good year. Why are you in the kitchens, by the by? In addition to arranging hair, do you also cook?"

She laughed at that. "I can't cook a thing. But you didn't answer my question. Why are you here?" The man seemed to get distracted easily. Noted.

"Because I owe you an apology." He turned back to face her, the bottle still in his hand.

"Did Lady Daphne send you?"

He threw back his head and laughed. "No. Contrary to what you might think, I'm not one to be ordered about by a woman. I'll leave that to my brother."

Trouble between the brothers? Also noted. And perhaps a slight unhappiness with women. Interesting.

"Don't care for your sister-in-law?" Danielle asked.

"I adore her. She's a wonderful little blue blood. I, however, don't care for domestication. Rafe's found it suits him."

Danielle unfolded her arms and leaned down and braced her palms on the tabletop, facing him. "What are you apologizing for, specifically?"

He lowered his voice. "Why, for insulting you, pulling you onto my lap, if that is indeed what happened, and for mentioning your backside. I meant it, of course, but I see now, in the light of day, the *sober* light of day, that it was indelicate of me to mention it."

She looked up at him through hooded eyes. She wanted to keep him off balance. Wanted him to wonder whether his apology was working. "What if I don't accept your apology?"

He studied the front of the wine bottle nonchalantly. "That would be a pity, because it's the only one you're likely to receive."

That made *her* laugh outright. "Not one for apologizing, are you?"

"So rarely I can't even tell you." He sighed.

"Then why begin now . . . with me?"

"Because you are gorgeous and I'm hoping you'll think better of me if we begin on a different foot. I'm also hoping you'll have a drink with me one night soon." He hefted the wine bottle in his hand.

Wait. What? She was gorgeous? When she dared to glance in the mirror, she saw a too-thin waif with dark smudges under her eyes, blue eyes that were far too large for her face, and a plethora of eyelashes that often made it difficult to convince anyone she was a lad. The man was either blind or a shameless flirt. Something told her it was the latter, but she wasn't about to let him see he'd flattered her. He was a bold one, telling her she was gorgeous and asking her to have a drink with him.

"A drink? Where?" She stood and crossed her arms over her chest, eyeing him down the length of her nose. She had a feeling things came too easily for this man when it came to the fairer sex and she wasn't about to make his apology or his request for a drink easy.

"Perhaps in the library? Rafe and Daphne go to bed hideously early. Newlyweds tend to." He leered at her.

She arched a brow at him for that cheeky remark.

"You don't seem to blush, mademoiselle."

"I've never seen the point in it."

He set the bottle on the table and braced his hands on the back of one of the chairs. "Why's that?"

She shrugged. "Perhaps because I'm French?"

"I don't think so." He was watching her carefully.

"Then why do you think?" she replied, doing her best to be nonchalant.

His eyes narrowed. "If I had to guess I'd say it's because you've seen too many things that would make you blush. You've grown inured."

Her gaze snapped to his. "Sir, are you questioning my morals?"

"Certainly not." He shook his head slowly.

"Good. Because I'll have you know, I'm not above slapping you if you get too far out of line." Cheeky was one thing. This man was hovering near the border of entirely inappropriate. She was even more disconcerted by the fact that she was . . . enjoying it. There was a third possibility. He could be blind, he could be a flirt, or he could be . . . testing her. If he was being watched by the likes of General Grimaldi, Cade might *know* he was being watched. Something told her he was no fool, and sparring with him was the most fun she'd had in an age.

"Sounds delightful." He grinned at her wolfishly. "So, will you?"

"Will I what? Slap you?" Oh, *mon dieu*. Was there anything this man wouldn't say? It reminded her a bit of . . . herself.

"No." He laughed. The corners of his eyes crinkled and his white teeth flashed. She found it entirely disarming.

"Have a drink with me?" he finished.

"You know that's completely improper. What if another one of the servants saw us?"

"Afraid they'd be jealous?" His eyes twinkled merrily.

"Afraid they'd tell Lady Daphne."

"Don't worry. I'll tell Daphne I made you do it."

"Why do I think that between her husband's brother and her new lady's maid, I would be the one tossed out if she thought something untoward was going on?"

"Who said anything untoward would be going on?" This time he studied his nails. More nonchalance. Why did she like that so much even while it was driving her mad?

She needed to be nonchalant, too. She made her way over to the corner and pretended to study the wine bottles. "You know as well as I that Society's rules are about perception, not reality."

"Fine. What if I promised you no one will ever find out, servant or master?"

"No." She tossed the word over her shoulder.

"No, because you don't accept my apology?" he asked.

"I accept your apology." She continued to fake-study the wine.

"Excellent," came his reply. "I'm ready to entertain yours now."

Her mouth nearly fell open. She was glad she wasn't facing him. Surprise and nonchalance were pure enemies. "Mine?" she managed finally.

"Yes."

She turned to see him clasp his arms behind his back and wait.

"My what?" She placed one fist on her hip.

"Your apology, of course." He leaned back against the wall and crossed his feet at the ankles.

"My apology to *you*?" Her fist remained primed on her hip. What could he possibly believe she owed *him* an apology for?

"Yes." He blinked at her slowly, a pleasant smile on his distracting lips.

"For what?"

"For calling me an ass. Though I'll admit it sounds much better when done in French." He tilted his head to the side. He was boyishly charming when he tilted his head to the side. Especially when paired with the appearance of that adorable dimple in his cheek. But she was still angry.

"I'm not about to apologize to you," she announced in as sweet a voice as she could muster.

"Why ever not?" He looked truly inquisitive.

"Because I'm not sorry. You *were* being an ass." Then

she cursed in a string of a French that caused him to put his hands in the air as if in surrender. He pushed himself off the wall and stepped toward her.

"Why do I have the feeling if I'd turned out to be Rafe last night you'd be apologizing now?"

Nonchalance be damned. This time her mouth truly did drop open. "If you'd turned out to be the viscount I wouldn't be here right now. I'd be looking for another position."

"That's heartening, I suppose. So, you'll accept impropriety from the brother of a lord but not the lord himself?"

She snapped her mouth shut. "I'll take it from a bachelor and a houseguest who had too much to drink but not from a married man who employs me."

"More heartening still. Very well, I suppose I shall be mollified by the fact that you accepted my apology at least. But why would you accept my apology and say no to my proposal to have a drink with me?"

This answer was simple. "Because I don't make it a habit to have drinks with strange men at inappropriate times." Of course she had every intention of having a drink with him. A drink would be the best way to ask him questions while his inhibitions were lowered. But she mustn't seem too *eager* to have a drink with him. This was the kind of man who wouldn't value a drink with a woman who agreed to it too readily.

"Who's strange?" Cade replied. "You've known me since *yesterday*. Besides, the best types of drinks are had at inappropriate times. Often with inappropriate people."

Danielle bit her lip but couldn't entirely hide her smile. She'd never met anyone like him. Not in England at least. He was inappropriate. He was incorrigible. And he was entirely too handsome for his own good. Or hers. "You make me laugh, Mr. Cavendish. I will admit that much."

"Excellent. I promise to make you laugh more when you and I drink this fine bottle of Madeira later this week." He stepped forward and plucked the bottle of wine back off the table.

"I'll *consider* it," she said, sweeping past him to step toward the door.

"Ah, we've gone from 'no' to 'I'll consider it.' Progress." He grinned at her.

Her fingers on the door handle, Danielle turned back to contemplate him. My, but he was a fine-looking man. Mrs. Huckleberry was right. "No is boring. I don't like to be boring."

With the wine bottle still in his hand, he bowed. "I assure you, mademoiselle, you are anything but."

CHAPTER TWELVE

Rafe Cavendish pulled off first one glove and then the other before tossing them upon the table in the reading salon at Brooks's. His friends, Derek Hunt, the Duke of Claringdon, and Julian Swift, the Earl of Swifdon, both gave him a once-over while he sighed and scrubbed a hand through his hair.

"Bad day, Cavendish?" Claringdon asked, gesturing to a footman to bring another brandy for his friend.

"Bloody awful day," Rafe replied. He pulled out the chair next to his friends and slumped into it.

"Why's that?" Swifdon, his brother-in-law, replied.

"Why do you think?" Rafe asked.

"Well, if history has any bearing on the matter, I'd guess it has something to do with your twin," Claringdon drawled.

"Precisely," Rafe replied with a tight smile. "How did you guess?"

"What's Cade done this time?" Swifdon asked.

"That's the problem," Rafe replied. "I have no idea."

"I'm not following." Claringdon settled his large frame into his seat.

"That makes two of us," Rafe replied. "Cade came home the other night foxed and with a black eye."

"Doesn't seem particularly out of character," Claringdon replied.

"No, but he left the theater not halfway through the first act and I got the impression he was meeting someone."

"Why did you think that?" Swifdon asked, his brow furrowed.

Rafe shrugged. "Kept checking his timepiece, that sort of thing."

"And?" Claringdon prompted.

"And the next time I saw him, he was three sheets to the wind and his eye was black and purple."

Swifdon shook his head. "He's always had a penchant for trouble."

"Not this kind of trouble." Rafe pulled a newspaper from his coat pocket and tossed it onto the table.

Swifdon unfolded it and spread it out in front of them. " 'The Black Fox Strikes Again!' Yes. I read this the other day. What does it have to do with your bro—?"

"You don't think?" Claringdon's eyebrows shot up.

"Yes, I do bloody well think," Rafe replied. "At least I suspect."

"Cade? Hasn't he been more into tavern-room brawls and keeping company with loose women"—Swifdon gestured to the paper—"than something like this?"

"He has been in the past," Rafe said. "But he's been

acting strange lately. Remember when he left us here last night?"

"Yes." Claringdon nodded. "He mentioned he was going to Madame Turlington's."

"Precisely," Rafe replied. "But when I got home after leaving you two, Cade was already there."

"At home?" Swifdon did a double-take.

"Yes. I noticed candlelight under the door to his room. When I knocked, he was in there blacking his boots."

"The chap needs a valet," Swifdon breathed.

"I asked him why he'd come home and he said he'd decided better of it."

"Decided better of going to a brothel? Cade?" Claringdon asked.

"Exactly," Rafe replied. "And think about it. The Black Fox has been in the papers again since Cade has been in town. He's been accused of half a dozen crimes in the last six months. The night after the chap was supposedly out on ship in the harbor stealing jewels from the French, my brother comes home with a black eye."

"Does seem like a string of coincidences? Don't it?" Swifdon said.

Rafe set his jaw. "I always knew Cade was up to more than just some innocent fun, but I had no idea he was into this much trouble. I mean, the fake names, the pretend death. He's probably wanted by the law in half a dozen other countries."

"If this is true . . ." Swifdon eyed Rafe carefully.

Rafe let out a deep breath and lowered his voice. "Gentlemen, I'm afraid my twin brother is the Black Fox. If it's true, I cannot keep it a secret. Not even for family."

CHAPTER THIRTEEN

Danielle darted behind the carriage wheels, her boots sucked into the mud. Trailing a person was never simple. It was much easier, however, when one dressed as a male. It had been sheer torture, these last few days, being trussed up in stays and forced to wear bonnets when she left the house. She was convinced the garment was waging a constant battle to strangle her.

She'd left the house ostensibly to run an errand. Then she'd hidden in an alleyway and changed as quickly as she could, stuffing the gown and other accoutrements behind a hedge. She could only hope the clothing remained where she left it. If not, she'd be forced to crawl back to Grimaldi and ask for new things. *That* would be awkward.

Now that she was wearing a flowy gray shirt, breeches, and boots, she felt better than she had all week. Pretending to be male had many advantages and one of them was the ease and comfort of breeches.

She hurried across the road and braced her back against the wall of a nearby shop, turning and tugging down the brim of her cap in an effort to disguise herself. She'd trailed a great many people in her day and if she didn't mistake her guess, Cade knew, or at least suspected, he was being followed. He stopped too often, glanced around too much. Either that or he was hoping to ensure he wasn't being followed and of course *that* was a fruitless hope.

Danielle had tracked him from Mayfair to a section of town she'd rarely been to before. It was a rookery. St. Giles. She was familiar with seedy parts of London, but the wharves were more her stomping grounds. The rookeries were unfamiliar territory and completely unsafe for a woman alone. Another advantage to dressing like a male. Still it was a good thing she knew how to take care of herself.

She followed Cade down one dark, dank alleyway after another in a zigzag pattern, one that clearly indicated he was suspicious. He was good. She'd allow him that. But she was better. She ducked into storefronts and hid in the shadows, while allowing him to maintain a sizable lead.

Where was he going? What was he doing? Was this why Grimaldi wanted her to watch him? To discover who he was meeting with and why?

Finally, Cade came to a stop in front of a questionable-looking tavern. The Bear's Paw. He ducked inside, doffing his hat. Danielle waited an interminable five minutes before ducking in herself. It didn't take her long to spy Cade in the back, sitting at a table with a swarthy-looking man. She sidled up as near as she dared and leaned back to listen. Good thing she had the hearing of a bat.

"*Bonjour, Monsieur Duhaime,*" the man said, greeting Cade. If she hadn't already seen him sit down, she might've checked to ensure she'd followed the right man. Why was this man calling him Duhaime? She slid onto a nearby stool.

"How do you do, Moreau?" Cade replied.

"I cannot complain," Moreau replied. "Care for a drink?"

"Do I ever refuse a drink?" Cade replied.

Moreau laughed and called to the barmaid who soon returned with two mugs of ale.

"Do you have it?" Cade asked after the barmaid slid the mug in front of him.

"*Oui,*" came Moreau's answer.

Danielle leaned closer. She waved the barmaid away from herself. There was some movement and rustling, but their coats hid whatever they were trading off. *Maudit.* She couldn't see.

"This is the original?" Cade asked.

"*Absolument.*"

Danielle pretended to be preoccupied with tying her boot.

"And the payment?" Moreau asked.

This time Danielle heard coins jingle. She surreptitiously glanced over her shoulder at the men, but couldn't see how much was being exchanged. They were stealthy, which meant they were up to no good.

"Have you heard anything about *le Renard Noir*?"

Danielle blinked rapidly, her heart pounded. The Black Fox? She leaned closer to hear the answer. The stool tipped, apparently one of its legs was shorter than the others. Danielle nearly toppled to the ground. She righted herself and slapped her hands on the table in front of her to keep steady. So. Poorly. Done. By the time she could pick up the thread of conversation again, it had drifted to pleasantries and bawdy jokes. *Maudit*. She'd missed whatever they'd said about the Black Fox. As they spoke, she took note of some of the other patrons and her environment. She didn't have long before the barmaid returned and demanded an order or made her leave.

It wasn't until many minutes later that she finally realized it. This entire time . . . Cade had been speaking in flawless, fluent French.

CHAPTER FOURTEEN

Cade hoped the boy who'd been following him got an earful. It was not particularly unusual to speak French, but he had no way of knowing whether the lad did. He didn't look like a particularly well-educated sort, but Cade had to be certain his conversation hadn't been overheard. There was one way to find out. Unfortunately, the boy had not removed his cap and Cade had yet to get a good look at his face. He'd been an excellent tracker. But Cade was an even better evader. He'd allowed the boy to follow him.

"Do you see that boy?" he asked Moreau in French. "The one with the blue cap behind you?"

Moreau glanced furtively back at the lad.

Cade winked at his friend, who quickly caught on to his ploy. The boy was doing a fair job of pretending as if he were simply another tavern patron.

"*Oui*," Moreau replied.

"He looks like a strong, healthy boy," Cade continued in French. "What say you and I press him into service?"

The side of the boy's cap tilted slightly, but otherwise, he remained rooted to the spot.

"Take him to the ships, you mean?" Moreau asked.

"Yes. No one here will care much if we drag him out kicking and screaming," Cade continued. "We might just make a bit of coin tonight." Another wink to his friend and Cade pushed back his chair with great aplomb, allowing the legs of the chair to drag dramatically across the wooden planks so the boy would hear.

By the time Cade stood and turned toward him, the boy had fled, silent as a wraith. Cade glanced around. The lad was nowhere to be seen. The front door was swinging as if it had recently been used. He ran to the door and out into the street. It was empty save for some urchins playing nearby, a mangy-looking dog, and a drunk, sleeping off his stupor on a nearby doorstep. Whoever the lad was, he was good. Better than Cade had thought. He'd had every intention of collaring him and taking him into the alley to garner some answers. No matter. Cade had discerned what he'd wanted to know. The lad, whoever he was, knew French. His tracker was no English urchin.

Danielle had to force herself not to run all the way back to Mayfair. Cade had been onto her. It wasn't unusual that he spoke French, of course. She already knew he understood the language. It was the *way* he spoke it that intrigued her. Intrigued her and surprised her. He spoke with the fluid ease of a native, something most Englishmen never accomplished. It was clear Cade had spent some time in her native country. Considerable time, if she didn't mistake her guess, and *that* was interesting indeed.

What was his story? The man wanted people to think he was the gadabout brother of a newly minted viscount, but there was more to him than that. She wanted to find out all of it. Such as what in the *nom de dieu* was he doing speaking with a Frenchman about the Black Fox? Grimaldi was right to be suspicious of him.

Cade had been aware that he was being followed and even worse, he'd known it was her (or the lad she'd pretended to be) and had said those things in French to let her know. He wasn't going to pull a boy out of a tavern and press him into the English Navy. She knew he'd been jesting, but she also couldn't risk him discovering her identity. She would be completely without an explanation had he discovered his sister-in-law's maid chasing him across town. Dressed as a lad!

Thank goodness her clothing was where she'd left it. She dressed quickly and with relative ease after a great deal of practice in her bedchamber last night. Now she knew for certain that Cade Cavendish had secrets she desperately wanted to discover.

CHAPTER FIFTEEN

Cade slid his key into the lock on the front door of Rafe's town house. He winced. The click echoed in the hallway and the rattle of the door sounded like a bloody racket in the stillness of the night. It was long past midnight and the place was dark and quiet. No doubt he'd wake the entire household.

He hadn't got far today. He'd been certain Moreau would have more information about what the French knew about the Black Fox. Absolutely nothing. He also hadn't been successful in locating the man who had sucker punched him. After leaving Moreau at the tavern, he'd gone to a few of his favorite haunts, keeping an eye out for the chap. The lad who'd followed him to the Bear's Paw today certainly wasn't the man who'd jumped him at the theater, but no doubt the boy worked for him.

Cade wasn't any closer to finding out who had been

after him, or why. He cursed himself for the hundredth time for hitting the scoundrel so hard he'd passed out. Blast it. He should have dragged the man into an alley and tried to revive him.

Cade stole across the darkened foyer. His hand was on the balustrade when a sultry female voice drifted toward him.

"Late night, no?"

Danielle. He smiled in the darkness before turning to face her. "Waiting up for me, eh?"

She strolled out of the shadows beneath the stairs. "I was helping myself to a nightcap."

He arched a brow. "Tsk. Tsk. Tsk. What would my brother say if he knew you were tipping back his port?"

She gave him a challenging stare. "Are you going to tell him?"

"Not if you share."

She was wearing the same white gown he'd seen her in yesterday but her hair was loose in a chignon, a few dark tendrils brushing her creamy shoulders. "What about the Madeira you promised me?"

"Funny you should mention it. I stashed it in the library. Care to join me?"

Her answer was to give him her arm. He put her hand on his sleeve and escorted her down the corridor and around the corner to the library. He opened the door quietly, pulled her through, and shut it. He led her over to the settee and saw her settled. Then he left to light a candle that sat on a nearby table. Next, he strolled over to a far bookshelf where he rummaged behind some books before producing the bottle of wine.

"You weren't jesting when you said you stashed it."

He grinned at her. "Couldn't risk some efficient maid finding it and putting it back in the kitchens. Mary, perhaps?"

From the sideboard he pulled out two wineglasses. Popping the cork off the bottle, he poured the dark red liquid before coming back to join Danielle on the settee. He handed her a glass.

She took a sip. "This is quite good."

"Better than the port?" he asked.

"I don't know. You came in before I had any of the port."

"If I didn't know any better, I'd wonder if you *had* been waiting up for me."

She laughed. "Don't flatter yourself, Mr. Cavendish."

He tipped his head to the side. "Half of my day would be in ruins if I stopped flattering myself."

"Why do I not doubt that?" She leaned back, took a long drink, and sighed.

"Long day?" he asked.

"Not any longer than any of the others," she said in voice that sounded weary.

"Why are you wearing those clothes?"

Cade glanced down at himself. He was wearing the same coarse woollen breeches, cheap burgundy waistcoat, and scuffed boots he'd had on all day. The clothes Monsieur Duhaime could afford. "What do you mean?" Better to play dumb than to explain himself.

"I don't know. You seem a bit . . . underdressed for a Mayfair drawing room."

He held up his glass to the firelight. "I prefer to find my amusements in parts of town outside of Mayfair."

Danielle raised her glass, too. "I can drink to that."

She took a sip. "What do you think your brother would say if he found us here?"

Cade pushed out his long legs and leaned his head back against the settee next to hers. She didn't admonish him for it. Progress. "Ah, no doubt there would be scolding and reprimands. Perhaps a lecture. Don't worry. It would all be on my head, not yours."

"And Lady Daphne?" Danielle asked.

He groaned. "She'd no doubt be embarrassed by her incorrigible brother-in-law's outlandish behavior."

"Incorrigible? Outlandish? Is that what you are?"

"You haven't learned that about me yet?"

"Oh, I knew. I just didn't realize that's how you would describe yourself."

He was impressed with her honesty. "I've never put much stock in pretending to be something I'm not."

"Such as?"

"Such as an honorable gentleman."

"You're not honorable?"

"I suppose I have some honor but it's not the kind that gets you a viscountcy. Called a paragon."

"Like your brother?"

"Exactly like my brother." He took another long sip.

Danielle turned to face him, propping her elbow against the back of the settee. Her other hand swirled the wine in her glass. "Why are you and your brother so different?"

Cade laid his head back against the settee and squeezed his eyes shut. "Ah, that is the question worth a hundred-thousand pounds."

"So much?"

He opened his eyes again and turned his head to face

her. "Yes. That and more. No one knows, my dear girl, but everyone asks."

"Do *you* know?" she asked, studying him with an intensity that made him uneasy.

He faced forward again, staring into the shadows beyond the candlelight. "Yes."

"What's the answer then?" came her soft voice.

He forced himself to relax his grip on his wineglass. It wouldn't do to crack the thing in his fist. More blood. A mess to clean up. And he'd already got this far with the beautiful maid. Only why was she asking him about his brother of all bloody topics? "It's . . . complicated."

She took another sip. "Complicated things make the best stories."

Cade scrubbed a hand through his hair. "Rafe and I . . . We didn't grow up like this." He flourished his hand in the air to indicate the room.

"A house like this, you mean?"

"A house like this. Mayfair. Servants. He didn't inherit the title, you know."

"Yes. Mary said something about it."

"Rafe joined the Navy when he was young and worked his way up. He worked hard, honestly, and fought for every single thing he has. He's earned every bit of it, viscountcy and all."

"And you?" She nodded toward him.

"Me?" He smiled a humorless half-smile. "I'm just the good-for-nothing brother, leeching off my twin's good fortune."

Cade had the distinct impression she could see through him, that she could tell he wasn't being honest with her. "*Est-ce vrai?*" she said so softly he almost didn't hear her.

"Yes, it's so." He stood, cleared his throat, and took her glass. Then he moved back to the sideboard to refill both glasses.

"Is that where you were tonight? Out leeching off your brother's good fortune?"

He hesitated, then turned to her with a grin. "Of course."

"And what does your brother think of you?"

"Our relationship is strained to say the least." Why had he just told her that? Why was he telling her any of this? He never discussed his business with anyone, not even his two closest friends. He made a point of it. Granted, no one ever asked but he never told, either.

"I always wished I had a sister," Danielle said. "It sounds foolish, but I used to pretend I was twins when I was a girl."

He wrinkled his brow. Pretended to be twins? She'd surprised him. Again. He found himself looking forward to the next words out of her mouth. That never happened with women he attempted to woo. "How did you do that?" he asked.

"In the looking glass," she replied. "It was ridiculous but also quite amusing. I cannot tell you how often I wished it wasn't just a game. I wanted a sister to play with, to talk to." She sighed. "And to have a sister who is the exact same age, who looks like me? Why, I can only imagine how close we'd be. I can't imagine how different my life might have been if I'd had someone else to rely on. Or someone else to worry about."

Cade snorted. "You have no idea how wrong you are."

"Wrong?" She shook her head.

Cade moved back over the settee to join her again. He handed her the refilled glass. "Careful what you wish for."

She took another sip. "Why do you say that?"

He lowered himself to sit, closer this time. She smelled like lavender. He leaned toward her, his mouth only inches from hers. "Can't we talk about something else? Like how perfectly gorgeous your mouth is."

Her face looked flushed, but he suspected it was from the wine. He remembered she didn't embarrass easily.

"Oh, no," she replied, scooting away from him. "You're not about to ply me with wine and try to kiss me."

"I'm not?" He blinked, for that was exactly what he'd been planning.

"No."

"Care to tell me why I'm not?" he asked, nonplussed. He was never nonplussed.

"Because that is far beneath your skill level."

"It is?" More blinking. He needed to stop blinking like an idiot.

"A master like you can think of a much better way to seduce a woman than to hand her a glass of wine and sit too close on a settee."

"I can?" He could?

"Do you doubt your own prowess?"

Cade scratched his head. In all of his years seducing women—he had lost count—he had never encountered one who had so subtly and completely turned the tables on him. Was he truly that obvious? It was time to change tactics. "Are you saying you don't *want* to kiss me?"

Her tinkling laughter followed. "Don't be petulant. It doesn't suit you."

Petulant? No one had *ever* called him petulant. "Very well, mademoiselle, why don't you tell me what you'd like?"

"I'd like for you to answer my question."

Question? Had she asked him a question? "Which was?"

"I told you I wanted a sister and you said, 'Careful what you wish for.' Then I asked why you said that."

Oh, that. Cade frowned. She still wanted to talk about *that*? Very well. He studied the liquid in his glass. "The truth is . . . my brother doesn't trust me."

"Have you given him reasons not to?"

This woman had a penchant for asking probing questions. It was as if she knew the exact thing to say to poke a hole through his armor. Cade thought about what Tomlinson had said, *"You wouldn't happen to be the Black Fox, would you?"* Cade knew Rafe suspected him. Had known it since the moment Rafe had seen the paper at the club the other day and turned his gaze on Cade with suspicion in his familiar blue eyes.

"Plenty of them," he whispered.

CHAPTER SIXTEEN

"Name one," Danielle whispered back. This was a dangerous game, asking Cade Cavendish for his secrets. Her stomach clenched. He wasn't about to reveal his without dragging out a few of hers. She would have to expose something to this man.

She had a job to do, she reminded herself. Grimaldi wanted to know why the self-proclaimed black sheep of his family was in London. Who was he meeting with, and why? That was the reason she'd been sent to this house, after all. Not to be mesmerized by the man's crystal-blue eyes and the scent of him, like wood smoke and soap. Nor the way he was tilting his head toward her and watching her lips. Nor the charming dimple in his cheek. *Mon dieu,* this wasn't helping.

"I've been gone for years," Cade replied in a deep, smooth voice. "Until I returned to London last year, my brother thought I was dead."

"Dead?" The word startled her. She sat up a bit straighter. "Why?" She took another sip of wine, trying to make sense of this latest revelation.

Cade reached out and traced the line of her décolletage against her skin with the tip of one finger. "Let's just say in my line of work, I'm sometimes better off dead."

"What in the world does that mean?" But her words came out a bit rushed and slurred, given the distraction of his finger tracing her neckline.

"I haven't always been . . . on the right side of the law," he finished, his finger tracing up the vein in her neck to her ear. She closed her eyes. The man knew where to touch a woman. She had never imagined that a simple stroke of her earlobe could feel so . . . good.

"What have you done?" she whispered.

"Ah, ah, ah, I'm not about to spill all my secrets, mademoiselle. Not without a bit of . . . impetus."

"What sort of impetus?" Her words came out in a breathy rush.

He leaned forward to set his wineglass on the table behind her head. "I could ask for a kiss, but you were right about me," he whispered back, his mouth mere inches from hers.

"How? When?" His gaze was mesmerizing her.

"When you said I wasn't about to ply you with wine and try to kiss you."

"You're not?" Oh, *why* did the news disappoint her?

"No. I'm not the type to *try*. I prefer action." He pulled her into his arms, his mouth hovering just above hers.

Danielle's wineglass nearly toppled out of her hand, but Cade managed to grab it and place it on the table, too. He was going to kiss her, wasn't he? Why didn't he? She wanted to sob.

"When I kiss you," he drawled, his breath hot on her lips. "You'll welcome it and wine won't be involved." He pushed himself away from her and moved back against the settee, a smug look on his face.

He could tell she was disappointed. She knew he could tell. It was sitting there, obvious, in the pompous smile on his handsome face. She did her best to right her skirts and appear completely unaffected but oh, how she had wanted his kiss.

"Why did you come back? Why are you here?" she asked in an effort to distract herself.

"Miss LaCrosse, you're going to have to do a lot more than almost kiss me to get me to answer *that*." He stood, winked at her wickedly, and exited the room.

One hour later, Danielle slipped into bed still replaying her conversation with Cade in the library. The man had many secrets. And that was coming from a woman who had many secrets. He seemed discomfited by the fact that his brother was a viscount. While he apparently enjoyed the fine things his brother's new life had to offer, something about it didn't sit well with him.

That near-kiss had been enough to scorch off her stockings. The most shocking part was that when he'd told her she'd have to do more than kiss him to get him to answer her other questions, her first thought had been to ask what. And then to do it. The man was tempting. It would be a pleasure to trade kisses for secrets. In fact, they might make a game of it. Ooh la la.

She suspected he'd left, however, because she'd asked

questions that made him uncomfortable. She had to be less forthright in the future.

A knock sounded at the door, interrupting her thoughts. Quiet. Soft. At first she was certain she'd imagined it. She sat up and listened. It came again a moment later, followed by Mary's voice floating through the wood. "Mademoiselle?"

Danielle lit the candle on the bedside table, tossed aside the quilt, and hurried to the door. Mary stood in the corridor in her night rail, a dressing gown wrapped over her thin shoulders.

"Mary? Is everything all right?"

Mary nodded. "Yes. Yes. I just thought we might . . ." The girl looked a bit sheepish. She pressed one bare foot atop the other and squeezed her hands together tightly. "Talk for a bit."

Danielle blinked. "Talk?"

"Yes." Mary's freckled face looked hopeful.

"Oh, well, of course," Danielle replied, remembering her manners. The ones her mother had tried to instill in her before her whole world changed.

"Come in." Danielle stepped back to allow the younger woman to enter.

"Gor," Mary exclaimed as she made her way over to the window and sat in the cushioned chair nearby. "Ye have yer own chair and wardrobe. And a dressing table? And a desk!"

"Yes. Don't you?"

Mary shook her head. "No. I room down the hall with Molly and all's we got is two beds and a few pegs fer our gowns."

"Oh," Danielle replied, not certain what else to say.

"Housemaids don't get their own fancy rooms with desk and chair," Mary continued. "I guess it don't matter none. What would me and Molly do with a fine desk like that? It's not like we can write." Mary snorted.

Danielle shut the door carefully and took a seat on the edge of the mattress facing Mary. "You can't write?"

Mary shook her head again. "Not at all." She scratched her nose. "Well, I surely can write me name, but that's all."

Danielle couldn't imagine not being able to write. Her father had taught her, her lovely French father. He'd been a professor of English and had met her beautiful mama during his extensive travels in England in his youth. Mama had run off with him, scandalized her family, caused an outrageous uproar—or so her aunt Madeline had once told her. They'd gone to France and lived until Papa was killed, Mama was imprisoned, and Danielle had been cast out on the streets.

She'd tried to find Aunt Madeline, but her aunt had been traveling. Her mama, she learned, had been sent back to England, a prisoner, for the murder of her husband. She'd been traded for a French prisoner. Danielle needed to get to London to plead with the judge. She'd seen the man who had killed her father, and she'd learned his name years later. Lafayette Baptiste. She'd spent her life hunting the man. She knew he was a sailor, the captain of a ship. She'd traced him to the docks, located his ship, and followed him. She'd tracked him, trailed him, knew all his secrets.

Then Grimaldi had found her, offered her another life in exchange for keeping her from gaol on the charge of smuggling. She was no fool. She'd taken his offer.

Grimaldi had offered her training, skills, a respectable position, and most importantly, he'd promised to find and help her mother.

And he had. Grimaldi was a man of his word. A man of honor. A man, perhaps the only man living, whom she could trust. A vision of Cade Cavendish flashed through her mind. No, she couldn't trust Cade. He saw her only as a pretty face. Another in a long string of women to seduce. Though he had answered her questions. And she suspected she'd flustered him.

"Mademoiselle?" Mary murmured, snapping Danielle out of her thoughts.

Danielle smiled at the girl. "You must call me Danielle."

Mary's grin widened, a charming gap-toothed smile. "Well, thank ye, madam—I mean, Danielle. Thank ye, kindly."

"No need to thank me, Mary. Now tell me, what did you wish to talk about?"

Mary blushed a beautiful rose color that highlighted the fine freckles on her cheeks.

"Tell me." Danielle tucked her feet beneath her and leaned toward Mary, even more eager to hear the subject that had made the girl blush so adorably.

Mary clasped her hands together and took a deep breath. "Oh, Danielle, ye're so poised and yer hair is so well done and ye're so lovely and—"

Danielle would have blushed if she was a blusher. "That's quite kind of you, but I hardly think that I—"

"Don't deny it. I've seen how the footmen look at ye and how Mr. Cavendish looks at ye and—"

"Oh, no, no, no. Surely you're mistaken." But then,

"Mr. Cavendish looks at me?" *Mon dieu,* she couldn't keep herself from asking.

"Like he can't take his eyes off o' ye." Mary sighed, a dreamlike expression on her face.

Danielle blinked. Could that amazing news possibly be true? "Oh, but I—"

"Ye're so kind, well-spoken, and have such gracious manners and . . ."

A lump formed in Danielle's throat. She'd never been told any of these things. Kind? It certainly wasn't something she aspired to. Treating people well was second nature. Who would be mean for mean's sake? Besides, was it kind of her to be lying to these good people about being a lady's maid while spying on her employer's brother?

Well-spoken? Perhaps. If that were true, it was thanks to the education at her parents' knees. Papa had taught her flawless French and Mama had taught her the perfect English-cultured tones. She'd taught herself the less refined accents of both languages.

As for gracious manners, she had her mother to thank. She supposed she had Aunt Madeline to thank for showing her how to arrange hair and how to toss on clothing that was fashionable, though she'd had precious little time for fashion and loveliness. And of course she'd undertaken a fortnight of training at the hands of one of London's most popular lady's maids. This position in Lady Daphne's household felt like a whole new world to her, one that, to her surprise, she was quite enjoying. Nevertheless it was kind of Mary to pay her such lovely compliments.

"Ye're just so . . . perfect," Mary continued.

Danielle waved her hands in front of her to stop the girl from saying more. "Now wait a moment. I'm far from perfect . . ." Danielle chuckled. If only Mary knew how imperfect she was. Guilt tugged at her. She bit her lip.

"You seem quite perfect ta me," Mary insisted. "I wanted ta ask if ye would perhaps . . . see fit ta . . ." The girl's blush returned. She seemed hesitant to continue.

"Yes?" Danielle prompted, nodding to encourage her.

"See fit ta give me some guidance," Mary finally blurted.

Danielle sat back, a hand to her chest. "Guidance?"

Mary smoothed her skirts. "Yes. Ye see, there's a boy I fancy and—"

Danielle lifted her brows. "A boy?" A smile spread across her face.

Mary giggled and nodded.

Danielle pushed her shoulder against Mary's thin one. "Anyone I know?"

Mary's blush deepened. "It's . . . Trevor."

Danielle blinked. "Trevor? The footman?"

Mary wrung her hands and nodded.

"You fancy Trevor?" Danielle clarified.

"He's so tall and handsome and he's been so sweet ta me." Mary sighed again, a starry look in her eyes.

Danielle considered the lanky footman. He was well over six feet tall, had a shock of white-blond hair, pale blue eyes, and as many freckles as Mary. It was utterly adorable that the maid should fancy him.

"What sort of advice are you looking for?" Danielle

couldn't imagine what she might be able to offer. When it came to someone fancying someone else, she'd had too little experience in that quarter herself.

"I thought ye might be able ta help me with me hair," Mary squeaked.

Danielle breathed a sigh of relief. "That is no problem whatsoever. I'd be happy to. Your hair is lovely, you know."

The girl self-consciously touched the braid wrapped around her head. "I . . . I noticed you had a . . . a vial o' perfume." She nodded toward the dressing table.

Danielle's gaze fell on the vial, too. Her French *grandmere* had given it to her. Lavender. "I could help you with your hair and I am certainly happy to share a bit of my perfume but—"

"Oh, no." Mary shook her head and turned pale. "I should never be so bold as ta ask ye for *yer* perfume. I was hoping ye would go with me ta choose some fer meself. I've been saving me wages and finally have enough ta purchase a small amount. I want some perfume that will drive Trevor mad with longing."

"Mad?" Danielle watched the girl's face. She was perfectly serious.

"Yes. Mrs. Huckleberry says perfume has been known ta drive men mad. Especially *French* perfume."

Danielle contemplated that for a moment. It sounded like something the cheeky housekeeper might say. A Frenchwoman was rarely without her perfume. The English must have decided it was the secret to attracting a man's attention. At least this English girl had. "I can help you with your hair and perhaps the perfume, but why do you think I would know much about . . . men?"

"Have ye never fancied a boy before?"

A boy? A vision flashed through her mind, one she hadn't contemplated in nearly a decade. A vision of a boy and a night and an uncomfortable act she didn't enjoy, fumbling hands and sweat and grunting. She shuddered. "I can't say I have."

"Don't ye fancy Mr. Cavendish?"

A vision of Cade Cavendish's enticing visage replaced the bad memory. "Ah, but Mr. Cavendish is no boy. He's all man." As soon as the words left her mouth, Danielle regretted them. She cleared her throat. "That is to say . . . I mean . . ."

"Ye don't have ta explain yerself." Mary nodded sagely. "I *quite* agree."

"But I don't know that I'd say I *fancy* him," Danielle rushed to add.

"He surely is handsome," Mary pointed out.

"Yes, he is that," Danielle agreed.

"And he has a fine body," Mary continued, hugging herself.

"It's true." Danielle couldn't argue that point.

"And he is ever so charming if ye ask me."

"Charming is an apt word," Danielle agreed.

Mary put her small hand on Danielle's and Danielle allowed it to stay.

"I've never been good at maths, mademoiselle," Mary said. "But I say when ye add up all o' them things, ye've got one fine specimen o' a man and one wot is quite worthy o' being fancied."

A small spattering of laugher spilled from Danielle's lips. *Mon dieu*. Was that? It couldn't be. A giggle? A giggle? When in her *entire* life had she ever giggled?

"You make a fine point, Mary. I cannot disagree with you."

Mary grinned and elbowed her and the two giggled again. It was an oddly comforting, sharing secrets with Mary.

"I'm happy to help," Danielle said, awkwardly patting Mary's hand.

Mary grabbed her hand and squeezed it. "Oh, Danielle, thank ye so much. I'm ever so glad we're friends."

Friends? The word rang in Danielle's head. "Friends?" She echoed without thinking about it.

A frown marred Mary's brow. "We are friends, ain't we?"

Danielle thought about it. Is this what it was like, having a friend? Was this sense of fun and belonging, talking and sharing secrets, what being a friend meant? She'd never had a friend before. She'd been born an only child, was never schooled with other children her own age, and then she'd gone to work on ships and pretended to be a boy. She couldn't make a friend during those years. She hadn't been able to share her secret with anyone. Well, unless you counted Robert, and he had left her soon after the one awful night they'd spent together.

"Yes," she replied, a wide smile spreading across her face. "Yes, Mary, we're friends."

"I'm so glad." Mary stood and moved toward the door. "And just think . . . after ye help me win Trevor, perhaps I can help ye win Mr. Cavendish."

CHAPTER SEVENTEEN

Danielle spent the next several days in a flurry of activity. In the mornings she served Lady Daphne her breakfast. Then she helped Mary and Molly with their reading. After that, she helped Lady Daphne dress and arranged her hair for her afternoon calls. Later, she prepared Lady Daphne's clothing and jewels for the endless rounds of balls, or the opera, or dinner parties. While Lady Daphne was out, if Mary wasn't busy with chores, Danielle taught the girl how to do her hair and answered her many questions about France. Danielle's days fell into a comfortable routine.

Much to her surprise, she found that in just a few days' time, she had grown fond of both Mary and Mrs. Huckleberry. Mary asked her about her day, saved her bits of cake if she wasn't present when it was served, and answered any questions she had about the household. If Mary didn't know the answer, then Mrs. Huckleberry did. The housekeeper proved a ready and willing ally. The two were friendlier than anyone Danielle had ever known. *Friendly and trusting.* A knot tightened in Danielle's chest each time she thought about it.

The other surprising thing was how much she enjoyed spending time in Lady Daphne's company. Danielle had assumed before she'd arrived that Lady Daphne would be a spoiled, pampered, demanding aristocrat who cared about nothing more than her clothing and hair. Danielle's mother had told stories of the kinds of ladies she'd grown up around. The infamous ladies of the *ton*.

Lady Daphne turned out to be the opposite. The viscountess spent many of her days helping at an orphanage. She cared little for social gatherings and seemed to attend such events only as obligations. She preferred visiting with friends and family, wanted to spend as little time as possible seeing to her hair and clothing, and was interested in the lives of her servants. She was kind and friendly and lovely, just as Mary said.

Danielle found that she, Mary, Mrs. Huckleberry, and Lady Daphne could talk and laugh much like . . . *friends*. The word still felt foreign to Danielle, but she embraced it more each day. But always, niggling in the back of her mind, was the fact that someday soon she'd have to leave these people and this life. Would they learn she'd been a fake? Would they hate her for it?

To her chagrin, Danielle didn't see Cade at all. She'd left off attempting to follow him after the first debacle. Instead, she turned her attention to eavesdropping. But the man stayed out until all hours, slept until afternoon, ate, dressed, and left. There wasn't much to eavesdrop upon and Danielle grew more frustrated by the day.

In addition to her busy days, at night, after Lady Daphne and Lord Cavendish went out to Society events, Danielle visited her mother. It was during those quiet moments, after her mother had fallen asleep and she listened to her labored breathing, that Danielle had a chance to contemplate her encounter with Cade. She'd been surprised at their conversation in the library. He'd seemed open and honest with her until he'd shut down and stopped answering questions. His charming veneer had returned and he'd done nothing but offer her more wine and tease her.

Why hadn't he kissed her? She honestly couldn't say that she wouldn't have allowed it had he tried. The man could tempt a saint. But when she wasn't drinking wine and wasn't in a romantically lit room with a handsome man, she realized it had been for the better. She suspected he relished his reputation as a rogue more than he actually deserved it. Or perhaps he had merely thought better of himself because he was in his brother's house and seducing one of the maids would be considered bad form. He'd mentioned that he and his brother hadn't been raised in Mayfair. Where had they been raised? Surely not too far away or his brother wouldn't be a viscount now. Some sort of gentry perhaps? Lady Daphne and Lord Rafe both seemed perfectly civilized and proper like the other members of the *ton* she'd met, but Cade, Cade seemed different. He didn't have a valet. Didn't seem to have a profession. He wanted her to think he was living off his brother. But why? Or was he living off his brother? That would certainly explain why the man might possibly turn to crime. Was he feeding secrets about his brother to someone, or group of someones, who wanted to hurt Rafe? Was that possible?

"There ye are." Mary's voice came floating down the servant's corridor.

Danielle turned to see Mary and Mrs. Huckleberry bustling toward her.

"We're off ta bed soon," Mrs. Huckleberry announced. "Care ta walk up with us?"

"I'd love it," Danielle replied. She needed to retrieve her shawl and reticule from her bedchamber before she hired a hack to go to her mother's.

The three of them made their way along the corridor toward the servants' staircase at the back of the kitchens.

"What's wrong, me dear? Why da ye seem so . . . well, sad, if you don't mind me askin'?" Mrs. Huckleberry held the candle high so they could navigate the steep, narrow stairs.

Danielle's chest felt heavy, as if Cook's iron cauldron were sitting on it. And *mon dieu,* were those . . . tears? She'd never had anyone ask her such a question before. Never had anyone else care or be so friendly or helpful or . . . nice. Not since she'd been on her own. Mother had cared once. Before she got sick. Now all she could do was care for her mother.

She took a deep breath. "It's my mother. She's sick." Now why had she gone and done that? Before she'd come here, she'd never told anyone about her mother.

Mary gasped and tears filled her eyes, too. She put her small pale hand on Danielle's shoulder. Danielle allowed it. It felt unexpectedly good to be touched, to be comforted. She didn't realize how much she'd been missing it.

"What's wrong with her, me dear?" Mrs. Huckleberry pulled Danielle down to sit next to her on the stair.

"Consumption." Danielle wiped away tears with the handkerchief Mary pressed into her hand.

"Oh, no." Mrs. Huckleberry shook her head.

"It's where I go to, at night, when I sneak away."

"I wasn't going ta say anything, me dear," Mrs. Huckleberry said.

"I know you weren't, and that's why I'm telling you. Thank you for understanding."

"We all have our problems in this life, me dear, and there's no sense in judging others fer how they handle theirs."

"Is there nothing we can do?" Mary's hazel eyes searched Danielle's face.

"Not much, I'm afraid," Danielle replied.

"There's always something, however small. You stay here." Mrs. Huckleberry hefted herself up and hurried back down the stairs.

Mary took Mrs. Huckleberry's seat and squeezed Danielle's hand again. "I'm sorry about yer mum, Danielle."

"It's all right. Thank you for listening to me."

"Me mum always says if ye want ta feel better, turn yer sights to some other topic."

"It's good advice." Danielle managed a smile for the maid. "What shall we talk about?"

Mary turned to Danielle with a gamine grin. "I'm glad Mrs. Huck is gone fer the moment. I've been meaning ta ask ye about yer drink with Mr. Cavendish the other night."

Danielle gasped. "You know about that?"

"With all me talk about Trevor I completely forgot ta ask about it when I came ta yer bedchamber. Don't worry. Mrs. Huckleberry has me see ta the fires in the big rooms in the middle of the night. I'm the only one up, I swear. I heard ye two talking in the library and sneaked away. I promise I didn't eavesdrop."

Danielle laughed. "It's all right. I believe you. If you had eavesdropped, you would have known that we had some wine and he told me about himself and his brother."

Mary's eyebrows shot up. "Wine? Do ye think he was trying ta get ye foxed ta have his way with ye?"

"Mary Hartfield, think what you're saying." Danielle couldn't help but laugh at the girl's obvious enjoyment of it though.

"Gor, I'd like that man ta get me foxed and have his way with me," Mary said, still grinning.

Danielle shook her head. "He did say a few cheeky things."

"He could be as cheeky as he pleased with me. Did he try ta steal a kiss?"

I wish. "I'll leave that to your imagination."

"Oy, I don't know if ye should do that. My imagination is cheeky, too." The maid paused for a moment. "Ye didn't get foxed?"

"I'm afraid not. I'd have to drink a sight more than two glasses of wine to get foxed."

Mary's face scrunched up. "What da ye mean?" Then she gasped. "Ye've been drunk afore, mademoiselle?"

Danielle laughed again. "Yes, lots of times, I'm afraid." With smugglers, drunkenness was a way of life.

"I suppose the French are more free with the wine than we are."

"Oh, I've found that both countries love wine and spirits equally."

Mary leaned forward and braced her hands on her knees. "What does it feel like ta get foxed?"

Danielle tilted her head to the side and contemplated that. "It feels like you haven't got a care in the world. And everything is funny."

"Funny?"

"For me it's funny. I've known other people who drink to excess and are angry or sad or just sleepy."

Mary blinked at her. "Ye mean it's different for everyone?"

"I think it can be. My father used to say a drunken man says a sober man's thoughts."

"Oy, that's mighty interestin', mademoiselle."

"It is, isn't it?"

"What did ye mean when ye said it would take more than two glasses of wine? How much does it take ta get foxed?"

"That also depends," Danielle replied.

"On what?"

"On how accustomed to drinking you are. I used to drink quite a lot with the sorts of people who drink quite a lot." And she'd had to learn quickly how to handle spirits to keep her identity secret.

"Who did ye drink with?"

"That's a story for another time, but suffice it to say I learned how to handle my liquor and now, it's not possible for two glasses of wine to get me foxed."

"I want ta get Trevor foxed and ask him if he fancies me." Mary giggled. "If I get him foxed will he tell me what he really thinks?"

Danielle laughed. "There's only one way to find out."

There was no time to discuss *that* plan before Mrs. Huckleberry came huffing back up the stairs. "I've put on a pot o' me garlic soup fer ye ta bring with ye ta yer mum's tonight."

Danielle started. "You didn't have to—"

"I've been told it helps with the cough and the tight chest." A kind smile wrinkled the housekeeper's face.

"Oh, yes," Mary said, nodding emphatically. "Mrs. Huck's garlic soup is legendary. It's sure ta make yer mum feel better."

"I'll send Trevor with ye ta carry it," Mrs. Huckleberry added.

"That's far too kind of you." Danielle's chest still felt tight. She twined her fingers together and stared down at her slippers. She'd never felt more guilty for deceiving these nice women. "I . . . I don't understand why you're helping me." She dared a glance up.

Mary's nose scrunched up and she gave Danielle the cutest little grin. "Oh, Mademoiselle Danielle, ye've never had friends afore, have ye?"

There was that word again. *Friends.* It hung in the air like a cloud of coal dust. No. She had never had friends before. This was what it felt like. To have people to talk to. People to ask questions of. People willing to make your sick *mere* garlic soup.

What sort of a friend was she? One who was lying to them? Deceiving them? A friend who would have to leave one day without so much as telling them where she'd gone or why? She was a horrible friend, which was exactly why she'd never had any. She didn't deserve one, let alone these two.

"I don't know what to say," Danielle murmured.

"There's nothing ta say, me dear, except . . . thank ye," Mrs. Huckleberry replied.

Thank you. Those, too, weren't words she'd used often. She'd never had anyone to thank but herself. No one aside from Grimaldi had done anything for her, but he didn't require thanks. She'd worked to pay him back. She hadn't asked anyone for help and they hadn't offered, which was exactly the way she liked it. No commitments. No obligations. Long ago, two people she trusted had betrayed her, but something told her Mary and Mrs. Huckleberry never would.

"Thank you for the soup," she whispered, standing so the three could continue their walk upstairs.

"It's me pleasure," Mrs. Huckleberry replied. "Now, hurry home tonight after yer visit, ye hear? Ye'll need ta get some sleep. Tomorrow's ta be a busy day."

"Yes, tomorrow's going ta be especially busy," Mary echoed.

Danielle paused. "Why? What's happening tomorrow?"

"Didn't Lady Daphne tell ye?" Mrs. Huckleberry asked. "She's planning a ball."

CHAPTER EIGHTEEN

Danielle had paid Nigel, the footman, to ensure the back door near the servants' staircase was left open. Having told Trevor he didn't need to wait after assisting her with the soup, she'd spent the entire evening reading to her mother. Mama had enjoyed the soup. It made her feel better. Danielle had stayed longer, reading to her until after midnight.

Back at Lord Cavendish's property, she flew across the alleyway like a wraith, up the back stoop, and slipped silently through the unlocked door. She was about to place her foot on the first step of the servants' staircase when a deep voice sounded from the shadows.

"Late night, eh?"

Instinct took over. She whipped a knife from her walking boot, spun around, and braced her arm against the throat of the man standing in the darkness not a pace away from her.

"I can honestly say I've never in my life been more aroused than I am at this moment."

Several seconds passed before Danielle managed to calm her pounding heart. Cade. Of course. Who else would it be?

"What are you doing here?" she demanded.

"I'd like to ask you the same question. The other night you were merely getting a nightcap. Now you're pulling knives? You're an anxious one, aren't you?" Cade drawled.

"*Je suis desole.*" She pulled her arm away from him, stepped back, and slipped the knife back into her boot.

"Don't apologize. I thoroughly enjoyed it."

"Did you?" She crossed her arms over her chest. She could see his smile in a beam of moonlight that shone through the window behind her.

"I don't know many lady's maids who are so—ahem—proficient with a knife. I clearly need to get out more."

"How many lady's maids do you know?"

"Enough."

"Perhaps you don't know them *well* enough. A female has to be able to defend herself on the streets of London. Especially at night."

"Which begs the next question. What were you doing out on the streets at this hour?"

Danielle sighed. "It's a long story."

"I have time." He pressed a shoulder against the wall and crossed his booted feet at the ankles.

She tilted her head. "What if I'd rather not tell it?"

"I'd respect that, but I'd ask if I could ask a different question."

"Which is?" She pressed her hands behind her and leaned back against the door.

"Where did you learn to handle a knife like that?"

A half-smile touched her lips. "Seems we both have our secrets."

"Secrets?"

"Where have you been tonight?" she asked.

"Ah, well, if you're going to pry into my secrets, at least come to the library and have another drink."

Ten minutes later, Danielle sat curled on the settee in the library across from Cade, who sat in a large leather chair. She swirled the liquid in the glass and stared into it.

"So," he began. "How about if I promise to tell you where I was this evening if you tell me where you were?"

Did she dare tell him the truth? What if he asked questions about her mother? She'd never told anyone about her mother's past. No one had ever asked. Cade was asking now. "Very well, you go first."

Cade lifted his glass in a toast. "How did I know you were going to say that?"

"A *tres* lucky guess?"

"I was out having drinks with friends," he said.

"That's vague. Where? With whom?"

"I doubt you'd know them, sweetheart."

"That's probably true, but you could at least tell me where."

"The Curious Goat Inn."

"A favorite haunt of yours?"

"I suppose you could say that. Enough stalling, where do you go?"

"I went to visit my mother." Even as the words left her mouth, she was surprised she'd said them.

"Your mother?" He seemed surprised as well.

"Yes, she's . . . unwell."

"What's wrong with her?"

"She has . . . consumption. She's not expected to live more than a year." Saying it aloud felt freeing. Danielle had lived with this fact every day, but allowing herself to speak it felt unexpectedly comforting.

She glanced at Cade. The man was handsome, but there was something more to him. Some bit of . . . dare she think it, *sensitivity* that made him easy to talk to. He was charming, yes, but it was more than that. He was also . . . friendly to her. Kind. Yes, that was it. Kind. It was unexpected. The truth was that she was falling for his charm a little. She was attracted to him, liked talking to him. But she couldn't allow herself to get too close. Cade might seem nice but he was also a job. Not to mention he might be a spy for the French along with the sin of stabbing his brother in the back. She didn't know for certain.

All she did know was that he was the key to finally getting her mother to the cottage by the sea she'd been saving most of her life for. If she finished this last mission, Grimaldi had promised she would finally be free for as much time as she needed to see to her mother. He'd personally give her the money she needed.

Everything was at stake here. Her mother's final days and her reaching her personal dream. She'd never had friends, never needed them, but she shouldn't confuse friendship with work. This was a job and she'd do well to remember that. Friends weren't real. Friends didn't matter. They'd reject her when they learned of her duplicity in the house. Only family was real. Only family mattered.

"How often do you visit her?" He pulled her back to their conversation.

"Every night. I try to take the burden off her nurse." Danielle sipped the wine he'd given her.

"As well as your father?"

"My father is dead." The last word stuck in her throat like hardtack.

"I'm sorry." His words were steady, even. Without a hint of pity. She appreciated that.

"So am I," she said.

"You loved your father then?"

"Very much." Odd that he'd asked that. Didn't everyone love their parents?

"How long ago did he die?" Cade asked.

"I was a child." Her heart was being squeezed. She shouldn't have told him. "It's late. I should go to bed."

"I'm sorry, Danielle. Don't go."

The words were uttered with such simple, unabashed honesty. She couldn't look at him.

"It's not that. I have a busy day tomorrow."

"What are you doing tomorrow?" The lightness was back in his tone. *This* was a conversation she could have with him.

"I'm taking Mary to find perfume and then I'm helping Lady Daphne plan a ball."

"Perfume?" His brow furrowed.

"She wants to purchase a small vial of French perfume and I've agreed to help her."

"May I escort you?"

If he'd announced he was Poseidon she couldn't have been more surprised. "Escort two maids? To purchase perfume? Are you quite serious?"

"Do I look as if I'm jesting?" Cade drained his wineglass.

Danielle eyed him. "Actually, no."

"Excellent. We'll take Rafe's coach. There must be some use for that expensive box of wood."

Danielle put her hand to her throat. "Oh, no. I could not go shopping in Lord Cavendish's fine carriage."

Cade peered at her, a questioning look on his face. "Why not?"

"It wouldn't be proper. Everyone would see."

Cade's laughter filled the room. "You have confused me with someone who cares about being proper or what anyone else thinks."

Danielle contemplated her options. On one hand, it was ludicrous to have a viscount's brother escort her and Mary to Bond Street to purchase perfume. On the other hand, perhaps she could find out more about him during the shopping expedition. "Are you quite certain you want to go?"

"Entirely."

"Very well, then. One o'clock?"

Cade pressed the palm of one hand against an eye. "That's quite early."

"Not for normal people."

"Fine," he replied, grinning at her. "I'll make the sacrifice . . . for you."

"Thank you." Their gazes met and Danielle had to swallow the lump in her throat. "I should go now."

"I'm sorry for bringing up your father." His voice was kind. Gone was the usual teasing tone.

She bit her lip. "You told me you didn't grow up like this? Well, I . . . I was supposed to."

He searched her face. "What do you mean?"

"My father is French and I was raised in France. But my mother, she's English, and has ties to the aristocracy. She used to tell me when I was young that I'd travel here, have a coming-out party, wear fancy gowns, and find a proper gentleman to marry."

His brow was furrowed. "Who is your mother?"

The hint of a smile passed over Danielle's lips. "It doesn't matter. That was a lifetime ago. Everything's changed. My father is dead. My mother is dying, disowned by her family. And I . . . I'm a . . . lady's maid."

"What happened, Danielle?" This time his voice was too kind. Too serious.

"I . . ." She couldn't tell him. She wanted to. A part of her really wanted to. She just . . . couldn't. "It's a long story. And I'm quite tired tonight." She stifled a yawn. Her eyes were heavy-lidded. She stood and he stood, too.

She turned toward the door but his voice stopped her.

"I came back to settle a score."

She turned back to face him. "Pardon?"

"You asked me the other night why I returned to London. I'm here to make something right."

"What sort of thing?"

He grinned at her. "We're sharing secrets, mademoiselle, not laying *all* of our cards on the table. The rest is a story for another time."

She nodded. That made sense. They were opening up

to each other. Slowly. She turned toward the door again before his voice stopped her one more time.

"Suffice it to say, I'm here to finally do the right thing by my brother."

"*Le mouton noir?*"

"Yes, it's time I made things right."

"Does your brother know you're helping him?"

"Absolutely not." His grin was unrepentant. "I trust you to keep my secret."

Danielle contemplated that for a moment. Whatever he was up to, he thought he was helping Rafe. Was he lying to her? Either could be true. She eyed him carefully. For the first time in a long time, she couldn't read someone. She took a step toward the door.

"Did you want those things?" he asked.

She paused, not facing him. "What things?"

"A coming-out party? Pretty gowns? Beaux?"

She squeezed her eyes shut before turning back to face him. "I wouldn't know what to do with those things. I have no idea how to dance, carry a fan, or flirt with a beau."

"You're doing a fine job with me." He moved close, pulled her hand to his lips, and kissed it.

"You're not a beau." It was difficult to force those words from her throat.

"You know about arranging hair and taking care of gowns. Daphne's told me how skilled you are."

"All a lot of doing my best and guesswork, I assure you. I wouldn't know a waltz from a quadrille."

"Would you dance with me?" The words were soft and reverent.

"What?" she whispered.

"Dance with me?"

Her breath caught in her throat. "Here? Now?"

"You said it yourself, Daphne's planning a ball. There will be musicians, dancing. When is it?"

"Mrs. Huckleberry said something about next week."

"Perfect. Dance with me then."

Was he teasing her again? This time she didn't like it. Anger rose in her throat. "Oh, yes, I'll simply saunter onto the dance floor in my maid's gown with my employer's brother. It will be entirely proper and no one will raise an eyebrow."

"Not in the ballroom, of course," Cade continued. "The music will carry."

She narrowed her eyes. "You're serious."

"Entirely."

"I'll step on your toes."

"I can stand it."

"I might trip you."

"I'll take my chances."

"Where will we meet for this dance?" He couldn't possibly be serious.

"Meet me here. At midnight."

CHAPTER NINETEEN

True to his word, Cade was not only ready to go shopping at one o'clock the next day, he was standing in the foyer dressed in buckskin breeches, a gray waistcoat and a green overcoat with a white shirt and cravat, and black top boots. The man not only looked perfect for shopping, but far too good overall. Mary stammered and blushed the entire time he escorted them to the carriage and handed each of them in as if they were fine ladies.

"It was kind of Lady Daphne to give us this time and allow us to use the coach," Danielle murmured as she accepted Cade's hand, stepped up into the coach, and sat on the velvety emerald seat next to Mary.

"Lady Daphne's far too good to us," Mary agreed.

"Nonsense." Cade hoisted himself into the conveyance and took a seat across from them. "She agreed solely to get me out of the house."

"Is that how you managed to convince her?" Danielle shook her head and smiled at his outrageousness.

"She's warned me away from you," Cade replied. "But I convinced her I am merely being chivalrous. Couldn't I stand to be more chivalrous? Besides, I suspect she doesn't think I could do anything too untoward with Miss Hartfield accompanying us."

The coach took off at a brisk pace toward Bond Street, the three of them laughing inside. It soon became apparent that Mary would not be happy with only one perfumery. She wanted to visit every shop to ensure she sniffed all of her possible choices.

"I'll just pop into this one by meself," she said when they pulled to a stop in front of the fourth shop. "I can tell you're vexed with me."

"Not at all," Danielle replied. "I want to ensure you find the perfect scent."

"Be that as it may," Cade interjected. "I'm certain Miss Hartfield can spare us for the span of one small outing."

Danielle flared her eyes at him but said nothing. Truthfully, she was weary of smelling perfumes and her feet were aching. She wasn't used to tripping around for so long in dainty slippers. Boots were much more comfortable. Even more enticing, however, was the thought of speaking to Cade alone.

The groom let down the steps and helped Mary alight. After ensuring that the groom would escort Mary into the shop, Cade promptly and unabashedly pulled the coach door shut.

"Miss Hartfield is no longer with us," Danielle said. "Does that mean you'll stop being chivalrous?"

"If you're lucky," Cade replied with a grin. "Do you think she'll find the perfect scent in there?"

"Absolutely not." Danielle fiddled with the strings to her reticule. Now that they were alone, she was far too aware of his soap-like scent and his proximity.

"Neither do I."

"It was much easier for me. My *grandmere* chose my perfume for me when I was a girl."

He lounged back in his seat. "What were you like as a girl?"

Now *that* was an unexpected question. She continued to trace the reticule strings with her fingers as she contemplated it. "I suppose I was inquisitive, impatient."

"And?" he prompted.

"Always studying languages, devoted to my parents, desperate for a sibling. A little too apt to try something first before thinking about it."

He laughed at that.

"What were you like . . . as a boy?" she asked tentatively, finding that she was truly interested in the answer and it had nothing to do with her mission.

He pressed his head against the back of the seat and rocked his shoulders. "Let's see. Rowdy, angry, full of too much energy, always scrabbling with my twin."

"And?"

"Hated my father and frustrated with my mother."

The second half of that was *entirely* unexpected. "Hated your father?"

Cade's jaw was tight. "Yes."

She would leave that alone for the time being. Apparently, she'd been wrong. Not everyone loved their parents. "Why were you frustrated with your mother?"

Cade sighed and looked out the window as if conjuring memories of the past. "My mother was . . . weak. I used to beg her to leave my father. To stand up to him."

"Stand up to him?" Danielle's heart pounded.

"He drank excessively. He was violent when he was sober and even more violent when he was drunk."

Danielle swallowed and shook her head. She'd been around violence. Living on ships she'd seen her share of men and boys fighting one another, but they'd been equally matched for the most part. She couldn't imagine a grown man being violent with a small child or a woman. How terrified Cade and Rafe must have been. Small, vulnerable, and afraid. She thought about her own father. He'd been nothing but patient, loving, and kind. She couldn't imagine a child being fearful of his own parents.

"What did Rafe do?"

"He tried to fight my father, defend our mother. She was a saint as far as Rafe was concerned. He stayed there far too long in order to protect her."

"And you?"

A humorless grin spread across Cade's face. "I left the moment I could. I've always left the heroics to my brother."

The reticule was forgotten in her lap. "Where did you go? Who did you rely on?"

"I went everywhere. I relied on myself. And a few trusted friends."

"Friends?" There was that word again.

"I suppose you could say I have a great many good friends."

"How did you get so many friends?"

Cade tipped up the brim of his hat. "I doubt you'd believe me if I told you."

"Tell me and I promise I'll endeavor to believe you."

He eyed her carefully. "I met my very best ones in gaol."

"Gaol!" She sat up straight.

"Does that surprise you?" He crossed his arms over his chest.

"No. I . . . It's just that . . ."

"You want to ask what I did to land myself in gaol. Go ahead." He nodded toward her.

"What did you do?" she asked tentatively. No wonder Grimaldi wanted her to keep an eye on him.

"I stole. Some bread. Because I was starving. I stole some for myself and another starving boy. I don't regret a moment of it. I only regret being caught."

"They put you in gaol for that?"

"I'm lucky my hand wasn't cut off."

"How long were you in gaol?"

"Two years."

"Two years? That seems like quite a sentence for merely stealing bread."

"The sentence was ten years. I escaped in two."

"Escaped!" The word came out much more emphatically than she'd meant it to. She covered her mouth with her gloved hand and then slowly lowered it. "Escaped?" she whispered.

"That's right."

"What did you do after that?"

His roguish grin was back. "I learned to acquire things with much more stealth."

He wasn't joking, she could tell. The man was entirely

serious. It wasn't that she was scandalized by his behavior. She herself had come close to being put in gaol a time or two. She was simply shocked that he was so casually telling her about it. Here in his brother's fine carriage, in the middle of Bond Street. As if he weren't in the least concerned. He'd meant it when he said he didn't care what anyone thought of him.

"How did you escape?"

"That is a long story, but suffice it to say I did it with the help of my friends." He took a deep breath. Silence rested between them, giving her time to absorb everything. After several moments ticked by, he finally asked, "What about you? Do you have many friends?"

A fortnight ago, Danielle would have answered no to this question, but today she had a different answer. A newly discovered, if bittersweet one. "Mary is my friend."

"But you've only just met her."

"That doesn't matter, does it?" Now that he was asking her about herself, she went back to fiddling with the reticule strings. But she wasn't about to allow him to hide from additional questions. If he was in a talking mood, she should take full advantage. But it made her feel guilty. He'd opened up to her last night. He was opening up to her more today. Betraying his confidence to Grimaldi felt . . . wrong. "Does Rafe know you were in gaol?"

Cade rubbed a palm across his chin. "Come to think of it, I don't know."

"How could that be?"

"Rafe and I have never been close."

"You mentioned that before. Why not?"

"We're complete opposites. We have nothing in common. Other than our age, our parents, and our devastatingly good looks."

She couldn't help her crack of laughter. "Is *he* modest then?"

"Of course."

"How else are you different?"

"Rafe always wanted to please everyone, follow all the rules, be a bloody hero."

"And you?"

"Never met a rule I didn't break and I'm the furthest thing from a hero you'll ever meet."

"Are you a villain then?" she ventured.

His eyes narrowed as he contemplated that question. "I wouldn't say that precisely, but I'd warn you to stay away from me."

"That dangerous?" Her words were flirtatious, but a chill went up her spine. He was serious.

"And more so."

"What about wanting to please people?" she ventured.

"Entirely depends upon the person and what it takes to please them."

She met his gaze. There was no stopping now. "Me?"

"Oh, sweetheart, you don't know how much I could please you." He pulled her hand into his lap, slowly unbuttoned her glove and removed it, and even more slowly, pulled her hand up to his mouth and brushed his lips against her knuckles.

Another shudder raced down her spine, for an entirely different reason. Pleasure? In bed? With a man? Somehow she couldn't imagine it. "That doesn't seem possible." She didn't realize she'd said the words aloud until Cade put a hand over his heart.

"You wound me."

"It's just that . . . I doubt it's possible to have a pleasant experience in bed with a man."

His grin turned wolfish. "Care to go home with me right now so I can prove you wrong?"

A flicker of something indecent unfurled in her lower abdomen. "You shouldn't say such things," she warned him with a half-smile, excitement coursing through her veins.

"Didn't you hear it when I said I never met a rule I didn't break?"

She ignored him while she pulled on her glove again.

"What about you, mademoiselle? How do you feel about rules?"

She pressed her lips together. "I've broken my fair share of them, too."

His eyebrows jumped. "Have you?"

"Surprised? I've never been one to pass up a dare."

He stroked his chin. "Is that so?"

"Yes, but even for someone like you, you don't think seducing your brother's maid is too . . . too bad of you?"

He shrugged. "Only if it's working."

"And if it is?"

"Then it's entirely worth it."

"What would Lord Cavendish do to you if he found you with me?"

Cade sighed. "Attempt to thrash me."

"That doesn't give you pause?"

Another roguish grin. "As you can see, it wouldn't be

the first swing someone's taken at me recently." He pressed two fingertips to his bruised eye and winced.

Danielle winced, too. "Yes. How did the poultice work for it?"

"It's healing, but I daresay it would feel even better if you would . . . kiss it."

"Kiss it?"

"Have I shocked you?"

"No."

"Really?"

"Really."

"Then I dare you."

CHAPTER TWENTY

Cade was not expecting her to do it. He assumed she'd bat her eyelashes at him—and she had the most arresting eyelashes—and murmur a few charming words about how he shouldn't be so incorrigible. Perhaps she'd give him another of those sultry smiles that he was coming to covet. That would be that until Mary returned.

So he was surprised, shocked really, when Danielle moved from her seat to his in one fluid motion and gently tugged his injured hand into hers. The touch of her hand against his was the most erotic thing he'd felt in far too long. She smelled like lavender. Like the fragrant fields he'd once walked through in Provence. Damn, it was enticing.

Something about this woman made him do crazy things like admit he'd returned to town to help Rafe and share secrets about his childhood. He'd never told anyone about those things before. Ever. But something about her intelligence and savvy combined with her station in life made her seem . . . safe. It wasn't a feeling Cade was used to. The truth was that it terrified him, both how she made him feel and how he couldn't seem to leave her alone.

He didn't look at his hand. Or her dark head bent over it. Instead, he bit the inside of his cheek and prayed his cockstand wasn't noticeable. He raised his face to the coach ceiling and tried to think about other things. Fencing. Card games. Riding horses. Riding . . .

"It looks good," Danielle finally murmured.

If only she were referring to his cockstand. "Does it?"

"Yes, it's healing nicely."

"Glad to hear it." Was it his imagination or did his voice sound garbled? By God, he was sweating. It was official. This woman made him sweat. He'd like to return the favor.

He wiped his forehead with the back of his other hand.

Danielle remained bent over his lap. "Do you want me to kiss it now?"

He braced his booted foot against the floor of the coach. Hard. And swallowed. Dear lord, did the woman know what she was doing to him? "Kiss it?" He tugged at his cravat.

"Yes."

Yes, please, God. Bend down and kiss it.

"Your hand," she murmured.

"Kiss whatever you like." He couldn't help himself.

Her dark head bent farther and her lips brushed against his knuckles, then the sensitive skin between his thumb and forefinger.

He braced both boots against the floor. "Is that all you're interested in kissing?" he managed to ground out.

She lifted her head and the look on her face was positively wicked. "Do you have any suggestions?"

Did he have any—? *That* surprised him, too. He was used to dealing with forward women but usually the ones he knew had no modesty whatsoever. Danielle was an intriguing combination of innocence and forwardness that he found irresistible. "Oh, sweetheart, I have a list."

"Really?" she purred. "May I see it?"

"It's a mental list," he drawled.

"Then you must tell me."

"You can begin with . . . my lips."

Her eyes narrowed. "You don't think I'll do it. Do you?"

"I'm hoping to hell you will."

She settled her skirts around her and lifted her head to face him, blinking at him innocently. "I have kissed a man before. I already know what it's like."

"You haven't kissed *me* before."

She sat up, folded her arms across her chest, and shook her head. "You are the most arrogant man I've ever met."

He shrugged one shoulder. "It's not arrogance if it's true."

"According to *you*, it's true."

He traced a finger along her collar. "There's only one way to find out if I'm being arrogant."

She continued to narrow her eyes on him. She definitely looked as if she were considering all of the implications, weighing the positives and negatives. "Very well."

The next thing Cade knew, her mouth was on his. It was a quick smack, a bit of movement, the slightest swipe of her tongue against the outside of his lips and then she was gone. It was over in little more than a moment.

"What in the devil's name was that?" he asked, blinking. "I feel as if I've been assaulted."

"A kiss, you dolt." She was already resettling her skirts around her. "It wasn't particularly good."

"That was not a kiss. That was a physical attack."

She sighed. "It wasn't much better than what I remember."

"My dear girl." He pushed himself off the seat and loomed over her. "I refuse to take responsibility for *that,* whatever it was. If you want a proper kiss, come here."

Her hands froze on her skirts. She slowly tilted up her head, a challenging look in her eyes as if she were a wild animal daring a predator to come closer.

"I'm here," she whispered. "If you think you can do better." She pushed her hands behind her, bracing both palms against the seat. Her chest thrust forward to provide him with a stunning view of her décolletage. He moved forward, leaning over her, his mouth mere inches from hers.

"Do better?" He rolled his eyes heavenward. "If that is the standard against which I'm to be compared, *better* is not the correct word. There isn't one sufficient in the English language. You may need to root around in French for one."

She looked affronted. "Very well. I'm waiting."

Good. He would make her wait. Slowness was an asset when it came to such things. She obviously didn't know that yet. No wonder she didn't want to repeat it, if that nonsense had been her prior experience. Cade hooded his eyes and took his time lowering his mouth to hers. God knew what sort of fool the woman had been kissed by before, but quick, hard pecks were not his style. He liked to savor the moment. Take his time. Enjoy every second.

He let his mouth slowly drift over hers, warm skin to warm skin. When his lips finally met hers, he didn't press, didn't push.

"It's nice, but—" Danielle began, trying to move away.

"Stay there . . . and kindly shut up," he murmured against her lips.

She did as she was told, going rigid.

His mouth still on hers, Cade brought up one hand to cradle her face. He brushed his thumb against her soft cheek, traced the outline of her shell-like ear with his forefinger. She sighed. Good.

He pressed his lips to hers more firmly, tilted his head to the side to get a better angle, and slowly, oh, so slowly, nudged her lips open with the tip of his tongue.

As soon as Danielle opened for him, his tongue plunged inside. Their mouths slanted across each other's and one of her hands snaked up to reach around his neck. She clung to him. She moaned. His mouth plundered hers, again and again, until both of her arms were around his neck and she was supporting herself by clinging to his shoulders. He moved to the side of her mouth, her check, her ear. He rained kisses along her neck. She leaned her head back, allowing him to touch every part of her. God, how he wanted to rip open her bodice and put his mouth on her pert, delectable breasts.

He forced himself to move up again. His mouth returned to hers and he gently bit her plump bottom lip. He sucked on the edge of her lip before slowly slipping his tongue back inside. She cradled his head in her hands. His hands were on her waist, pulling her to him, his mouth never leaving hers. It was endless, drugging. One of his hands moved up to the back of her neck where he stroked gently, easing her head to the side to angle the kiss. The other hand moved to her back, pulling her body into ever-increasing contact with his.

When his mouth finally broke contact with hers, Danielle was panting, clinging to him. Her eyes looked wild and her hair was slightly mussed. And yes, by God, there was an unmistakable bead of sweat on her forehead. Mission accomplished.

With a smug, satisfied smile, his mouth moved to her delicate ear and he whispered huskily, *"That* was a kiss."

CHAPTER TWENTY-ONE

The sound of Mary's voice outside the coach snapped them both back to reality. Danielle hastily smoothed her hair and moved back to the opposite seat just before the coach door was wrenched open and Mary's smiling face was framed by the harsh sunlight streaming into the vehicle from behind her.

"Good news!" Mary announced, as Cade, who looked positively delectable with slightly mussed hair, helped her into the coach.

"You found a perfume?" Danielle asked as her friend slid into the seat next to her. Danielle steadfastly kept her gaze from Cade. She couldn't look at him. The man had told her kissing him would be different. *Mon dieu, that* was an understatement.

"No," Mary replied. "But I know which one I shall purchase."

"Which?" Danielle asked, self-consciously pushing the pins into her coiffure to ensure they remained tidy.

"The bergamot scent at the first shop. The one on the corner."

"Ah, excellent choice," Cade chimed in. Danielle dared a glance at him. He looked perfectly put together and unaffected. So that was that how rakes did things. Passionately kissing a woman one minute and completely unaffected the next. She, however, was never going to be the same. *Nom de dieu* she'd had no idea kissing could be like *that*.

"Did you smell it, Mr. Cavendish?" Mary asked.

"No, but I've always been partial to bergamot." He grinned at the maid and called to the groomsman who remained by the open door. "Back to LaFont's, if you please."

"Very well, sir," the groomsman replied.

Soon the coach was parked in front of the small shop. Cade alighted first, then turned to help Mary down. As he was helping Danielle, a shrill female voice sounded behind them from the bustle of the crowd on the street. "Cade Cavendish, is that you?"

Cade turned one shade paler, gave Danielle an apologetic look, and turned just as a gorgeous—if gaudily dressed—woman came stamping toward him. "Amanda?" he asked in a dismayed tone.

Danielle's eyebrow shot up at his use of the woman's Christian name.

"Of course it's Amanda." The woman wore rouge on her cheeks and pink paint on her pouty, full lips. She was tall, blond, and looked as if she were Venus and had just walked off the shell.

"Who's this?" Amanda demanded, waving her hand at Danielle and Mary simultaneously, as if they were one person.

"Friends of mine," Cade replied. "Allow me to introduce Miss Danielle LaCrosse and Miss Mary Hartfield." He turned to them. "Ladies, this is Miss Amanda . . ."

Amanda's gorgeous face crumpled in a fierce scowl. "Jones!" she announced.

"Of course. Jones. Amanda Jones."

Danielle tried to greet the woman but she completely ignored Danielle and continued in a rush of words. "Cade, if you were still in town, why didn't you tell me?" Another pretty pout appeared on her lips.

Danielle and Mary exchanged disapproving glances.

"My apologies. I've been busy," Cade replied.

"Busy with *these* ladies?" she asked, a skeptical note in her voice. She leaned up and whispered in Cade's ear loud enough for the others to hear. "I've missed you. We might have been having *fun* all this time."

Fun? Danielle blinked. Oh, good heavens, she was actually standing in the middle of the street being introduced to one of Cade's light-o'-loves. How entirely inappropriate. Not to mention awkward. It was all Danielle could do to keep from taking a step back and curling her lip in disgust.

Instead she clenched her jaw and said, "We'll just go inside." She nodded toward the perfumery, desperate to be anywhere but there.

"Yes!" Mary agreed a bit too loudly.

Danielle grabbed Mary's hand, flung a "Nice to meet you, Miss Jones," toward the woman, and took off toward the door of the shop.

Once inside, Mary flew away to find her bergamot while Danielle hid behind the curtains near the front window and peered outside to watch Cade and Miss Jones. The woman was clearly perturbed about something. What was this? More secrets from the man? Tempted by his charm and his looks, Danielle had forgotten herself when she'd decided to kiss him. She'd forgotten he was a mark and she was a spy. When his mouth had captured hers, she'd been a woman and he a man and nothing else had mattered.

Watching him out the window with his lover, for surely that's what Miss Jones was, Danielle realized the reason he knew how to kiss like that was because he'd had a great deal of practice. He was a full-blown, undeniable rake. Danielle would do well to remember it. No more kissing. She needed to discover his secrets and one of them was standing in the street with him, wearing a yellow day dress so tight in the décolletage, Danielle was almost embarrassed for the woman. Almost, although jealousy, not embarrassment, seemed to be her predominate emotion. *Mon dieu*. Jealous over a rake? *Such* a bad idea.

"Here it is," Mary called from behind her, pulling Danielle's attention back to the reason she'd left the house this afternoon.

She hurried over to her friend, who stood with a tiny glass vial in her hand. Mary had taken off the stopper and was busily sniffing the perfume. She held it up for Danielle to sample, too.

"It's perfect," Danielle declared. She had also decided to buy a new vial of perfume. An orchid scent that she'd found while shopping here earlier with Mary. Lady

Daphne had been kind enough to increase her wages after her first week, declaring she'd already done a better job than the erstwhile Miss Anderson. The increase was enough to purchase the perfume and ensure all her mother's medical bills were paid for the week.

Danielle had already pushed her coins to the proprietor and Mary was fishing the last of her monies out of her small change purse to pay when Cade strolled in. He strode over to the women, an inscrutable look on his face.

"Absolutely not," he declared when he saw the money on the counter.

Mary blinked at Cade, confused.

"I cannot allow you to purchase this perfume," he said. "I shall purchase it for you. For you both."

Mary blushed scarlet. "Oh, no. Mr. Cavendish. I could never—"

"Absolutely not," Danielle snapped.

It would be a gross impropriety for Cade to purchase such intimate gifts for unmarried ladies. That didn't dissuade him one bit.

"My nieces," Cade declared to the shopkeeper before pulling a purse from his coat pocket and tossing the necessary bills onto the counter.

"Thank you," the shopkeeper said. If the woman had any doubts that Mary and Danielle were his nieces she mercifully kept them to herself. "I'll just go fetch your change."

While the shopkeeper was gone, Mary and Danielle stared at Cade in wonder. "Mr. Cavendish, I cannot allow—" Mary began.

"Please, Miss Hartfield. It will bring me great pleasure. Don't speak another word about it."

Mary seemed as if she were about to argue more, but Danielle put her hand on the girl's arm. She was interested in something far more eyebrow-raising than whether Cade paid for a couple of vials of perfume. She'd seen the contents of his purse and the man was *tres* rich!

CHAPTER TWENTY-TWO

That evening, Danielle was in Lady Daphne's bedchamber helping her to prepare for the soiree she'd be attending that night. She'd just finished telling her mistress every detail about the girlish endeavor upon which she'd embarked this afternoon. Specifically, Mary's encounter downstairs with Trevor.

After she and Mary returned from their shopping adventure, Danielle and Mrs. Huckleberry had arranged Mary's hair in a sweeping chignon, applied a hint of her new perfume at her throat and wrists, and plied her with instructions. Mary had waited in the corridor for Trevor to come in from his afternoon chores.

"Mary looked absolutely lovely," Danielle finished. "When he saw her, Trevor nearly dropped the coal buckets. Then Mary worked up the nerve to ask him if he'd like to go walking in the park on Sunday and I'm happy to report, they have an appointment to do exactly *that*."

"I do love love," Lady Daphne said with a sigh. "Do you know Rafe once sent me a little ship?"

"A ship?"

"It was a replica of one we'd both spend time on. The *True Love.*"

"That sounds *tres romantique,*" Danielle replied. "Oh, I nearly forgot. I'll get your hair ribbon back tonight."

"Oh, no. Please tell Mary she can keep it. I've little use for it," Lady Daphne replied. "Why, I've got dozens of hair ribbons."

"That's kind of you, my lady."

Lady Daphne bit her lip. "I've been meaning to ask you . . ."

Danielle's hands paused on her hair. "Yes, my lady?"

"How was the shopping excursion with Cade?"

Danielle tried to concentrate on perfecting the chignon. "It was . . . fine, my lady."

"Fine?" Daphne stared at her in the mirror, one eyebrow cocked.

Was it getting hot in the room? Every time Danielle considered her shopping trip with Cade, she thought of three things. First, the smoldering kiss they'd shared in the coach. Second, the hideous encounter with Miss Jones. And third, the large sum of money she'd seen in his purse. That was not the kind of money a ne'er-do-well carried about, brother of a viscount or no. Was he a thief? A criminal? She doubted he'd robbed his brother. He claimed he was here to help him. But how? By doing something illegal? Cade had something up his sleeve and Danielle intended to find out what it was.

It only complicated matters that the man had given her the kind of kiss that could singe off your eyelashes.

"Mary found her perfume," Danielle offered instead.

"No. I mean did *Cade* do anything . . . untoward?"

A vision of his mouth on her neck flashed through Danielle's unhelpful mind. "I . . . er, wouldn't say that."

"Did he do anything indecent?" Lady Daphne asked.

The words, *"Is that all that you're interested in? Kissing?"* burned in her brain.

"No . . . certainly not," Danielle lied.

"I hesitated to allow him to escort you," Lady Daphne continued. "He promised to be on his best behavior. Was he?"

Danielle had to swallow the smile that popped to her lips. She suspected he *had* been on his best behavior. The man was a complete rogue. "Yes," she answered emphatically. "Of course. Though he did . . . meet a friend in the street."

"Oh, no!" Daphne turned in her seat to face Danielle. "Not some criminal or ne'er-do-well."

"I couldn't say, my lady," Danielle replied. "Her name was Miss Jones. She seemed to be . . ." Danielle cleared her throat. "Quite *close* to Mr. Cavendish."

Daphne shook her head. "Her Christian name wasn't Amanda, was it?"

Danielle's eyes widened. "You know her?"

"I'm sorry to say we've met once. Under some very trying circumstances. Suffice it to say that Miss Jones mistook Rafe for Cade and it was . . . quite distressing."

Danielle resumed the brushing. "Oh, my lady, I can only guess."

"I didn't care much for that tart," Lady Daphne continued. "I cannot believe she'd be bold enough to stop him in the street. Wait. Yes, I can. She was quite bold indeed."

"Agreed," Danielle murmured. "At any rate, it was kind of Mr. Cavendish to escort Mary and me to Bond Street."

Lady Daphne sighed. "I'm pleased to hear that you don't regret it. I do worry about him."

That was intriguing. "You worry about him, my lady?"

"Yes, quite a lot. When he first arrived in London we were shocked. You see, Rafe had believed his brother was dead."

"Is that so?" She continued to brush Lady Daphne's pretty hair.

"Rafe hadn't seen him in nearly a decade and had heard he'd been . . . I can trust you to keep this confidential, can't I?"

Danielle nodded but a vision of Grimaldi hovered in the back of her mind.

"Rafe had heard that Cade had been in gaol," Lady Daphne continued.

"Gaol?" Danielle did her best to feign surprise. Surely Grimaldi already knew that.

Lady Daphne wrinkled her nose. "Let's just say Cade hasn't always been on the correct side of the law."

Neither have I. "Yet you allow him into your home, my lady?"

"He's family. We would never shut him out. Besides, we don't know of anything he's done *lately*."

"I understand, my lady. I hope you don't think I'm prying." She wanted to ask Lady Daphne if she thought

Cade would steal from his own brother. "Do you know of any business ventures Mr. Cavendish is involved in?"

Daphne frowned. "Business? No. I mean we always assume he's up to something. Mostly gambling and the occasional fight, but I've never known him to have an occupation. Not a proper one at least. He and Rafe have a complicated relationship."

"What do *you* think of him, my lady?" Gambling *might* explain the large purse. Perhaps he was *tres, tres* good at gambling.

Lady Daphne tapped her cheek with one finger. "I think." She sighed again. "I think he's a good man who lost his way." She shook her head. "I'm sorry if he's been untoward to you, Danielle. If he bothers you, please do not hesitate to tell me or Lord Cavendish. I'd like to think we're friends and you can be honest with me."

Friends? Yet again, that word. Not only was Danielle pretending to be a maid and hiding in the woman's house, but she just might be trying to ruin her brother-in-law and send him back to gaol. There was no way beautiful, kind Lady Daphne wouldn't end up hating her.

"Mr. Cavendish has been no bother," Danielle said instead. "No bother at all."

CHAPTER TWENTY-THREE

Daphne Cavendish sat at the dressing table in her bed-chamber, staring at her reflection in the glass. She wore a dressing gown and her hair was mussed, having just been thoroughly ravished by her gorgeous husband. Rafe stood behind her, shrugging into his shirt.

"The servants are going to talk, you know, as many nights as we spend in here together," Daphne said, dragging a brush through her hair.

"Good. Let them talk," Rafe replied. "I refuse to leave your bed, my lady. Not after having to wait for so long to get back into it after we were married."

Daphne giggled. "Shh. We're not supposed to discuss that."

Rafe glanced around, grinning. "You may not have noticed but we're quite alone at the moment."

"That reminds me. We won't be alone for long. Delilah is coming to visit tomorrow. She insists she is coming to see the new house, but I have my suspicions she wants to sneak down to the ball." Delilah was Daphne's irascible thirteen-year-old cousin who had a penchant for matchmaking, speaking deplorable French, and causing mischief.

"Why don't you tell her she can't come until the week after?" Rafe asked, pulling on his breeches.

Daphne stared at him through the looking glass and shook her head. "You've met Delilah. One simply doesn't tell that girl no."

Rafe threw back his head and laughed. "Yes, well, let her sneak down to the ball then. What's the harm?"

"The harm is she'll get a reputation for being a heathen at the ripe old age of thirteen."

"Lord help the young men of the marriage mart five years from now."

Daphne nodded. "You're perfectly right. I'm already preparing myself for her debut."

Rafe sat on the edge of the bed to pull on his boots. He sighed loud and long.

"You look tired, darling. Is something the matter?" Daphne set the brush down and turned to face him.

Rafe left off with his boot and shrugged. His shoulders fell. "It's Cade."

Daphne pulled her dressing gown up higher. "What about Cade?"

"I want to know why he's come back."

"He said it's high time he paid a visit."

"It's never that simple with Cade. He's up to something. He's been going out until all hours. Meeting with people. And that fight the night of the theater."

"You said yourself that your brother's always been a bit of . . . trouble."

"This is more than trouble. He may be in something over his head."

"I know you're worried, darling, but try not to assume the worst."

"That's a difficult thing to do when Cade is involved."

Daphne stood, walked over to her husband, and bent down to kiss him. "Just try, darling. By the by, Cass tells me Lucy Hunt has her sights set on figuring out Cade's secrets. Perhaps she can inform you of them once she's done."

Rafe laughed. "Best of luck to her. I can't figure him out and *I'm* a spy."

Daphne rested a hand on his shoulder. "You don't suspect anything truly serious, do you?"

Cade scrubbed a hand across his forehead. "Have you heard of the Black Fox?"

CHAPTER TWENTY-FOUR

"The flowers will go there and the refreshments over there." Lady Daphne twirled around in the middle of the empty ballroom. "Oh, and we must remember to purchase more candles for the chandeliers."

Mr. Ayers, Lord Cavendish's personal secretary, busily scribbled notes in his ledger while following Lady Daphne as she flitted around the room like a butterfly. Danielle stood near the doors watching the proceedings. "Yes, my lady," Mr. Ayers said after every one of Lady Daphne's requests.

"The musicians will go over there, of course, and I want the dancing to be centered around this area here."

"Yes, my lady," Mr. Ayers replied breathlessly.

Lady Daphne turned to face him. "You look a bit flushed, Mr. Ayers. Are you quite all right?"

"I think I may need a drink of water, my lady," the poor man admitted.

Danielle hurried toward them. "By all means, go to the kitchens and Cook will get you some. I'll take over here. I'm more than happy to be of use."

"Thank you kindly, Miss LaCrosse." Mr. Ayers handed Danielle his ledger and quill and scurried from the room before Lady Daphne could stop him.

Danielle crossed over to the small table the man had set up and dunked the quill in the ink pot. The planning and executing of a ball was absolutely fascinating to her and she was interested in learning more. This was something she had been born to do. Something her mother would have shown her, something she might have had to do regularly if her life had been different. If Lafayette Baptiste hadn't stolen her childhood. Someday, she would make him pay. But today she had a ball to plan. She turned back to Lady Daphne. "Where were we?"

"I daresay I've lost my train of thought," Lady Daphne replied, blinking.

Danielle read from the bottom of the list. "The musicians will be located on the far left and the dancing will be concentrated here."

"Oh, yes, that's right," Lady Daphne replied with a wide smile, clapping her hands. "We must get the extra napkins out of storage and be sure Cook has everything she needs and—"

"And we mustn't forget to have the front steps scrubbed," Danielle added.

"Yes, of course."

"I've already asked Mrs. Huckleberry to see to the flower arrangements," Danielle said.

Lady Daphne smiled at her. "Have you helped plan balls before? In your other positions?"

"Not . . . precisely," Danielle replied. It would have been so easy to say yes. Why hadn't she just said yes?

"Then how do you know so much about it?"

"I . . . Oh, I shouldn't bother you with such unimportant nonsense, my lady."

"Nonsense? I hardly think it's nonsense, especially if you're able to help me."

Danielle hesitated. Did she dare to tell Lady Daphne? The truth was she desperately wanted to tell this secret, had been dying to since the moment she'd begun working with Lady Daphne on the arrangements for the ball. It was so rare that a spy was able to safely tell a secret. The temptation was overwhelming. "Well," she began, stepping closer to Lady Daphne and lowering her voice. "The truth is that my mother was part of the aristocracy. She taught me . . . a few things. Before she fell ill."

Any fears Danielle had about Lady Daphne's reaction were quickly put to rest when the lady smiled brightly and said, "The English aristocracy?"

Danielle nodded. "Yes."

"I had no idea. What is your mother's name?"

"It doesn't matter now," Danielle replied. "My mother was disowned by her family for marrying my father, who was a poor French professor."

Lady Daphne's face softened and she reached out to gingerly pat Danielle's shoulder. "I'm sorry, dear. I understand completely. My family wasn't particularly fond of Rafe until he quite unexpectedly became a viscount. We married, er, planned to marry regardless. Your mother had the right of it. One should only ever marry for love."

"I never had a coming-out party," Danielle replied, trying to dispel the sad tone in her voice. She'd never been one to feel sorry for herself. Her life was the way it was and she had accepted it long ago. However, the unfairness of it all washed over her from time to time. It was irresistible to admit she might have been a part of this world had things not happened the way they had.

"When did your mother get sick, dear?"

"Many years ago."

"Did you live with your father after that?"

"No, Father was . . . dead."

Lady Daphne's hand flew to her throat. "I'm so sorry."

"It's all right. It's been . . . a lifetime." She forced a smile to her lips.

Lady Daphne twined her arm through Danielle's and pulled her close. "I daresay, with our combined experience, we shall plan a magnificent ball."

CHAPTER TWENTY-FIVE

"Aye, there, Oakleaf, wot happened to yer eye?" a boom-ing voice called out to Cade.

Cade wore the common clothes of a dockworker, in-cluding a hat, white shirt, and coarse breeches. He'd traded in his boots from Hoby's for a decidedly less costly pair. There was only one more thing to do to fit in in this environment—change his voice. He needed to get this over with quickly. Daphne's ball was tonight and his sister-in-law wouldn't be pleased if he arrived late or say . . . bleeding.

"Why don't ye sit down and 'ave a drink wit me, O'Conner, and I'll tell ye the tale," Cade answered. He pulled his tricorn down over his forehead. The London docks were a teeming rabbit warren of taverns, alleys, and streets. Overall, the place wasn't large, however, and in these parts if someone saw him they might recognize him not only as Oakleaf but also as Eversby, Duhaime, or a variety of other names.

Tommy O'Conner had been out to sea for more years than Cade had been alive. The man knew the comings and goings along the docks better than most. He knew when every single ship put into port and when it was planning to leave. More importantly, he had a couple of the wharf police in his pocket. O'Conner was a good man to know.

"Someone didn't like the look o' ye, eh?" O'Conner pulled up a chair next to Cade's table and straddled it.

"Somethin' like that." Cade ordered a mug of ale from a young lady who leered at him with lust in her eyes.

"Evenin', guvna," she said, batting her eyelashes at him.

He was not interested. A vision of Danielle flashed through his mind. Which reminded him. He needed to get to business and leave this fine establishment. Alone. He'd promised Danielle a dance at midnight.

"Do ye 'ave the information I seek?" He nearly barked at O'Conner.

"So touchy tonight, is ye?"

Cade rubbed the back of his neck and took a quaff of the ale the barmaid brought him. "Just   busy."

"I see that, Cap'n. Got a fancy ball ta attend?" The man nearly laughed himself into stitches.

"Somethin' like that." Cade forced a smile.

O'Conner fished in his dirty coat pocket and brought out a sealed letter that he promptly handed to Cade. "Yer information, Cap'n."

Cade took the letter, stuffed it into his inside coat pocket, downed the rest of the ale with a grimace, and wiped the back of his mouth. He stood and tossed a few coins on the table to pay for both his and O'Conner's drinks. Then he pulled out another small but hefty bag of coins and threw it to O'Conner. "Your fee."

O'Conner caught the bag in one meaty hand and tested its weight. A slow smile spread across his weathered face. "A pleasure doin' bus'ness wit ye as usual, Cap'n." O'Conner's raucous laughter followed Cade out the door.

CHAPTER TWENTY-SIX

"Delilah, you know you're not supposed to be down here." Daphne shook her head at her cousin. The girl was sitting on a tufted ottoman in a corner of the ballroom, eating a tea cake. She wore her best pink gown with a wide pink bow on her head, and she swung her white stockinged feet in time to the music.

It was half past eleven and the ball was busy and crowded. Daphne was relieved the party had been a success, despite her cousin's sneaking about. She'd broken away from the large crowd in the ballroom to chastise Delilah whom she'd spotted in the corner. "You promised you'd stay upstairs and only peek down once in a while."

"I know, Cousin Daphne, but *j'adore* the music and *j'adore* the dancing and the beautiful gowns. I just couldn't *help* myself. Not to mention there are tea cakes down here and nary a one upstairs."

Daphne put her hands on her hips. "Despite the plethora of tea cakes, you shouldn't be here. I will send up a maid with some tea cakes for you."

"Why shouldn't I be here?" Delilah asked. "*J'adore* a ball." She took a large bite of tea cake.

"Your debut isn't for five more years." Daphne tapped her slipper against the floor.

Delilah finished chewing. Her subsequent sigh was long and exaggerated. "It might as well be five more decades for as successful as it's certain to be."

"Why do you say that?" Daphne asked, frowning.

"Allow me to call attention to the fact that my bow is askew." Delilah pointed at her head. "I cannot dance." She pointed at her feet. "And I have an unfortunate jelly stain on my bodice which I was hoping no one would notice but now I must reveal its existence in order to prove my point." She pointed at her bodice where, indeed, a dark red stain was visible.

"And what is your point?" Daphne asked.

"That I am a mess. I have no grace, no style, no bearing. Nor poise. I have absolutely no poise to speak of. And you're constantly telling me my French needs work."

"Well, it does. But I have an idea. My new maid is French. Perhaps she can help you learn more while you're here."

Delilah beamed at that. "Oh, *j'adore* that idea. Thank you very much, Cousin Daphne. I should quite like to meet your French maid." Then she frowned. "But it doesn't help with the poise nor the grace."

"Poise and grace? You think those things are important?" Daphne smiled down at her cousin.

"Of course. Look at Miss Pembrooke." Delilah nodded into the crowd where one of the Season's most coveted young ladies stood holding a flute of champagne in an elegant, gloved hand. "I am not elegant," Delilah said with a sigh. "And most of my gloves are stained."

"You have plenty of time to sort it out, Delilah. Don't be so harsh with yourself."

Just then, Daphne's friends Owen and Alexandra Monroe broke away from the crowd and came over to where Daphne and Delilah were talking. A young man was with them. He looked to be about seventeen, tall and straight-backed, completely at ease, if bored, in a ballroom. He was dark haired and blue eyed and ever so handsome.

Daphne turned to greet her new guests. "Lady Alexandra! Lord Owen! So good to see you again."

"Thank you for having us, Lady Daphne," Lady Alexandra said. "Have you met my brother, Lord Thomas?"

"Ah yes, your brother, the Marquess of Huntfield." Alexandra's father was a duke and her younger brother the heir.

"That's right." Alexandra smiled. "He's on leave from Oxford and I insisted on his coming with us this evening."

The young man bowed formally to Daphne. "A pleasure to meet you, Lady Daphne."

"I do hope you're not too bored by a stuffy old *ton* ball, Lord Thomas."

"On the contrary," he said smoothly. "I find it quite amusing. I've got a bet on how long it takes the middle button on Lord Hoppington's waistcoat to burst and

Lady Hammock's turban will certainly tumble from her head before the night is through. That ought to be a sight." There was a twinkle in his eye.

At this, Delilah let out a delighted burst of laughter. She promptly clasped her inappropriately ungloved hand over her mouth.

Daphne turned to her. There was no help for it. "Lord Thomas, may I introduce you to Lady Delilah Montebank? She shouldn't be here as she's yet to make her debut, but such rules don't daunt her, I'm afraid. Allow me to apologize in advance for anything inappropriate she says."

Delilah promptly rolled her eyes at Daphne and gave Thomas a wide grin before patting the seat next to her. "Oh, Lord Thomas. I do believe we are going to be fast friends. For I, too, have been eyeing Lord Hoppington's button and the precarious state of Lady Hammock's turban. If you've any more such delightful things to say, do come sit by me."

Thomas grinned in return and promptly took a seat.

"Do you like tea cake?" Delilah asked.

"Who doesn't?"

Daphne was immediately convinced the two were destined to be fast friends. She turned back to Alex and Owen and shook her head. "She's certain to be hideously inappropriate."

Alexandra waved a gloved hand in the air. "Thomas can be similarly inappropriate. It's Mother's despair that he spends more of his time gambling with stable grooms and racing his horses than preparing for the esteemed role of duke one day."

Daphne glanced at the two young people. They were

already engaged in a happy conversation, talking and laughing. Daphne would no doubt get written up in the papers tomorrow for letting her scandalous cousin into the ballroom, but she had more important things to worry about. At least Lord Thomas seemed to be keeping Delilah preoccupied. She threaded her arms through both Alexandra's and Owen's and walked away with them.

"There's something I wanted to ask you both about." She lowered her voice. "How well do either of you know my brother-in-law?"

CHAPTER TWENTY-SEVEN

Danielle was peeking into the crowded ballroom, her backside sticking out into the corridor when Trevor jogged up to her.

"A messenger brought this to the back door just now, miss. Said to deliver it to you personally as soon as possible," the footman said.

Danielle jumped. Then her heart dropped into her belly. The door to the ballroom closed and she was left standing in the darkened corridor, the strains of the music still floating in the air. Trevor had hurried away as quickly as he'd come. He was as busy as the rest of the staff ensuring the party was a success. It had been kind of him to take a moment to find her.

"Oh, God. Please don't let it be *Mere,*" she whispered to herself as her trembling hands ripped open the seal.

She unfolded the note and breathed a sigh of relief. It was from Grimaldi. And he . . . She continued to read, holding her breath again. He wanted her to pack her bags and meet him three streets over at midnight. Good God. That wasn't much time. There were a few more details, not many, but clearly she was meant to abandon her pretense of being Lady Daphne's maid. Immediately.

The momentary relief Danielle felt at realizing the note wasn't about her mother's health was quickly replaced with something else. Something foreign. Something that felt like . . . regret. She pressed the note to her chest and glanced around the corridor. It was all over? So soon? It seemed she'd only just arrived here to this happy household. She didn't want to go. Didn't want to never see Mrs. Huckleberry again. Didn't want to lose Lady Daphne's company. Didn't want to stop her talks with Mary. And . . . Cade. That was the worst part. She would miss her dance at midnight with Cade.

Cade waited in the *empty* library. It was nearly midnight. Where was Danielle? Had she decided the dance was pointless? Had she convinced herself he'd been jesting? He paced around. He would wait. She'd begun to mean something to him. Their talks. The questions she'd asked. They'd felt real, true. And that kiss in the coach. That had been unbelievable. It had been unfortunate that Amanda had arrived shortly after. He'd seen the look of hurt and accusation on Danielle's face when she'd realized Amanda was more than a casual acquaintance. After he'd dispatched the woman to hurry back to

Danielle's side, he'd been elated when she'd allowed him to purchase the perfume. He'd never felt that before, that desire to so please a woman, well, not outside of bed. Not since . . . his mother.

He'd actually admitted to Danielle that he was frustrated with his mother. That was something else that was surprising. He'd told Danielle more in the short time he'd known her than he'd ever told anyone. And he wasn't even sleeping with her. His mother had been the reason he'd left. He hadn't been able to stand watching her cower in fear of her husband any longer. He was tired of trying to talk her into leaving his father. Tired of trying to fight off a man who was twice as big as he was every time he laid into her. Finally, he'd left. And left Rafe to deal with it. Alone. It was the worst thing he'd ever done and for a man who'd stolen, lied, and fought countless people, that was saying something. Coming back to London had been his one chance to do right by his brother. He would if it was the last thing he did.

He hadn't expected to meet Danielle, however. Danielle had made him feel things he hadn't felt . . . ever. A part of him wanted to run, to leave London, to never look back. It was what he did best, after all. Another part of him wanted to stay, to lay down roots, to kiss Danielle again. To dance with her.

He paced over to the window and looked out into the darkened gardens. He glanced at the clock again. Damn it. Danielle wasn't coming and he was a fool to wait for her. He strode over to the desk, jerked open the drawer, and pulled out a sheet of paper. He fumbled in the side drawer for a quill and ink pot. He scribbled off a note and folded it. Then he headed for the door. He would go up the servants' staircase and leave the note on her pillow.

CHAPTER TWENTY-EIGHT

He'd promised her a dance at midnight. Just like a fairy tale. The idea of missing it tugged at her heart, but Danielle couldn't indulge in such foolishness. Not now that she knew what her mission was. Baptiste's ship was sailing tonight. Whatever Grimaldi suspected of Cade was not more important than trailing Baptiste. That was what they'd been waiting for.

She had to stow away aboard a ship called *The Elenor*, which would be following Lafayette's ship. She must once again dress as a cabin boy. No doubt the former cabin boy had recently resigned. Knowing Grimaldi, that had been no coincidence. More likely he'd paid off the young man. Grimaldi didn't take risks. But Danielle was about to. She was about to take a big one. She would have to pretend to be someone she was not with a lot of strangers, convince them, and follow Baptiste to his destination. She must leave immediately. She had no time for fairy tales.

She hurried up to her room, her feet nearly flying over the stairs. There wasn't much to pack and she'd be taking less on the ship as Cross. But for now, she would have to take it all with her so Mrs. Huckleberry and Lady Daphne weren't burdened with her things.

A pang of regret throbbed in Danielle's chest. She'd miss these people. Missing people other than her family was completely foreign to her. She'd missed her father desperately, but she no longer felt it as acutely as she once had. She'd missed her mother, too, but she'd never had *friends,* people whom she actually liked and who she believed liked her in return.

She would miss her talks with Mary and the outrageous things Mrs. Huckleberry said. She'd miss Lady Daphne, too. The woman had been so kind and helpful, treating her with nothing but respect. An unfamiliar sensation tugged at Danielle's chest. Regret. Another foreign emotion. Regret wasn't something she indulged in. It was too messy, too complicated, too rooted in the past and Danielle strove to live for the moment.

She would miss Cade, too, if she were honest, but she didn't have time to think about that. There would be time for memories later. This moment was all she was ever guaranteed. But she would feel regret. Regret that she couldn't say good-bye to Mary and Mrs. Huckleberry. Regret that she couldn't give Lady Daphne more notice, that she would be leaving her without a lady's maid so suddenly.

She was allowed to leave a note, Grimaldi had

informed her, as long as it revealed no details. She'd hurried to her writing desk and scribbled on a piece of paper. *I have to leave. I am sorry. Danielle.* She wrote two more notes. One for Cade and one for her mother.

She knew Grimaldi allowed this only because he didn't want them to look for her. Such a search would only end in failure or worse—disaster. She set the note on the center of the pillow that rested atop her neatly made bed. She shoved her two other gowns and all her other belongings including her hair ribbons, stockings, a packet of hair pins, the vial of her *grandmere*'s lavender perfume, and her new orchid perfume into her worn leather valise. Choking back something that felt suspiciously like tears, Danielle took one last look at the small room that had been hers for such a short time. That's how everything was in her life. Short. Temporary. No roots. No connections. It was easier that way.

She eyed the note she'd written for Cade. On her way out, she would sneak across the hall from Lady Daphne's room and slip it onto his pillow. For some unknown reason she felt as if she owed it to him to say good-bye.

She took a deep breath and spun around to leave, Cade's note in her hand. The second she opened the door, she gasped and the valise dropped from her numb fingers to sit lopsided next to her foot. Cade stood in the doorway, filling it with his presence. So tall and broad-shouldered, her heart leaped in her chest. "Cade," she whispered.

His hand hung arrested in midair. He had been about to knock. He pulled his fist behind his back and his brow arched sardonically. His eyes took in her pelisse and the valise at her feet. Then they studied her face. "Going somewhere?"

She swallowed hard, crumpling the note in her hand. "I—Why are you here? How did you know where my room—"

"I know a great many things," he said. "As to why I'm here, you owe me a dance."

"I . . ." She bit her lip. "I thought you were jesting about that," she admitted hesitantly.

"Jesting?" He braced an arm against the door frame. "Did *you* find the idea of us dancing to be amusing?"

The word lodged in her throat, a lump of regret before she forced it out. "No."

"Neither did I. I was waiting for you in the library, but it seems I've come at an inopportune time. You're leaving?" He glanced at the valise once again and back at her.

She might as well tell him. He'd find out soon enough. The note burned in her hand. "I'm . . . I'm . . . Yes." She nodded. "I am going, but I'm not at liberty to discuss where."

He narrowed his eyes on her. "Sweetheart, we're all at liberty to discuss our whereabouts. You simply mean you do not *want* to tell me."

She'd learned long ago that the best way to distract someone from a question she didn't want to answer was to ask a question of her own. "Where have you been tonight? Out with Miss Jones?"

His grin dissolved. "No. I made it clear to Miss Jones that our acquaintance was at an end."

Danielle crossed her arms over her chest. "Acquaintance? Is that what you call it?"

"She doesn't compare to you, Danielle," he said softly, a boyish look on his handsome face.

That stopped her. She shouldn't have asked him about it. She sounded like a jealous fishwife. Now he'd gone and said one of the loveliest things she'd ever heard. He'd actually rendered her speechless.

"You changed the subject," he continued. "I asked you where you're off to."

She rubbed the note still clutched in her hand. "It wouldn't matter if I told you. You wouldn't believe me."

"So little faith in me?"

"It would sound quite fantastic."

"Try." He leaned against the door frame, blocking her way.

She closed her eyes. "Please don't ask me to."

"Very well. A woman with secrets. I understand."

She nearly sighed with relief. She opened her eyes, surprised to feel them wet with unshed tears.

He stood up straight and held out his arms. "Do you have time for a dance?"

That caught her entirely off guard as well. Did she have time for a dance? Almost as if it had read her mind, a clock somewhere within the house began to chime the midnight hour. She and Cade stood stock-still, staring at each other, his hands in the air, reaching for her in silent invitation for a dance. Once the chimes finished, she whispered, "There is no music."

"Of course there is." He dropped his arms and entered the room, shutting the door behind him. In three long strides, he'd crossed to the window and slid it open. The musicians played at the back of the ballroom near the French doors leading out to the patio. A lovely melody floated up through the summer air to filter prettily into Danielle's fourth-floor bedchamber. It was a waltz.

Cade turned back to face her, his arms outstretched again.

Danielle nearly choked on the lump in her throat this time. "You don't have to do this." Along with the music, the breeze carried the scent of night-blooming jasmine. That, combined with the melody and the darkness of the room with only a single candle flickering on the bedside table, made the entire scene quite . . . *romantique.*

"Don't have to do what?" Cade's tone was unreadable.

She glanced down at her slippers. "Dance with a maid?" She hated how vulnerable her voice sounded. How small. How . . . lonely.

He glanced over both shoulders. "I don't see a maid here."

"No?" Her reply was faint.

"I see only a beautiful woman with whom I desperately want to dance."

Beautiful? Her? She was too thin, too straight, too short, too flat-chested, too—well, too anything to be called beautiful. She glanced over both of her own shoulders. "Where?" She did her best to hide her smile. She passed by the writing desk and laid the crumpled note on top. Cade's eyes missed nothing. She could tell he'd seen it. That and the other note resting on the pillow. He pretended not to notice it. Instead, he pulled her into his arms and said, "Here."

"I don't how know to dance," she whispered into his starch-scented shirtfront.

"I'm not particularly adroit at it myself, but I'll teach you." His voice was so calm, and smooth, and reassuring. Danielle sighed. It nearly made her forget for a moment. Forget that . . . She didn't have time for this. She shouldn't be indulging in such nonsense when she had a job to do. Grimaldi was waiting at their designated meeting location, three streets away in a hackney coach. He'd be checking his timepiece and cursing her.

She was being foolish. She was being selfish. She was being . . . a girl. By God, she'd had precious few moments when she could enjoy being a girl. She'd had precious few moments spent in the company of a handsome man who wanted her the way a man wanted a woman. Cade had looked at her that way since the beginning. Never looked at her any other way.

She was about to have to pull on breeches, wear a cap, and spend days, if not weeks, aboard a cramped ship with no French soap for bathing. No bathtub for bathing! She was about to spend time itching in places she rarely contemplated. She would never have a satin gown. Would never have a coming-out party or be pursued by eligible gentlemen. She would never own delicate kid gloves or carry a reticule full of dainty things like a vial of perfume and a handkerchief with roses embroidered near her initials. None of that was in her future. But like the fairy tales, she did have this one moment where she could pretend. Pretend to be a stunningly beautiful lady, pretend to be the belle of the ball. In this one moment, she could dance with a handsome gentleman. Perhaps Cade wasn't *precisely* a gentleman. He'd been to gaol. He had secrets. But she was no lady. And she had secrets, too. They made a good match.

She would take her moment. Grimaldi could wait.

She looked up into Cade's blue eyes and smiled at him. She lived in the moment and in this particular moment she was going to . . . dance. "Yes, Mr. Cavendish. I'll dance with you."

All of the servants were busy attending to the ball, which made it a perfect time for Danielle to escape. Now was also the perfect time to participate in a clandestine dance with an unmarried man in her bedchamber. She placed her small, cold hands in Cade's large, warm ones.

The smile he gave her turned her belly to jam. His fingers closed around her hands and the warmth and strength there reassured her. "Wait." She stepped back, unhooked the clasps on her pelisse and shrugged it off both shoulders. She tossed it on the bed, attempting to cover the note sitting on the pillow. If Cade noticed, he didn't react. She turned back to him and offered her hands again.

"It's a three-step process," he explained, claiming her hands again and pulling her indecently close. She stared into his blindingly white cravat, too overcome with emotion to look him in the eye. It was more than just the dancing. No one had ever treated her with such reverence. No one had ever taken the time to look at her. Not carefully. Not deeply. Not as if he was studying her the way Cade always seemed to be. Few things escaped his notice. She already knew that about him. Was it her imagination or was he breathing in the scent of her hair? She dared a glance up to see him inhale, his eyes closed. "Orchids," he said, in a low, deep voice.

"Pardon?"

"You smell like the orchids that grow out of the rock formation of the island of Elba."

"Elba?" She tilted her head to the side. "Have you been to Elba?"

"Many times."

She puzzled over that. "It's my new perfume," she breathed. And then, "I didn't know orchids grew in Elba."

"The *Spiranthes spiralis* does. It's subtle. Small. Its blooms are white. It seems insignificant, nearly invisible to those who don't pay attention, until you look closer. It's gorgeous and it smells heavenly."

How to reply to that? She didn't realize for several seconds that she was holding her breath. His words were so similar to what she'd been thinking a moment earlier. It was as if the man had read her mind. She didn't have to answer because Cade said, "Just follow my lead." He stepped forward, then back, then to the side.

Danielle felt herself swept into the easy, lilting rhythm with a partner who, despite claims to the contrary, obviously knew precisely what he was doing.

They turned in time to the music in the small space by the bed. For a moment Danielle felt like a young lady of the *ton* at her debut. She would pretend for just a few minutes more.

"You're a quick study." Cade smiled down at her.

"You're an effortless teacher." She paused before asking, "When were you in Elba?"

"Years ago."

"Why were you there?"

He contemplated that for several seconds before saying evenly, "I ran off from home and joined the Navy when I was thirteen."

"Thirteen!" She gasped. So young. But she'd run away herself at that age. Why did it seem so terribly young when someone else said it?

"When you come from the alleys of Seven Dials, a life in the Navy seems preferable, believe me."

Seven Dials? Is that where he and Rafe grew up? She'd never imagined. "Was it preferable?" Why couldn't she keep herself from asking these questions?

"In some ways, yes. In some ways, no."

"In what ways was it not?"

Still leading her in the dance, Cade scoffed. "Let's just say I didn't grow up with a healthy respect for authority, which is an essential trait in a sailor."

I didn't, either. "Did it end badly?"

He downright grinned at that. "Everything I've ever attempted has ended badly. That's the hallmark of a black sheep, don't you know?" He was silent for a second, "Except . . ."

She watched him carefully. "Except? Except what?"

"There are only two things I've ever been truly good at." His voice took on an almost wistful tone.

"What is the first one?" she asked, holding her breath.

His smile turned downright roguish. "Breaking the law."

Danielle nearly choked. She peered up at him, examining his face. "You must be joking."

"Absolutely not. I became proficient at it from a young age."

"When you were in Elba, were you in the Navy or breaking the law?"

His grin didn't diminish. "Both." His white teeth flashed in the darkness.

The strains of the waltz faded and the music went silent. The musicians were no doubt taking a break. Cade released Danielle's hand and with a small shiver she took a step back. She rubbed the gooseflesh that had popped up along her arms. Cade rubbed his hands along her arms, too. It was much too forward a gesture, but she couldn't bring herself to ask him to stop.

He lowered his mouth to her ear and whispered huskily, "Better?"

She shook her head. "No . . . no actually, your touch is making it worse." She dared a glance up at him. His brow furrowed.

"Worse?" The furrow deepened. "Why?"

"Because when you touch me . . . when you touch me, Cade . . ." She shook her head. "What's the second?" she asked, breaking the spell between them.

"The second?" He searched her face.

"The second thing you're truly good at."

This time his grin was positively wolfish. "This," he murmured right before he pulled her tightly against his body and his mouth descended to capture hers.

CHAPTER TWENTY-NINE

Their mouths tangled, his slanting over hers. Her arms went up to reach around his neck. She forgot all about Grimaldi and the mission as soon as Cade picked her up and laid her on the bed. He came down on top of her, his mouth never leaving hers. His tongue plunged again and again until she was moaning and mindless.

His hips settled in between her legs, which she opened for him. They were both still fully dressed. It was the most erotic thing she'd ever felt, his hardness pushing against her softness through their layers of clothes. He ground his hips against her and his mouth continued to shape and mold hers. He cradled her face in his hands, whispering words in her ear. Dirty words. Words about what he wanted to do to her *sans* clothing.

His hands snaked up to her décolletage and tugged down the front of both her gown and her shift. One of her breasts popped free and his mouth moved down to claim it. She gasped as soon as his lips found her nipple. He bit, he licked, he brushed his hot tongue across it, making her arch toward his mouth and moan. He sucked it and Danielle nearly sobbed. She held his head to her while zings of white heat shot from her breast to the intimate spot between her legs, the spot he was rubbing against. His hips levered against hers in a primitive rhythm she didn't want to end.

When Danielle finally found the will to push him away, his mouth came off her breast with a sucking sound. He released her arms, but continued to hold her close, his forehead pressed to hers, his breathing heavy, his shoulders heaving, his breath loud in the silence of the room. Tentatively, she raised her hand to his chest and pressed her palm against the soft linen of his shirt. His heart was pounding as crazily as hers was. *Bien*.

"Cade, I must go."

"Let me feel you for a moment. Give me something to remember you by." His hands moved over her shoulders and down to her bodice to cup her small breasts.

She didn't want to deny him, but a glance at the little clock that rested on the table told her it was nearly half past. Grimaldi would have her head for being so late.

She grabbed Cade's muscled upper arms and squeezed. In another time and place, in another world, she would do more than let him touch her. She'd have given herself to this man. If some madness overtook her and she married someday, her husband wouldn't be the type who would care whom she'd been with before.

"It's a pity," she murmured, cupping Cade's face with a still-trembling palm.

"What is?" He turned his rough cheek and kissed her palm, sending sparks shooting through her body.

She let out a throaty laugh. "I didn't realize I'd said that aloud."

"You did." Cade pulled her hand away from his face and threaded his fingers through hers. "Now you must tell me . . . what's a pity?"

They were holding hands. His strong fingers had captured hers and his thumb stroked against hers in a way that made all her thoughts scatter. What had he asked her? Oh, yes. What was a pity? What was a pity, indeed? She did her best to ignore the thrumming of her pulse and retraced her thoughts. What had she been thinking? Right. *That.* She arched her brow at him and gave him her naughtiest look.

"Now I *must* know," Cade demanded, a thunderous expression on his face. He pulled her hand to his lips and kissed it.

Danielle took a moment to think. It would not be proper to tell him what she'd been considering. But when had she given a damn about being proper? She popped her lips together as she contemplated it.

"Go on," he prompted, watching her carefully.

Danielle reluctantly and slowly pulled her hand from his grasp. She tried to memorize the details, what the rough calluses of his fingertips felt like, how his thumb turned out at the tip.

She rolled out from under him and stood up. Cade stood, too, and watched her as she dragged the pelisse she'd been laying on from the bed, straightened the coverlet, and repositioned the note on the pillow.

She arranged the garment over her shoulders, looked up at Cade, and blinked. "I must go."

Cade reached for her. "Not before you tell me what the pity is."

She sidestepped out of his reach and bit her lip to keep from smiling. She grabbed the crumpled note from the desk, took a few steps toward the door, and scooped up her valise.

"Danielle . . ." Cade drew out the word in a warning tone.

Her hand on the knob, she paused to look at him over her shoulder, a smile she just *knew* was impish resting on her lips. "I was going to say . . ." She paused, enjoying this moment of teasing him. "I was going to say it's a pity that we never spent the night together."

With that, she flew from the room.

CHAPTER THIRTY

Cade waited until the music began again. He waited until the breeze coming through the window took on a decided chill. He waited until the thrumming in his balls subsided and the cockstand he'd had since pulling Danielle into his embrace slowly descended.

Only then did he take a deep breath and move. Otherwise, he might have believed the last half hour was nothing more than a dream. Even worse, that the words the woman had said, the words that had sent blood rushing through his veins and heat pouring through his hardened body, was the notion that it had been a figment of his imagination.

"It's a pity that we never spent the night together." He'd heard it correctly, hadn't he? He wanted to ask the empty bedchamber. Never had he been more aroused by a woman's words, especially words that clearly indicated they were *not* going to sleep together. She was leaving

and, damn her, she hadn't explained where she was going or why. How in the devil's own bollocks had the woman been able to say something like that to him and then *leave*?

Cade shook his head. Under any other circumstances, he would not have let her leave the room and he certainly wouldn't have stood there for minutes afterward like a damn fool staring out the window into the green leaves of the elm tree outside. Under any other circumstances, had the woman he'd been fantasizing about for the past several days informed him she found it a *pity* that they hadn't spent the night together, he would have whirled around, slammed the damn door, and had her up against it, kissing her until she was out of her mind with lust and ready and willing to right that egregious wrong. That would have been his reaction had Danielle not so thoroughly distracted and surprised him, not just with her words but with the fact that she was leaving and refused to tell him why.

He shut the window, muffling the strains of music he'd been so keen to hear minutes earlier. He pushed a hand through his hair and turned back around, expelling a breath. His eyes fell on the note on the pillow. He'd noticed it earlier but hadn't said anything for fear Danielle would remove it. *Lady Daphne* was written on the outside and it was sealed. He should not read it.

Good thing he was a scoundrel. He smiled as he plucked the piece of parchment off the pillow and broke the seal with his finger. He unfolded it. His eyes scanned the words. Only two lines. Two scant, short lines that didn't offer much. Damn it. Where was she off to with such haste? Had she got news that her mother had taken a turn for the worse? He should have asked her, should have offered to help. But she wouldn't have told him, nor would she have accepted his help.

Danielle was fiercely independent. Fiercely independent and full of secrets. Most women of his acquaintance wanted something from him. They wanted him to stay, to commit, to promise things. Other women had been sources of pleasure but he never stayed long enough to form an attachment to any of them. The minute a woman wanted more, he took off, never to be seen or heard from again. Amanda had been particularly deft at hunting him down and she'd been amusing for a while, but she was the perfect example of why he should leave before either party formed an attachment. Things got messy after that.

Danielle, however, didn't want an attachment. Instead, she'd denied him her bed and she was the one running off and leaving him. The irony of *that* made him shake his head again. He folded the note and placed it back on the bedspread near the pillow where he'd found it.

Pausing, he picked up the pillow, put it to his nose, and breathed in deeply. Orchids. Like the ones in Elba. He'd hedged telling Danielle why he'd been to Elba. Mademoiselle LaCrosse wasn't the only one with secrets. The scent sent a wave of memories through him, most recently that of her dark hair. He'd never be able to smell orchids again without thinking of her. Good God, he was resembling a lovesick fool. He groaned and rubbed his forehead, letting the pillow fall back to the bed. He turned away from the letter before remembering a letter of his own. A completely different one. Not the note he'd written Danielle earlier in the library, but the one tucked away inside his coat pocket. The one O'Conner had given him at the tavern.

Cade pulled open the side of his coat and fished out the missive. He read it by the light of the small wax candle that had yet to burn out. *Bloody hell*. He should have read this blasted note earlier. Should not have allowed his promise of a dance with Danielle to distract him. He glanced at the clock. He was late. Quite late. He folded the paper, jammed it back inside his pocket, and took off toward the door with ground-devouring strides. Just as his hand touched the knob, he paused, jogged back to the bed, and grabbed the pillow. Seems tonight was also his last night in this house. *The Elenor* sailed with the dawn and he was her captain.

CHAPTER THIRTY-ONE

Danielle ran as fast as she could. Her slippers splashed in puddles, her stockings got muddied, her hair came loose from its pins and fell into her eyes, and the valise banged against her knees with each lunge, making them nearly buckle. Still, she didn't stop. She hoisted her skirts in one hand and ran blindly down two different alleys and three streets until she located the hackney on the corner where she'd been told to meet Grimaldi. Grimaldi was never late.

She glanced around. The light from nearby town houses highlighted the coach's silhouette across the muddy road. Gasping for breath, Danielle paused only long enough to yank up her skirts again with her left hand and readjust the valise with her right. She dashed across the road, nearly getting mowed down by a fine carriage no doubt on its way back from the theater or the opera or some other fine amusement the residents of Mayfair preferred.

Glancing up and nodding at the driver, she rapped twice on the door. It opened immediately and only a second ticked by before she found herself grabbed bodily and hoisted up, valise and all, into the interior of the rented coach. She found herself splayed across the seat opposite a furious General Grimaldi. His eyes blazed dark fire and his nostrils flared menacingly. "You're late."

Danielle scrambled into a sitting position. "I know." There was no use trying to explain. That would only end in embarrassment. Grimaldi didn't take kindly to excuses.

He tossed a bundle to her. She caught it in both hands with a decided *oompf* and fumbled to pull it apart. She already knew what it was. A shirt, breeches, cap, stockings, and shoes. The garb of a cabin boy.

"Get dressed," Grimaldi barked. He turned his back to her and pulled the brim of his hat down over his eyes to give her privacy. Danielle fought the urge to use the crude hand gesture a deckhand had taught her when she was fifteen. She'd found it useful on innumerable occasions. Grimaldi wouldn't see. He would never be so ungentlemanly as to peek. Not the stone man himself. Danielle doubted he'd had a moment of fun in his entire regimented life. He probably didn't even know the meaning of the word. He wouldn't look even if she informed him she was on fire. She was momentarily tempted to do so, if only to test her theory.

No. She didn't give the man a crude hand gesture because she was clearly in the wrong. She had been late and for a completely self-indulgent, ridiculous reason. But oh, it had been worth it to see the look on Cade's face when she'd told him it had been a pity they'd never spent the night together.

Mark Grimaldi wouldn't for a moment understand his top spy being late to a mission because she was dancing with a suspected criminal in the moonlight. As she kicked off her shoes and peeled off her muddy stockings, she amused herself with the thought of telling him. What would stick-up-the-arse Grimaldi reply to such an admission? A moment later, she was no longer smiling as she realized she had a . . . situation.

"I'll need help with my gown." She turned her back to him, exposing the buttons of her dress, and looked at him over her shoulder. "I could do it myself but it would take much longer."

He slowly tipped up his hat. A look of pure disgruntlement rested on his fine features. His lip was curled. Grimaldi would be downright handsome, Danielle thought wistfully, if he wasn't so . . . Grimaldi.

"Bloody hell," he mumbled, but his fingers went to the buttons and made quick work of them. Quite quick, Danielle noted with surprise. Hmm. Seemed the general knew his way around a woman's clothing. How very interesting. This discovery was further reinforced when Danielle was obliged to add, "And now my stays."

"Jesus Christ," Grimaldi ground out.

Danielle plunked her hands on her hips. "It's not my fault you had me traipsing around Mayfair dressed as a lady's maid. Had to look the part, didn't I?"

The only answer was a sort of unhappy grunt, but his deft fingers made quick work of the shift's laces as well.

"Anything else? Need help with your hair?" he grumbled.

"Why, General, did you just make a jest?"

"No." He shoved his hat back down and turned away again, folding his arms across his rigid chest.

"Don't worry," she called in a singsong voice. "I can manage the tapes of my drawers myself."

"That's a damn relief." The general grunted before rapping on the door that separated them from the driver. At the man's "Yes, guvna?" Grimaldi snapped, "The docks and make it lively."

The driver called to the horses and snapped the reins and the conveyance took off down the street.

Danielle spent the ride to the docks removing the rest of her maid's clothing and replacing it with the garments of a cabin boy. By the time her shoes were buckled and her hat placed atop her head, with her hair tucked up inside, the hackney was pulling to a stop near the docks. Danielle rolled up the clothing she'd been wearing and stuffed it into the valise.

"Make certain this gets back to my mother's flat," she said, pushing the valise toward Grimaldi with her foot. "Along with this." She handed him the note she'd written to her mother, telling her and Mrs. Horton she'd be gone for a while and would return as soon as possible.

"I will," Grimaldi said with a curt nod. "I'll also ensure they have enough money while you're gone."

"Thank you," she managed.

Realizing she was fully dressed, Grimaldi turned back toward her and pushed up his hat. All business again.

"What are my orders?" She pulled her short leather

vest tightly against her shoulders. She glanced down to ensure that her breasts weren't—ahem—noticeable. Thankfully, she wasn't well-endowed enough to require much binding there. A cotton tunic beneath her shirt was all she needed.

"*The Elenor* sails at dawn," Grimaldi said. "It's chasing Capitan Baptiste."

Danielle nodded. Exactly as she had suspected. She was meant to follow Lafayette Baptiste. It was time for a reckoning. "Is *The Elenor* friendly to the Crown?"

He studied her face. "It's a privateer, friendly enough. I just learned tonight, it's on the same mission we are."

She turned her head to look out the window, searching the dark waterline for any sign of the vessel. "I suppose I'm to be a cabin boy."

"No."

The one word stopped her. Her hands dropped away from her vest and her head snapped up to face the general.

"There wasn't an opening for a cabin boy. You're to be the cook's assistant this time."

"Cook's assistant?" Her mouth fell open. "But I can't cook a bloody thing!"

"You didn't know how to be a cabin boy once upon a time, either, but I daresay you'll learn. You've always been a quick study, Cross. Besides, how difficult could it be?"

She pushed a couple of wayward strands of hair up into her cap. "Did you tell them I have experience as a cook's assistant?"

Grimaldi smirked. "Of course I did."

She scowled at him. "What do you think they'll do when they find out I don't know a potato from a carrot?"

He eyed her in that condescending way of his. "Potatoes are white. Carrots are orange. Any other questions?"

Danielle clamped her mouth shut and glared at him. Grimaldi did exactly as he pleased whenever he pleased and she and the other poor sops in his employ were left to make do the best they were able. All in a day's work of being one of the Home Office's best. "Fine. I'm a cook's assistant," she muttered. "Anything else I need to know?"

"Not at the moment. We'll have another ship following you a day or so behind. I'll be on it. You know what you need to do."

She nodded once. There was only one more thing she wanted to clarify. "This is it, Grimaldi. My last mission. You promised. For my mother's sake, I'm settling on the coast and living a life of peace and quiet."

"You know I'm a man of my word," he said. "I promised you."

That was all she needed to hear. She nodded once. "Very well." She finished tucking her hair into her cap. "You're not going to ask me what I learned about Cade Cavendish?"

"No. I've recently received some additional intelligence about him. Cade is no longer our mark."

"Who is?"

"Baptiste, of course."

Grimaldi let down the opposite canvas window and pointed into the inky darkness. The light from the nearly full moon illuminated the water and the large ship that rested at anchor in front of them.

"There she is." Grimaldi nodded toward the ship. *The*

Elenor. She follows *The French Secret* on the dawn tide."

Danielle could see enough of the ship to tell it was a sight better than many of the vessels she'd crewed over the years. Perhaps it wouldn't be so horrible. A thought of Lady Daphne and Mary flashed across her mind. Had they discovered her absence yet? Were they angry with her? She tamped down the thought. No looking back. She nodded to the ship, too. "Are they going where I think they're going?"

Grimaldi's eyes glinted in the dark of the coach. "Yes."

CHAPTER THIRTY-TWO

Barely more than an hour after watching Danielle leave his brother's house in Mayfair, Cade was sitting in his captain's cabin aboard *The Elenor*. He'd traded his fine black evening attire for breeches, boots, and a loose white linen shirt. Bloody hell, he was much more comfortable and at ease. He'd always felt at home on the sea.

He didn't belong in a town house at a stuffy *ton* ball. He'd left them a note, of course, Daphne and Rafe. They wouldn't be surprised. The good thing about being the black sheep was you rarely let anyone down. They didn't expect much from you. Who knew how long it would be before he saw his brother again, if ever.

Cade stood with his legs braced apart, breathing in the sea air and shaking his head. A vision of Danielle flashed unbidden through his mind. Normally, when he left a woman, he didn't think of her again. Not so soon, at least.

This was different. This time Danielle had been the one to leave, and she'd left him a note. He'd found it there, sitting on his pillow when he'd gone to his room to pack his things. It was crumpled and the ink was smeared. It was what she'd been holding in her hands when he'd come to her bedchamber.

A bloody good-bye note that had barely mentioned she was leaving, let alone why. The woman had gone and she hadn't looked back. Damned frustrating. Even more frustrating, they hadn't even really had a dalliance. His balls still throbbed at the thought of what he *hadn't* had.

Cade studied the map with one ripped corner that rested on the table in front of him.

St. Helena.

Lafayette Baptiste, the captain of *The French Secret,* was in charge of the latest plot to liberate Napoleon from his second island prison and return him to power. Again.

A knock sounded at the door. "Cap'n," came the muffled voice of his first mate, Danny McCummins. Cade had met the man on a prison ship years ago. Danny had been about to have his hand sliced off for stealing from another man on the ship. Cade had helped the Irishman escape and they'd taken off together. Later, Danny had met up with one his mates, another Irishman named Sean O'Malley. They two had sworn their allegiance to Cade.

For his part, Cade trusted no one more than Danny and Sean. Together with their penchant for getting into trouble, exacerbated by their love of women and their perhaps even greater love of ale, Cade had bailed the both of them out of a fair number of scrapes over the years.

"Come in." Cade rolled up the map and stuck it under his arm.

Danny came strolling in, humming a sailor's tune, the remnants of last night's supper smeared on his coarse shirt. That was typical for Danny McCummins. Danny. Damn. The name reminded Cade of Danielle. He couldn't get her out of his thoughts.

"Are we ready to sail, McCummins?"

"Aye, Cap'n," the first mate replied.

"Were you able to round up the rest of the crew on such short notice?"

"Aye, Cap'n. Everyone excepting Billy."

Cade turned to face him. "Where's Billy?"

McCummins's smile revealed a hodgepodge of ill-tended teeth. "If'n I knew that, Cap'n, I daresay he'd be here."

Cade cracked a smile. "I suppose we can make do without a cook's assistant." He strode to his desk, opened a drawer, and placed the map there. He shut the drawer and locked it.

"We don't have ta, Cap'n," McCummins replied, obviously pleased with himself, judging from the size of his grin. "O'Malley found us a replacement at the tavern last night. A chap what was looking fer work fer his son."

"Son?" Cade narrowed his eyes.

"Aye. Says he's sailed afore and knows his way 'round a ship."

"Does he know how to cook?"

"Enough ta be an assistant, or so his da says."

"You haven't met the boy?"

"Not me'self. O'Malley seems ta think the lad might

well be on the wrong side o' the wharf police. Apparently, he's looking ta set sail immediately."

Cade sighed. It was a story he'd heard before. Often. Most of *The Elenor*'s crew had been on the wrong side of the law, himself included. Cade was more worried about O'Malley hiring the boy sight unseen. What if he was an opium addict or riddled with vermin? *That* wouldn't do for a cook's assistant. "Very well," Cade replied. "Tell O'Malley it's on his head if the lad is of no use."

McCummins nodded. "He's here now, Cap'n. O'Malley says he's a right energetic thing, ready and willin' ta work hard."

"Is that so?" Cade stood looking out the window above his bed. "What's his name?" he asked, not particularly interested in the answer.

"I believe it's Cross," McCummins replied. "Yeah, that's the one. Cross."

"Cross?" Cade narrowed his eyes at the skyline. Cross? LaCrosse. He shook his head. Damn. Was he to be plagued with thoughts of that woman forever? Would everything remind him of her? For how long? Bloody nuisance.

Dawn was beginning to break. It was time to leave. He grabbed up his spyglass from a hook on the bulk head and focused it on *The French Secret* anchored far across the harbor but still within view. The French ship was hauling up its anchor. Cade spun around. "Weigh anchor!"

"Aye, aye, Cap'n." McCummins headed for the door to issue the orders across the ship.

"McCummins," Cade called.

The older man paused, his foot on the first step leading up the ladder. "Yes, Cap'n?"

"Not too close to *The French Secret*. Give it a sizeable lead, then . . ."

McCummins nodded. "Yes, Cap'n?"

"Bring the new cook's assistant to me."

CHAPTER THIRTY-THREE

"Then there was the time the captain gave the order to throw half the guns over the starboard bow and focus the rest on the masts of the *Devil's Joke*. Why, we routed those blighters in less than an hour and they took off toward Portugal with a busted mizzen, limping like a three-legged dog." Danielle listened attentively as this diatribe was proudly uttered by the first mate, a man named Danny McCummins.

It was yet another in a parade of stories featuring the captain's heroics. In her short time on *The Elanor*, she'd already learned that these men were loyal, committed, and completely adoring of their captain. He had apparently fought traitors, saved helpless children, and even rescued a wounded dog from an enemy ship during hand-to-hand combat in the middle of the sea. The only thing she hadn't heard so far was a tale about the captain wrestling a shark—though she'd little doubt that particular story would soon be told if she listened long enough.

She didn't mind the stories. They served to distract the crew from asking her questions about herself and that was exactly how she wanted to keep it.

Bells sounded and Danny and the rest of the crew raced away. Danielle was left alone with the cook, a middle-aged man of few words who possessed a nearly bald head, a sturdy paunch, and spent most of his time rattling around in the pantry. She sat on a stool at the rickety galley table and dropped her head into her hands and allowed herself to expel her breath. It was the first moment she'd had alone since she'd been rowed out to the ship in a dinghy manned by Sean O'Malley, the second mate.

"I've never known an Irishman ta be second mate afore," she'd said as she and O'Malley rowed toward *The Elenor*. She'd been attempting to make small talk with the man but it was true. She'd never known an Irish second mate, not on an English ship, with their prejudice against the Irish.

"Then ye'll be even more surprised when ye learn the first mate is also an Irishman. McCummins is 'is name. Ye'll be meetin' 'im soon enough."

"Is the captain Irish, too?"

O'Malley snort-laughed at that. "Nah, Cap'n is an English bloke. Oakleaf's 'is name."

Oakleaf? That sounded solidly English. Not that Danielle cared one whit. She'd been treated badly by both the French and the English at times. She knew the sting of prejudice. The captain of *The Elenor* seemed more kind to Irish than some of the French had been to her poor mother.

Danielle enjoyed her moments alone, for surely they would be brief and rare. All the other moments since she'd arrived on the ship had been fraught with tension as she hoped the crew believed she was a boy. Despite all the years she'd spent successfully pretending to be a boy and her familiarity with the role, she always experienced that moment when meeting a new person when she feared he'd see through her disguise and recognize her for a young woman instantly. Thankfully, that hadn't happened after her advent to *The Elenor*. They'd all believed she was a lad. She'd held her breath at first. But she'd found over the years that most men didn't stare too long or too closely at grubby little urchin boys, and the ones who did she'd long-ago learned to keep her distance from.

She'd spent the last hour after they'd got underway being regaled with distasteful jokes by the cook and a rotating cast of other crew members who made brief appearances in the kitchen after seeing to their chores. The galley, she learned, was the social hub of this particular ship. It was also hot as Hades with a constantly boiling pot over an open fire and a cookstove that belched black smoke into the air. The smoke leisurely dissipated through a dark hole that obviously wasn't large enough in the deck above. The crew seemed a friendly, if bawdy lot and she'd already begun to feel she might fit in.

The door swung open and O'Malley came barreling into the galley. "Get up, Cross," he barked at her. "The cap'n wants ta see ye."

Danielle's head snapped up. She'd expected to meet the captain eventually, of course, perhaps at dinnertime when she was serving him a meal, but to have a request for a private audience . . . that was rare. Her stomach dropped. Captains were often the most astute people on ships. If this one wasn't just meeting her quickly in passing, but actually studying her, asking her questions . . . she didn't even want to think about what might happen.

"Yes, yes. O' course," she replied in her best deckhand's voice, using the common English accent she'd perfected over the years. She had a penchant for mimicking language that had served her well. She'd simply listened to a few of the younger males on a ship for a while and then said what they said just as they'd said it as if she were a quick-witted parrot. She'd blended right in.

"Come with me," O'Malley said, gesturing over his shoulder.

Danielle followed him out of the kitchen, up the ladder, over the deck, and across the planks into a gangway where they descended another ladder into a darkened, cool space near the aft of the ship. Danielle pulled her sweaty shirt away from her tunic. No matter how this meeting went, at least she'd have a few blissful minutes away from the searing heat of the galley. Grimaldi was going to get an earful about forcing her to pose as a cook's assistant.

O'Malley rapped twice upon the large wooden door to the captain's cabin.

"Come in," came a muffled deep male voice. The captain sounded young.

Danielle held her breath while O'Malley pushed open the door. The second mate stepped inside first. Danielle followed him. She'd never seen a captain's cabin so grand. It must have taken up the whole aft of the ship. There was a desk, a set of chairs, and a brass bathtub of all things, with buckets hung on pegs near it. A large bed dominated the rear of the space, with emerald-green satin sheets covering it. No small bunk for *this* captain. The room smelled like lemon wax and a spicy mix of cigar smoke and something else vaguely familiar that Danielle couldn't quite place. She glanced around, curious for a glimpse of the man who inhabited such a grand space.

"Here's the new cook's assistant," O'Malley said, doffing his hat and gesturing back toward Danielle. O'Malley was a large man. Given her lack of height, Danielle couldn't see around him.

"Captain Oakleaf," she intoned. She hoped to *dieu* he didn't question why she didn't doff her hat, too.

"Cross, did you say?" the captain asked.

There was something familiar about that voice. Fear snaked up Danielle's spine.

"Aye, Cap'n," O'Malley replied. The larger man stepped to the side just then and Danielle was afforded an unencumbered view of the captain's tall, broad-shouldered form. He stood with his back to her, but his physique caused the hairs on the back of her neck to stand up. He seemed so . . . familiar.

"Welcome, Mr. Cross," the captain said, turning to face her.

Their eyes met and Danielle had to brace her hand against the bulkhead to keep herself steady. Time stopped.

Whatever O'Malley was saying was unintelligible noise in her ears. She blinked twice, trying to make sense of what she was seeing. It couldn't be . . . Cade. Cade was Captain Oakleaf?

She had fooled the others, but there was no fooling Cade Cavendish. She sucked in her breath and with a small gasp, took an instinctive step back.

Cade betrayed her by neither word nor deed. His eyes didn't blink, his brows didn't rise, and there was no gasp, small or otherwise, from his quarter. He stood there, outwardly calm and entirely in control. Damn him. He had to be surprised, didn't he? He couldn't have possibly known. The implications of that line of logic raced through Danielle's brain at a speed that made her head ache. No. No. He couldn't possibly have known.

"Don't be afeered o' the cap'n," O'Malley said, poking Danielle in the ribs with his elbow and laughing. "He's a large man, ta be sure, but I promise he won't beat ye. Unless ye steal sumpin' o' don't do yer duties. Then it's the cat-o-nine fer ye," O'Malley continued, still laughing good-naturedly.

All Danielle could do was nod. Nod and stare at Cade, willing him not to reveal her secret in front of O'Malley. She plucked at her shirt again. It was practically plastered to her chest. Had she really ever thought it was cooler here than the galley? Ridiculous.

"Would you care for a drink, *Mister* Cross?" Cade asked smoothly.

Danielle did not mistake the emphasis he placed on her name. She closed her eyes briefly, praying. How long had it been since she'd prayed? No time like the present to begin again.

After a quick knock, the door swung open again and this time McCummins strolled in. The first mate was usually humming and this time was no exception. He stopped as soon as he saw them. "Ah, there ye be, Cross. I was looking fer ye ta bring ye here ta meet the cap'n. Seems me matey Seanny beat me ta it."

"That's what ye get fer snoozin' on the job," O'Malley replied, still laughing.

McCummins grabbed his tricorn off his balding head and slapped at the other man with it. O'Malley followed suit and a good-natured tussle ensued before Cade ended it with one word that shot through the cabin like the crack of a pistol. "Enough."

Both men fell into line next to each other and jammed their hats back on their heads. Cade smiled. "I was just about to ask Cross here if he'd like a drink." He made his way toward the desk. "Where did you say you found Cross again?"

Nearly panting from fear, Danielle couldn't look away from him. It was as if their gazes were melded together. Would he betray her? Would he? Sweat trickled between her breasts. She clenched her jaw. Why was there a tiny part of her that was . . . glad to see him?

"I told ye, Cap'n," McCummins began. "O'Malley met his pa in—"

"No." Another crack like a pistol. "I'd like *Cross* to tell the story."

Danielle sucked in her breath. She could do this. Grimaldi wasn't a fool. He'd prepared her well by explaining how she'd come to be on the boat. She expelled a breath and focused on her earlier conversation with the general. It was not possible Grimaldi hadn't known Cade was the captain of this ship. Known and not seen fit—for some godforsaken reason—to tell her. She was going to gut the general from ear to navel when next they met. Ironic, considering he'd been the one to teach her how to use a knife so deftly. There would be time later to fantasize about how she'd murder Grimaldi.

At the moment, her only concern, her greatest concern, was ensuring that Cade kept her secret. She'd be no better than horsemeat on a ship like this within minutes if word got out she was a woman.

She kept her eyes trained on Cade. "I've done a few things I ain't proud of, Cap'n," she said, silently willing him to hold his tongue.

His brows rose when he heard her accent. A quirk of amusement? She deftly continued. "Me pa were looking out fer me, wanted ta find me a spot on the first ship what was leaving 'arbor."

"And that was my ship?" Cade drawled. He crossed over to a cupboard near the desk and took out two glasses. Next, he pulled a bottle of whiskey from the cupboard. He splashed a healthy portion of the brown liquid into both glasses.

"Aye." She still eyed him warily.

He held up both glasses. "Care for a drink, Cross?"

"No, thank ye, Cap'n," she answered politely, folding her hands together in front of her.

"Ah, come now, Cross," he replied, a lazy smile covering his handsome features. "On this ship it's bad luck not to drink a toast to the newest member of the crew. How else will we thank you for coming to our rescue when we so desperately needed a cook's assistant?"

She shifted uncomfortably on both feet. "If it's all the

same ta ye, Cap'n, I don't like ta take spirits whilst I'm workin'."

That statement sent Danny and Sean into peals of laughter.

Cade arched one blond brow. "It isn't all the same to me, Cross. As I'm certain you know from *all* your *experience* on ships. We sailors are quite odd about our superstitions . . . the things we consider bad luck. Not drinking a toast to a new crew member's health is considered extremely bad luck on *The Elenor*. Isn't it, lads?" He directed his words to McCummins and O'Malley but his eyes remained locked with Danielle's.

"That 'tis," McCummins agreed. "I, fer one, am quite willin' ta drink ta yer health, Cross, me boy."

"Aye," O'Malley added with a resolute nod.

"It's nearly as bad of luck as say, killing an albatross or having a *woman* aboard," Cade drawled.

Both O'Malley and McCummins gasped and both men quickly crossed themselves. "Oy, Cap'n, don't say somethin' like that even in jest," O'Malley pleaded, shaking his head.

Cade held the whiskey glass at arm's length to Danielle.

With tight lips, she took it. "I wouldn't want ta cause no bad luck, Cap'n," she ground out, giving him a withering glare.

"Excellent." Cade replaced the stopper on the bottle and put it back in the cabinet.

"None for us, Cap'n?" O'Malley looked hopefully toward the bottle and licked his lips.

Danielle eyed Cade. He was toying with her. Letting her know he held the power in this exchange of wills because he knew her secret. She squared her shoulders and took a swig from the glass. She'd had whiskey before. This was some *maudit* fine whiskey, but she mustn't drink too much. She needed to keep her wits about her. Cade may have scored the first blow, but she wasn't about to let him win the battle. It was time to fight back.

"Yes, Captain *Oakleaf*. None fer the others?" She blinked at him innocently. "Oakleaf is a mighty interestin' name, by the by. Who are yer kinsfolk if'n ye don't mind me askin'?"

Cade's gaze narrowed on her and he tilted his head to the side almost imperceptibly as if acknowledging the point she'd just made. He turned to his first and second mates. "McCummins, go see to it that we're on course. O'Malley, climb up to the eagle's nest and get a report."

"But Cap'n, Hendricks usually gets the rep—"

"Now!" With that one word, both men scrambled toward the door. "I'd like to speak to Cross alone."

CHAPTER THIRTY-FOUR

A deafening silence ensued once the two men had gone. Danielle couldn't decide which was louder, the ticking of the gilded clock anchored to the desk, or the beating of her own heart. Cade faced away from her the entire time. It lasted until she wanted to scream, "Say something! Do something!"

Finally he turned, stared at her, and drained his glass in one large gulp. "I'm only going to ask you one time and if you know what's good for you, you'll tell the truth." His voice was more deadly calm and filled with anger than she'd ever heard it. "What the hell are you doing here?"

"I have the same question for you." She tossed her head, though admittedly the effect was ruined with her hair tucked into her hat. She'd never noticed until recently how effective a good head toss could be for a woman.

"You want to know why I'm on my own ship?" He scoffed. "That's rich. Why did you follow me here?"

"Follow you? Don't flatter yourself. I'm not here for you. I needed the passage."

He snorted. "Important lady's maid business, is it?"

She rolled her eyes. "If you haven't figured it out by now, I'm not a lady's maid."

"And I'm the bloody prince."

"Your highness." She bowed.

His eyes narrowed on her. "Are you seriously trying to convince me that you're actually a ship's cook's assistant? I happen to know you make more money seeing to my sister-in-law's hair."

"Of course I'm not going to try to convince you I'm a cook's assistant. I'm going to succeed in convincing you that I know General Grimaldi."

Cade's eyes flashed blue fire before narrowing on her closely. "What did you say?"

"Don't deny that you know him, too. He's obviously thrown us together for this little adventure."

Cade opened his mouth to say something, closed it, pulled out the whiskey bottle, splashed more into this glass, and tossed that back, too. "What the hell are you talking about?"

"General Grimaldi, my superior."

"You report to Grim?" Cade asked in a way that made Danielle realize he was trying to convince himself he wasn't in the middle of a dream. Perhaps a nightmare.

Grim? She'd never heard her stately boss referred to by that nickname, but she wasn't about to admit it to Cade. "Yes. If I don't mistake my guess, you do, too."

"You're serious. You didn't follow me. You're really here because Grim sent you?"

"Yes."

"Why are you dressed like a boy?

"Because women aren't usually welcome aboard ships."

"Why is a lady's maid pretending to be a cook's assistant?"

Danielle took a deep breath. Obviously, Grimaldi had meant for them to discover each other. There was hardly any use in prevaricating. "The truth is, I'm a pirate."

"*You're* a pirate?"

"A smuggler really. Reformed at times." She nodded toward him. "And you?"

"Also a pirate. Who do you think I am?"

She nearly stamped her foot. "At the moment I don't care if you're the ghost of Horatio Nelson. I need passage to where this pile of wood is going."

"Pile of wood?" His voice was outraged.

She shrugged. "Very well. She's actually a fine ship. Beautiful lines. This cabin is particularly impressive. It's positively grand."

"Thank you. Now, tell me what the bloody hell you were doing in my brother's house posing as a lady's maid? Were you spying on Rafe?"

"I was spying on you."

"Me? You were spying on *me*? That's why you were at Rafe's house?"

"Why were you staying with your brother?"

Cade slammed his fist on the table. "Damn it. Stop answering questions with questions."

"Or what? You'll toss me overboard? You'll have to answer to Grimaldi for that and he's not a day behind us."

Cade paced across the cabin and back, scrubbing his hand through his hair. "What in the devil's name is going on?"

"I'd like to know as well. Do you want to slow the ship and wait to ask the general?"

"No."

"Neither do I. Baptiste might outrun us."

Cade's eyes were as wide as the bottom of the whiskey glasses. "You know about Baptiste?"

"Among other things," Danielle replied with a sigh.

Cade's nostrils flared. "What the hell am I supposed to do with a *woman* on my ship?"

"I know my way around a ship probably better than you do."

"How is that possible? You're a bloody lady's maid."

"In case it *still* hasn't sunk in, you lug-headed brute, I'm *not* a lady's maid. Just like *you're* not a London gadabout leeching off his brother's money, or named Captain *Oakleaf* for that matter."

He narrowed his eyes at her, apparently not believing any of it. "This ship isn't going to France if that's what you think."

"I know. You're following Lafayette Baptiste to St. Helena, which is where I'm going, too. Stay out of my way and I'll stay out of yours, and perhaps Grimaldi can explain this mess when we get there."

Cade looked positively dumbfounded. "There's no possibility I'm allowing you to remain pretending to be this ship's cook's assistant. Not even for one night."

She smiled at him smugly and crossed her arms over her chest. "What do you intend to do, toss me overboard?"

He gripped the back of the chair so tightly his knuckles turned white. "No. If Grim put you here, as you said, you must stay. But I also cannot allow you to go gallivanting around the ship unprotected, either."

"No one but you knows I'm a woman."

His gaze traced her up and down, a sultry look in his eyes. "I find that difficult to believe."

She gave him a tight smile. "Believe it."

"*I* happen to know the truth and I won't allow you to go about. The more interaction you have with the crew, the more chance they'll discover your sex."

She groaned and rubbed her temples. "I don't expect you'll believe this, but I've made my way on ships, convincing everyone I was male, since I was thirteen."

He gave her a tight-lipped smile. "You're right. I don't believe you."

"You're a stubborn ass."

"And you are my responsibility now."

"I can take care of myself."

He planted both fists on his hips. "I will not take the risk."

"What do you intend to do? Store me in a trunk in this cabin?"

"You're partially right. I do intend to keep you in this cabin."

"What!" Her eyes flew wide.

"My cabin boy will take over as cook's assistant."

"That makes no sense. What will you tell everyone?"

"I'll tell them Martin wants to try his hand at

cooking. I'll tell them I want to keep an eye on you because I don't trust you. I'll tell them I bloody well made a ruling decision. It doesn't matter what I tell them. I'm the captain and what I say goes."

She glared at him, nearly spitting out of anger. "Have I told you you're a stubborn ass?"

"Not in the last five seconds."

"Well, you are."

"I'll take that as a compliment." He called out, "McCummins!"

The first mate arrived in seconds, doffing his cap. "Yes, Cap'n?"

"Tell Martin he'll be taking over as cook's assistant. I'm going to teach Cross here how to be a proper cabin boy."

If the first mate thought the order odd, he didn't betray it. "Yes, Cap'n." He nodded before hurrying off to inform Martin.

"Perfect," Danielle said. "Now the entire ship will be talking about me."

"Make no mistake, they already were."

"And you think this makes it better?"

"I think it makes you safer."

"I already told you, I—"

"Can take care of yourself. I've heard that before, along with something about my being a stubborn ass. Regardless, my decision is final."

She wanted to kick him, hit him, throw something at his big, overly confident head.

He slowly, deliberately crossed over to the door, shut it, and made his way back to the table that stood between them. "Tell me, Cross," he drawled. "Do you know anything about being a cabin boy?"

"Oh, only *everything*."

A roguish grin spread across his face. "Excellent. That means we can spend our time on things other than your lessons."

She raised a brow. Her stomach lurched. "Other things?"

"Yes."

"Such as?"

He leaned over, braced both hands on the table, and arched a brow. "I believe the last time we saw each other, you said it was a pity we hadn't spent the night together." He grinned, his eyes gleaming wickedly. "I'm willing to rectify that mistake, if you are."

CHAPTER THIRTY-FIVE

Cade pulled the cabin door closed behind him and stood in the corridor outside. He scrubbed a hand through his hair and paced back and forth in the small space. What in the name of God was going on? He didn't work for anyone, let alone Mark Grimaldi. It was true that the general and he had worked together in the past, but that was because they had a shared goal and it suited both men's purposes. Cade's preoccupation with Baptiste wasn't something the law-abiding Grimaldi would approve of. But Grimaldi was after Baptiste, too, if Danielle was to be believed. Her story was outlandish enough to be true. But why the hell had she been spying on *him*?

Damn. He already knew the answer. Grimaldi didn't trust him. He should have guessed. It all made sense. No doubt Daphne's former lady's maid had been well paid to leave town.

There was nothing left to do. Until they put into

port—and according to O'Conner's information they wouldn't do that until they reached the coast of Spain—Cade had to keep an eye on Danielle. He must wait to get the answers he needed from Grimaldi. That bastard better have some damn good ones.

Danielle spent the time since Cade had left the cabin poking around through his belongings. It served to distract her from what he'd said. *Mon dieu.* The man knew how to say the most provocative things. Spend the night together? Here on this ship? After . . . ? After what? What in the *nom de dieu* was happening here? She paced back and forth in front of the massive bed, trying to ignore the tingles Cade's offer sparked in her belly.

She'd known all along that Baptiste had been the ultimate goal. But what did Cade have to do with it?

What exactly was Grimaldi up to? Why had he sent her to watch Cade to begin with? He had to have known they would recognize each other immediately on this ship. Why wouldn't he have told her? What sort of sick, twisted game was all of this?

She knew from her training, the weeks she'd spent studying, running, lifting heavy objects, learning to fight, throwing knives, rowing oars, remaining silent, hiding, waiting, listening, watching. She'd been trained by the best. Mark Grimaldi. The first week of spy training he'd informed her over and over until the words blurred in her head. The mission always came first.

Maudit. She'd been put on this ship with Cade for some reason. Apparently they were meant to work together. But could she trust him? He certainly wouldn't trust *her* now. Not after she'd lied to him. But they each had a mission to complete. They might be on this ship together for weeks. She refused to be cowed by him. Now that he'd deprived her of her duties as cook's assistant, she'd be damned if she'd run around catering to his every whim.

She inspected the glorious cabin. Cade's shaving utensils were lined up perfectly in the cabinet by the washbasin. His shirts were folded perfectly in the wardrobe. The man didn't need a valet; why in heaven's name did he need a cabin boy? She wrenched open the desk drawer. It held a sextant, a small spyglass, some paperwork, and . . . a map.

She unfurled it, studied it, but she already knew what it contained. She'd already discussed it with Grimaldi. It was a map of their destination. St. Helena.

She found an assortment of books on a shelf on a far wall, a collection of philosophy, history, science, and nautical topics. She hadn't figured Cade for a scholar. If he'd read even a quarter of the books here, he'd be considered well-read, surprising for someone who'd been raised in Seven Dials.

She, too, had always tried to educate herself by reading, but there were several volumes here she hadn't read before. Shucking her boots and stockings, she plucked a copy of *The Life and Death of Cardinal Wolsey* off the shelf and padded over to the giant bed. She slid onto the jade-colored satin sheets and luxuriated in the feel of them beneath her feet. The mattress was soft and fluffy, filled with down. She glanced over.

One pillow didn't match the others. It was covered in white linen as opposed to green satin. There was something familiar about it. She crawled across the sprawling bed and pulled the pillow into her lap. It looked much like the one she'd used at Lady Daphne's house. She put it to her nose and sniffed. *Her orchid perfume.*

Could it be? Was it possible Cade had taken the pillow from her bedchamber? He had been in her bedchamber the last time she'd seen him, after all. But why had he taken it? To remember her by? Contemplating the enormity of that thought, she snuggled into the sheets and laid her head on the pillow. Her yawn was so big her ears popped. The fact that she hadn't slept all night, combined with the gentle rocking of the ship and the supreme comfort of the bed conspired to lull her to sleep.

The next thing Danielle knew, she was awakened by a husky male voice near her ear. "In my bed, I see. Does that mean you've decided to take me up on my offer?"

CHAPTER THIRTY-SIX

Danielle's eyes flew open and she scrambled up, her back against the luxurious pillows, instinctively pulling the covers to her chin even though she was still fully dressed. "Wha-what?"

Cade stood over the bed, his hands on his hips, laughing. "Sorry to wake you so suddenly. I didn't mean to startle you."

Danielle rubbed the sleep from her eyes and glanced around. It was dark outside the windows and only moonlight and the brace of candles sitting on the desk illuminated the room.

Had she truly slept all day? "What time is it?"

Eight bells sounded. "It's the dog watch," Cade said with a grin.

"Eight o'clock," she whispered.

"No," he replied, still grinning.

"Surely it's not twelve?" Her eyes went wide.

His brows rose. "You know time on a ship?"

She rolled her eyes. "I already informed you that I know quite a lot about ships."

"You did." His grin was positively wolfish. "And yes, it's twelve."

"I can't believe I slept all day," she said.

"Well, we didn't exactly get much sleep last night."

She eyed him warily. "Don't say it like *that*."

"Like what?"

"Like we . . . spent the night together."

"Didn't we?"

"No! Not like *that*. You know we didn't."

"Ah, that's right. You only told me you *wished* it had been like that. Right before you took off to stow aboard my ship."

She scrambled off the bed and stood next to it, sheepishly, her feet bare and her hair, which had come free of the cap, streaming over her shoulders.

"You look absolutely nothing like a boy right now, by the by," he informed her. "What do you think would happen to you if you were in the bunks with the others?"

"If I were a cook's assistant I wouldn't have been asleep. I'd have been working."

"A convenient answer."

"A truthful one."

He sat on the fur edge of the bed and began shucking off his boots. "Would you like to help?" he asked. "I seem to remember you have some experience in this quarter."

"You're endlessly amusing," she shot back.

Ignoring that, he stood and began to take off his shirt, unbuttoning it and pulling it over one shoulder.

Her eyes flared. "What are you doing?"

His grin was wicked. "Undressing. Care to help?"

"No!"

"You're not a particularly helpful cabin boy."

She smirked at him. "About that. I thought you said you didn't need a valet, yet you have a cabin boy?"

"A cabin boy is entirely different from a valet," Cade replied.

"How so?"

"Less picky. Less exacting. Someone you can yell at to bloody well get out and leave you alone when you choose."

"You have an answer for everything." She rolled her eyes.

"Of course I do. At any rate, unlike you, I don't sleep fully dressed and don't intend to begin now to accommodate you."

When he began to unbutton his breeches, Danielle spun around and crossed her arms over her chest, facing away from him. She waited a few minutes, trying not to imagine him undressed. "Finished?" She hated the fact that her voice shook.

"Not until I'm nude," he replied in far too jovial of a tone.

Her mouth fell open. And went dry. "Am I to understand that you—" She snapped her mouth shut again as his breeches came flying past her shoulder to land in a heap on the wood planks in front of her.

"You'll see to those, won't you, *boy*?"

Danielle gritted her teeth. "Yes, Cap'n." She grabbed the breeches from the floor, still facing away from him, and spent an inordinate amount of time shaking them out and folding them. They smelled like him, spicy cologne and a hint of soap. *Nom de dieu*. Why did they have to *smell* like him? If they didn't, she'd have a much easier time ignoring the fact that the man who owned them and had recently occupied them was standing five paces behind her completely naked.

"Are you decent?" she finally asked in a much sharper voice than she'd meant to.

"I'm never decent," came his laughter-tinged reply. "I thought you knew that about me."

She closed her eyes and pinched the bridge of her nose. "I meant are you clothed?"

"No," came the succinct reply.

"No?" she echoed. Before she had a chance to inquire as to whether he meant to stand there unclothed all night, he continued, "I sleep in the nude."

"You sleep in the—?" A string of French curse words flew through her head.

"However, I am covered, if that's what you're worried about, though I can uncover myself again if you'd like."

That was it. She was through playing word games with him. She'd seen a lot on ships. A naked man wasn't about to intimidate her. She would call his bluff. She spun on her heel to face the bed again. He was in it, covered by the sheets from the waist down. From the waist up, however, the man was fully, gloriously undressed. The bare expanse of his chest was on display. His muscled arms were crossed behind his head and he had a roguish grin on his face.

Danielle had seen her fair share of male chests before. Working on ships, she'd been careful to keep herself covered, but she'd seen and heard it all. Every inch of the male anatomy and every word they used to describe their . . . parts. And there were a great many words, to be sure. Nothing in her experience had prepared her for the sight of Cade Cavendish's bare chest. Broad, muscled, ripped, hairless. She longed to run her fingers across the smooth expanse of skin. Her mouth watered. She pressed her lips together and forced herself to drag her eyes away from his chest and meet his gaze.

"Care to join me?" He patted the empty space next to him.

She ignored the invitation, instead marching past the bed to open the wardrobe and carefully set the breeches inside. She located his discarded shirt and shook it out before hanging it in the wardrobe, too. Next, she gathered his boots and made her way to the cabinet where she'd located the polishing items earlier. She set about dusting the boots with a horsehair brush.

The entire time he watched her with an unabashed grin on his face. "Hmm. Seems you do know the duties of a good cabin boy."

She forced herself to bite back the I-told-you-so on her lips. Finally, she finished her ministrations and faced him again. "Where does—did—Martin sleep?"

"In here."

"Where?" she bit out. He wasn't about to make this any easier for her, was he?

"If you're asking where *you* should sleep, may I suggest the bed?" He blinked at her innocently and patted the empty space next to him.

"Will you be in the bed if I sleep there?"

"Of course I will. It's my bed." His grin was unrepentant. "It's far more comfortable than where Martin slept, however."

She tapped her booted foot on the ground. "Which was?"

Cade sighed and pointed. "On a pallet on the floor in the corner."

She hadn't seen a pallet during her earlier explorations. "Where is it?"

"Look, Danielle, I won't touch you. I promise. No one needs to know we share this bed. I can't stand to think of you sleeping on the floor."

"Where's the pallet?" she asked calmly.

He sighed again. "In the cabinet near the bookshelf."

She marched over to the cabinet, opened it, and knelt down to pull out the pallet. It consisted of a small pad filled with old hay by the smell of it, and a rough woolen blanket. No pillow. She wrangled it out of the cabinet and spread it on the floor nearby. It was perfectly acceptable. She'd slept on worse. Many times.

Cade got up to blow out the candles. She turned her head to the wall and concentrated on trying to get comfortable on the pallet. A pillow, the one she'd used at Lady Daphne's house, came sailing through the air and landed near her. The man was a good shot. She smiled and pulled the pillow close, snuggling her head upon it. It was nice to have this one memory of her time at Lady Daphne's. She wondered how much Mary and Mrs. Huckleberry hated her now, and what Lady Daphne thought. She hoped the poor woman didn't think her brother-in-law and her maid had run off together. Only they had. Sort of. *Mon dieu,* it was complicated. She'd think about it tomorrow.

The last words she heard before she fell asleep were, "Good night, Cross. If you change your mind, the bed remains available."

CHAPTER THIRTY-SEVEN

Danielle woke the next morning to the smell of sea air and . . . an aching back. Not just an aching back—an *excruciatingly* aching back. It had been a long while since she'd slept on the floor. How long *had* it been? She'd got her sea legs back so quickly. She'd assumed all the other aspects of life aboard a ship would come back to her immediately. She sat up, braced her hands behind her on the planks, and groaned. Sunlight streamed through the windows. She glanced over at the bed. Cade was gone and his bed was neat as a pin.

She made her way slowly to her feet, groaning again as she stood. The pallet was even thinner than she'd thought. She stretched and rubbed the small of her back. Then she raised her arms to the sky. First things first. She needed to answer the call of nature.

She tiptoed—she didn't know why she tiptoed—over to the washbasin and peered down into the chamber pot.

Empty. She breathed a sigh of relief. *Merci dieu* for small favors. At least Cade didn't expect her to perform *that* odious part of the job of cabin boy. She did her business quickly, hoping against hope that Cade didn't return while she was in the middle of it.

Thankfully, she was left alone and when she finished she was left with the chamber pot filled with the contents of her bladder. She tiptoed to the window, careful not to splash. She couldn't toss it out because the side of the ship jutted out too far. *Maudit*. She'd have to find another place to dispose of it. She closed her eyes. Why did she have a feeling this was going to end in nothing but embarrassment?

Ensuring her hair was properly tucked into her hat, she tentatively opened the door to the captain's cabin and peered out. No one there. She managed to climb the stairs to the quarterdeck without spilling on herself. Well done, Cross!

She scurried across the deck to the lee side, the wind at her back. She'd just finished tossing the lot into the water when a voice startled her.

"Cross, there ye be." O'Malley's jovial voice rang across the deck. "How did ye manage to get a demotion in the span o' one night's time?" The man laughed.

Still clutching the chamber pot, Danielle turned to face the second mate and lifted her chin. She was prepared for this question. Had been planning for it all night. "The cap'n decided he didn't believe me credentials as a cook's assistant."

O'Malley laughed again and slapped his thigh. "Ye can't be no worse than Martin. Boy don't know a spoon from a fork."

Danielle shrugged. "I don't much care what I do as long as I'm out o' London."

O'Malley laughed more and clapped her on the back. "I hear that, lad. I hear that."

Danielle was still clutching the thankfully empty chamber pot minutes later when Cade's booming voice rang out. "Cross! What are you doing there?"

She jumped and turned, clutching the pot to her middle. Cade strode toward them.

"I hope I don't have ta explain, sir." She glanced down at the pot.

She could tell he was fighting a smile. "I see. Are you finished?"

If she were a blusher, now would be an *excellent* time to blush. "Aye, Cap'n," she managed.

"Then get back to the cabin."

Danielle ground her teeth. To defy a direct order from the captain was a whipping offense on a ship.

He must have seen the hesitation in her eyes because he gave her an intimidating stare and put his hands on his hips. "Thinking about disobeying me, Cross?"

She choked down the sassy reply that was on her lips. "Never, Cap'n."

By the time Cade returned to the cabin hours later, Danielle was fuming. She was also nearly starving. She had inventoried the entire contents of the large room, inspected all of Cade's clothing, studied every square inch of the torn map, and washed the blasted chamber pot until it shone. When he waltzed into the room, she nearly threw it at his too-handsome head.

"How dare you order me down here and leave me to

rot?" she demanded, setting the pot back in the cabinet so forcefully it nearly cracked.

He lifted a brow in a questioning manner. "I'm *trying* to keep you safe. What else do you think you should be doing?"

"Being the cook's assistant!"

He crossed his arms over his chest. "Weren't you the one who told me you can't cook a thing?"

She plunked her hands on her hips. "Yes, but you're not supposed to know that."

"That's a ridiculous excuse."

"At least I could be learning a new trade."

"To cook? Are you serious?"

"Why wouldn't I be?"

Cade strode over and stood in front of her, trailing his finger along her arm. "If you're bored, I have a suggestion for what we could do to pass the time."

A thrill shot through her belly, but she forced herself to look away. He was too tempting. "What would that accomplish?"

"Accomplish? If I have to explain it to you . . ." He sighed. "The point is that it's fun. It's a much better time than cleaning chamber pots."

"Confident, are you?"

"Exceedingly. Besides, you were interested the other night. What's changed?"

She took several steps away from him so she could think better. There was a very good reason why they couldn't have "fun" and she needed to remember it. "It's obvious Grimaldi wants us to work together."

"And?"

"And if we sleep together that will complicate everything."

"I haven't agreed to work with you or Grimaldi," Cade replied. "Even if I did, it would still be fun."

Mon dieu. The man personified the word *incorrigible*. Was he seriously *arguing* with her about this? "I've little doubt, but having fun is not always the most important thing."

"You've little doubt? Oh, sweetheart, you just sealed your fate."

She scowled at him. "What does that mean?"

A knock sounded at the door.

"Captain, I have your dinner," Martin's voice announced through the wood.

The smile faded from Cade's face. He strode over to open the door. Martin marched in. He was a medium-sized boy with dark brown hair and dark eyes and a pair of silver spectacles rested on his cheeks. He looked intelligent and seemed pleasant. He had a towel over his arm and a platter balanced in his hand. He eyed Danielle carefully while he set about efficiently preparing the place for Cade at the dining table in the center of the room. The smell of the meal nearly sent Danielle to her knees.

"How are you enjoying your new position?" Cade asked him.

"I'm happy to learn something new, Captain," the boy replied, looking perfectly pleased.

Maudit. Martin was apparently content with his new role. If that were true, he wouldn't prove an ally in switching back. She'd been planning to speak with him and ask him to try to convince Cade he'd made a mistake.

"Glad to hear it," Cade replied.

Martin glanced at Danielle again, obviously interested in the person who'd replaced him.

"Anything else, Captain?" Martin asked.

"Yes, Martin. Will you please bring a meal for Cross here as well?"

Danielle started. "I can eat in the galley with—"

"No. You can't," Cade said calmly but firmly. "Martin, another plate, if you please."

"Right away, Captain." The boy bowed and hurried away back to the galley.

As soon as Martin had quit the room, Danielle turned on Cade. "Are you mad? Now they'll all think—"

"They'll all think something preferable to discovering you're a beautiful woman."

That knocked the anger out of her. She couldn't help it. "Beautiful?"

The shadow of a frown crossed his face. "Quite beautiful."

She snapped her mouth shut. She couldn't stay angry with him after he'd called her beautiful and added a "quite" to it. She was seriously trying and having no luck. Not to mention she was famished. Perhaps eating in the captain's cabin would be preferable to scrounging for seconds in the galley with the rest of the crew. She took a seat across from him and waited patiently until Martin returned with her plate. Danielle pulled the cover from the meal and stared down at white fish, green beans, and fried apples. It smelled heavenly. Her stomach growled like the traitor it apparently was. She snatched up her fork and took the first delicious bite. The food on *The Elenor* was a sight better than on most of the ships she'd worked. Probably best that she wasn't in the galley to make it worse, but she'd hang from the mast before she admitted that to Cade.

She waited until Martin had left before speaking again. "So, I'm beautiful, eh?" She stabbed her fork into a plump apple slice swimming in cinnamon.

"Fishing for compliments?" he replied.

"Never. I don't fish . . . or swim."

One of his eyebrows arched. "A sailor who doesn't swim?"

"I know many who don't."

"And fishing?"

"Never tried."

"Care for a drink?" Cade stood and pulled the bottle of whiskey down from the cabinet.

"I already had my inaugural toast," she replied.

"That's no reason to stop drinking."

"If I didn't know better I'd wonder if you're trying to get me foxed."

"And if I didn't know better, I'd think you were trying to avoid it. It's fortunate that I do know better."

The man was outrageous. "How do you know better?"

"Because we've had drinks before, you and I. Don't you remember? The library? The wine?"

Her eyes flashed. "That was . . . before."

"Before what, love? Before you were working? We both know that that's not true."

She lifted her chin. She wouldn't insult his intelligence by claiming that wasn't true. "So." He handed her a half-full glass of whiskey. "Are you ready to have a drink with me or are you still pretending you don't want to? I, for one, could use a drink after today's events. I'm guessing you could, too."

The man had a point. She took the glass and knocked back a healthy portion.

"Excellent." He grinned at her. "Now, should we discuss whether we will spend the night together?"

The man was incorrigible. Very well. She'd play into his little game. Her grin was devilish. "How about a proposition?"

"A proposition? I love the sound of that."

Danielle contemplated her options. Her conversation with Mary flashed through her mind. She'd told Mary that a drunken man's words were a sober man's thoughts. The idea had merit. Cade seemed intent upon trying to get her foxed. He deserved it, really. Danielle nodded and gave Cade a catlike grin. "If you can outdrink me, I'll go to bed with you tonight."

Two hours and many, many drinks later, Cade set his empty glass on the table and wiped his mouth with the back of his arm. The two had managed to drink an entire bottle of whiskey.

"By God, woman, aren't you foxed yet?"

She wasn't entirely sober, but she was also a long way from being door-knobbed. Besides, Cade had yet to tell her how he really felt about her. It was time to begin asking questions. He was at least as drunk as she was. Not the type of drunk that caused a man to pass out, but certainly in a state that would have him speaking a bit of truth were she to ask the right questions.

Might as well get right to it. She propped her chin on her fist atop the table and blinked at him. "So, you said I'm beautiful. What else do you think about me?"

He narrowed his eyes. "I think you're the most confounding woman I've ever met."

Confounding? That was hardly satisfying. "And?"

"And I want to kiss you."

"Because?"

"Because you simultaneously drive me mad by degrees and make me want you."

She narrowed her eyes back at him. "Are you foxed?"

"Are you?"

"I've been drinking since I was thirteen. I know how to handle my alcohol like a true sailor."

He snort-laughed at that. "Better than a true sailor if Danny and Sean are the comparisons. Those two are cockeyed every time they're in port."

"Be that as it may, if I decide to spend the night with you, Captain, it won't be because I'm intoxicated."

Cade opened his mouth to make some sort of retort, no doubt, but a knock on the door interrupted their conversation. McCummins came bowling in to consult Cade about the navigation.

"We're on course, Cap'n," the first mate announced. "Baptiste's ship is at least two leagues ahead."

"And Spain?"

"We should be there in two days at most."

"Excellent."

The men spoke of a few other things while Danielle cleared the table and prepared her pallet on the floor. When McCummins left, Danielle glanced back at Cade.

He stood in the candlelight, staring at her intently. The strains of some music floated up from the hold where the majority of the sailors slept in wooden bunks. Someone was playing the harmonica. It was a long, slow, pretty song. She stood and made her way over to the wardrobe and prepared to put away his clothing as he flung them at her like he had last night.

"Care to dance?" Cade whispered as she passed by. She stopped, closed her eyes, and breathed in the scent of him just behind her.

She was being churlish. Had been since she'd come aboard. Cade hadn't known she would be here any more than she'd known he was the captain. If she was angry with anyone it should be Grimaldi but he wasn't here right now and it was easier to take out her anger on Cade.

A memory of their dance in her bedchamber floated through her mind. It had been romantic and candlelit and dreamlike. She'd been forced to cut short that magical night. She would not have to cut short this one.

She faced him, curtsied in her boots and breeches, glided into his arms, and danced with him.

"I cannot tell you how fetching you look in those breeches." He smiled down at her.

"You don't look half bad in yours," she admitted, returning his smile.

He pulled her close and she breathed in his scent. His lips brushed her forehead.

"Are you foxed?" she asked.

"No." He sighed. "I, too, have been drinking far too often for far too long. It takes a lot more whiskey than we had tonight to do the job. I was merely hoping to get *you* foxed." His grin was roguish.

"Sorry to disappoint." She laid her head against his chest.

"Not to worry. I'll just have to rely on my charm instead of my alcohol."

They both laughed at that, his chuckle rumbling in his chest, vibrating against her cheek. They danced for the next several moments, Danielle memorizing his heartbeat beneath his shirt. She closed her eyes and imagined he was her beau and they were at a beautiful London ball. The song came to an end and she pulled away from him.

"Thank you," she whispered.

"Thank me?" His voice held a note of surprise. "For what?"

"For dancing with me. Twice. I've never danced with anyone before I met you. I probably will never dance with anyone else again."

He pulled her back to him. "Nonsense." He smiled at her. "We can dance whenever we like. It's an advantage of being a pirate." He slowly pulled her back into his arms and they gently swayed together in silence.

Warning bells sounded in Danielle's head. It was one thing to stop being so churlish. It was another to get so close to him that his arms were around her waist and she was breathing in his musky scent. Nothing good could come of this. Nothing but . . .

His voice sounded huskily in her ear. "I'm going to kiss you now."

She sighed and tipped back her head. "What took you so long?"

CHAPTER THIRTY-EIGHT

His hands went to her hair first. Plucking the cap from her head, he sent the hat spinning into the corner. She tried not to laugh. All right, perhaps she was a *touch* foxed. He pushed his hands through her hair, letting the locks fall over her shoulders. She tossed her head back to shake it out.

"Do you know how long I've wanted to run my fingers through your hair?" he asked against her mouth.

"As long as I've wanted to run my fingers through yours?" She pulled his head down to hers and let her fingers tug at the strands of hair at his nape.

He kissed her temple, her cheek, the side of her lips, before returning his attention to her mouth. He cradled her face in his palms while his lips brushed against her, his tongue plunging, then another brush, and another plunge in a rhythm that slowly drove Danielle mad. She pressed both palms to his shirtfront, feeling his muscled chest through the cloth.

"Do you know how long I've wanted to touch you here?" she asked between kisses.

"Are you certain you're not foxed?" he asked, with a smile against her lips.

"Mmm hmm," she murmured. "When I saw you without your shirt last night, I nearly climbed into bed with you."

"Why didn't you?" He stepped back, quickly unwound his cravat, and used both hands to pull his shirt over his head. He tossed the garment on the floor. Instinctively, she reached for it.

"Leave it."

She turned back to stare at the gloriousness that was his chest. She ran her fingers over it, marveling, watching the muscles jump and flex in reaction to her touch. "You look like you're made from stone."

"Is that a good thing?" He kissed her again and her legs felt wobbly.

"Like you're unreal. A statue."

"A statue wouldn't be able to take off his boots," he murmured. "Help me?"

She nodded.

He sat on the edge of the bed and she promptly slid onto his lap. Hmm. She was feeling the whiskeys she'd had earlier after all. She might not be foxed but she was deliciously light-headed and sitting on Cade's hard lap, feeling the length of his arousal and the warmth coming off his bare chest. Heat pooled between her legs and an ache began to spread there, too. She leaned down to tug at his boot, just like she had the night they'd met. The first boot came off without incident. The second one came off with a pop and she flew backward on top of him.

"Another boot trick to get me into bed with you?"

He quickly changed their positions and pushed her beneath him. He slid down her body and pulled off her boots, too.

"Yes," he said. "Your shirt next."

She nodded again. This heady feeling spreading through her veins was pure elation. She was no virgin. She'd had an awful time the first and only time she'd ever given herself to a man, well, a boy really. Robert. Since her first kiss had been entirely different from the one Cade had given her, she knew making love with him would be an experience she would never forget. First she had to make certain they both understood what this was . . . and what it wasn't. She didn't want a repeat of the last time she'd done this.

"Wait."

His hand arrested at the top of her shirt. "What? Are you all right?"

"Yes, it's just that . . . I must tell you something."

"What's that, love?" He kissed her neck. She couldn't think when he kissed her neck, let alone speak. She forced herself to push him to arm's length.

He stopped and searched her face. "What is it?"

"I need you to listen to me."

He braced his arms behind him on the mattress. "I'm listening."

She brushed a swath of her hair over her shoulder. "Before we do this, I need you to agree to two things."

"Sweetheart, right now I'd agree with you if you told me to move to Russia."

She laughed at that. "Nothing that drastic."

"Good, because I don't speak the language. Though Daphne does."

"She does?"

"Love, I need you to focus."

"Right. The first thing you must agree to is that we'll . . . you'll . . . take precautions. I do not want a child to result from this."

He nodded. "I understand. I know what to do. I don't have any bastards to my knowledge."

That made her feel much better. "Thank you."

"And the second thing?"

"We must both agree that . . . this doesn't mean anything."

"Doesn't mean anything?" He frowned at her. "I'm afraid I'm not following."

"I mean that we both need to understand that this is . . . just for fun. We're not making any promises to each other. This is not a commitment."

"If you insist," he said with nonchalance, but his countenance betrayed a hint of disgruntlement. "Now may I get back to the business of removing your shirt?"

"Yes," she said, relieved that he'd so readily agreed to both of her requests. Perhaps this might be pleasurable and simple after all. Perhaps they wouldn't have to worry about working together (if indeed that was Grimaldi's plan) after having had a naked romp in bed. Perhaps it really was possible to keep the two things separate. All she knew was she had to try.

Men left after sex. They were no longer interested. She didn't want that inevitability to keep Cade from helping Grimaldi. By establishing this boundary, she was ensuring there would be no awkwardness later. It would simply be business after this. She settled back into the mattress and let out a sigh. Now she could enjoy herself.

Cade took his time unbuttoning her shirt. There was no frantic pushing or tugging like last time. No sweaty grabbing or stale ale breath, only the spicy scent of Cade's cologne near her ear and the slight shake of his hand going from button to button of her shirt. Knowing that his hand was shaking made her heady with power. Did she do that to him? Well, she was shaking, too. Would he find her naked body beautiful? He'd said she was beautiful, but would he truly think so when she was fully bared to his discerning eye? The man had been with ladies as gorgeous as the tall, ethereal Amanda Jones. There was no way Danielle's short, hardly buxom body could compare.

"You're gorgeous," he whispered into her hair as if he'd read her mind.

The last button gave way and he pushed off her shirt first from one shoulder and then the other. The tunic she wore beneath to conceal her small breasts was next to go. He pulled it over her head and tossed it onto the floor with the rest of the clothing. He stared at her breasts with pure reverence in his eyes.

"Are they . . . ?" She bit her lip. "Acceptable?"

"Acceptable?" He looked horrified by the question, then gave her a wolfish grin. "Sweetheart, they're magnificent."

She couldn't help but smile at that.

His hand went to her waist to begin unbuttoning her breeches but she stopped him. "You first."

"With pleasure." He winked at her. She shook her head. She should have known he'd be fine with showing off his—ahem—assets first. The man was pure confidence. From what she'd seen so far, he had a lot to be confident about. Apparently, when you were built like Michelangelo's *David,* embarrassment wasn't a word in your vocabulary. Even his feet were perfect. She'd dared a glance at them. They were arched and long with beautifully shaped toes. It was entirely unfair. Her own toes could be described as positively plain.

He rolled over onto his back, unbuttoned his breeches, and pushed them down his hips and legs. The garment became a ball in the corner with the rest of the clothing. Danielle was in awe of how quickly he'd done it. She swallowed.

Ooh la la. The sight of an entirely nude Cade was something for which she was *simplement* not prepared. Narrow hips; lean, muscled legs; and a cock that would make other sailors jealous. The size of their members was exceedingly important to men. Cade's was thick and strong and long, jutting out from a patch of dark golden hair between his muscular thighs. She stared at it, mesmerized. She wanted to touch it. She reached out, but snatched her hand away.

"Go ahead," he prompted. He lay on his back and crossed his hands beneath his head, proud and calm at the notion that his naked body was on full display.

Still wearing her breeches and nothing else, she crawled toward him and lay at his side. She reached out and stroked his member. Cade groaned. She turned to watch his face. His eyes were closed. His face was pinched in pleasure. His mouth slightly open, panting. She reveled in the power she had over him. With every flick of her wrist, his hips arched and the look of ecstasy mixed with pain on his face intensified.

"I could give you pleasure," she said. "With my hand. I've heard of that." She'd heard of a lot of things on ships in the middle of the night.

"You could," Cade said, his breathing heavy. He opened his eyes and rolled on his side to face her. "But I want to take you and when I take you it's going to be unbelievable, and I'm not about to do that until you've experienced pleasure that will make you half mad."

"Half mad?" she whispered, a thrill shooting down between her legs.

He was already looming above her, on his knees. He pushed her onto her back and his gaze held hers in its sultry embrace while he unbuttoned her breeches with excruciating slowness. "I believe a man shouldn't take his pleasure until his woman is fully satisfied."

"Hurry," she pleaded, desperately wanting to feel him.

"No," he teased. His face was tender. His eyes were soft. "I refuse to hurry."

The third button came undone and his fingers brushed against the private skin beneath. She shuddered. His hand moved lower, unbuttoning the fourth button. At the fifth button she tried to do it herself, but he pushed her hands away and waved a finger at her. "Don't try to rush me. I've been waiting a long time for this."

She squirmed beneath him. *Mon dieu*. The man was maddening.

He finally unbuttoned all of them and slid down to the end of the bed where he neatly tugged at the ankles of her breeches. They magically flew off after only a few gentle tugs. "You seem quite good at that," she said.

He winked at her again. "I'm better with gowns, but I happen to know my way around breeches because of my own use."

At the moment, she didn't care what he knew about her breeches. She was much more interested in what he knew about her naked body. He took his time looking at her. His gaze started at her head and traveled down to her shoulders, her chest, her belly, pausing at the juncture between her thighs. His fingers traveled the path his eyes took and she bucked at the new sensation when he gently stroked her hip and the side of her leg. He stopped at her knee. "So beautiful," he whispered. "Danielle."

"Touch me," she begged, trying to guide his hand to where she wanted it.

But he eluded her grasp. His hand moved slowly, too slowly, back up her leg until it found the juncture between her thighs. Her legs spread open of their own accord. Maddeningly, he only touched her there for barely a moment before his mouth descended to capture one of her nipples. She gasped and her fingers tangled in his hair, holding his head to her chest. "Cade!"

"Oh, darling, you can't be calling my name *yet*. We've barely started. Let me do something to truly earn it."

Her panting breath was her only response to that exasperating statement. He traveled down, raining kisses on her belly, and lower, lower until his mouth was positioned just above her sex. He pulled her knees apart with his strong hands and wrapped his arms beneath them, leaving her open to him.

Cade breathed in Danielle's womanly scent. His cock was so hard it was painful. He clenched his jaw. Never in his life had he wanted a woman as badly as he wanted Danielle. Never in his life had he taken such care and time preparing a woman for his lovemaking. He wanted his partners to enjoy themselves, of course, but it had never mattered more to him. He wanted her to come so hard, she wouldn't be the same. Why? He didn't want to examine that question at the moment. All he knew was that tonight her pleasure was his pleasure and he was about to make her explode with it.

His tongue dipped into her cleft. She clamped her thighs against his head. He smiled and pulled them away with his hands at her knees. "Shh," he murmured, blowing softly into her sex. She gasped. His tongue dipped a second time and she moaned. It was the most erotic sound he'd ever heard. He was dizzy with the sight and sound and smell and taste of her. He swiped his tongue along the seam of her sex. Again, he burrowed his tongue between the cleft, finding the nub of pleasure. Her feet pushed against the bed and her hips arched off the mattress.

"Shh. No." He pulled her hips back down.

"I can't." Her head fell back against the sheets, tossing from side to side.

"Relax," he murmured against her soft, wet, hot skin.

He pushed his tongue between her cleft again and nudged at the bud. Her fingers tangled in his hair. He glanced up at her. She was mindless with want, her head thrown back, her beautiful dark hair splayed out behind her, her eyes closed. She wriggled beneath him but he held her thighs tightly with both hands, not letting her slip away. All the while he kept up the pressure with his tongue, nudging at the bud between her legs, moving in small circles as her panting increased and her thighs tensed. She bit her lip so hard, it turned bloodred and still he didn't stop, lapping at her, licking her in long strokes until she finally took a deep breath to scream his name. His hand shot up to cover her mouth and muffle her scream.

She lay panting for several moments, her eyes wide, unfocused. "Cade, did I just . . . ? Was that what I . . . ? I never knew my body was capable of . . ."

"Now, *that* was something to scream my name for," he said, pleased with himself. "Though I daresay you'll need to be more careful next time. You'll bring the entire crew running."

"Next time." Her brow furrowed. "Oh, but I said there might not be a next—"

"Of course there's going to be a next time." He moved up her body and covered her with his own. "Because I'm not done making you come."

His words made Danielle wet all over again. She had no vocabulary in French or English for the pleasure she'd just experienced. It was mind-numbing, indescribable. She didn't think her body could take it again, but when Cade began kissing her neck, she was more than willing to try. Besides, she knew he hadn't been satisfied. After the pleasure he'd just given her, she wanted to return the *faveur*.

"Love?" he asked, rising up on his elbow, his finger tracing her cheekbone.

"Yes?" Her lust haze still hadn't cleared and she felt a huge smile sitting on her face like a well-fed cat.

"Forgive me for asking, but . . . are you a virgin?"

This was it. The moment of truth. She'd decided long ago to refuse to be ashamed of her past choices. Besides, he'd been with other women. Well, she'd been with another man. One. One inexperienced one. She'd chosen poorly the first time. She was about to make up for it now.

"No," she said, shaking her head. "Does that make a difference to you?"

"Not at all. In fact, it's a huge relief." An honest look of contentment covered his face.

"A relief?" she murmured against his head. His hand was making its way between her legs and touching her in that same indescribable spot again, making it difficult to think. "Why?"

"Because." He kissed her eye, her ear. "When I slide into you there will be only pleasure. No pain."

She shivered at those words and when one of his fingers slipped inside, her eyes fluttered back into her head. "*Mon dieu*," she whispered. She hadn't known that. She had assumed it would hurt every time. She sighed and allowed her eyes to flutter closed.

"That's right." He pulled out his finger and pushed it in again. "Tell me how much you want me. In French."

"*J'ai envie de toi*," she murmured.

"I want you, too. I'm going to make you come again so hard you see stars."

"*Baise-moi.*"

"Oh, sweetheart, with pleasure," he whispered. "First, touch me."

Danielle reached down to close her hand around him.

"That's right," he said, his eyes closed. "Stroke me." Then, "Show me where you want me."

She guided him to the cradle between her legs. There was a hot pressure, a prodding for a moment, and then he slid slowly inside her.

"*Mon dieu!*" She shouted into the pillow to muffle the noise.

Cade stopped. He was entirely still. Sweat beaded on his brow but still he didn't move. The unholy torture of being sheathed to the hilt inside Danielle was too much to bear. If he moved he wasn't certain he wouldn't spend himself like an untried lad. He bit the inside of his cheek to control himself. Danielle wasn't helping. She was frantically kissing him, her body straining up to reach his, her hips rocking against his. She murmured French love words in his ear and that alone was enough to make him come. She'd asked him to ensure there was no baby. He had no French letters with him. The only choice was to pull out. This was going to be a bloody act of heroism.

He wanted her so badly he couldn't see straight. His entire body shook with pent-up longing. He'd never experienced anything like it. His intense desire to make her happy. His overwhelming need to ensure she took her pleasure first. His body thrummed with unreleased passion. He forced himself to count to ten, hovering above her, his arms braced against the mattress on either side of her body. His lowered his mouth to hers and kissed her with all the pent-up desire he felt for her.

When Cade began to move, Danielle went mindless. The feel of him inside her was nearly too much to bear. It was nothing like the painful poking she'd experienced with Robert all those years ago. This time, she was filled entirely by Cade's big cock and she was pinned beneath his gorgeous body while he pumped into her. Her knees clamped against his sides and she bit her lip to keep from crying out. *Mon dieu*. The man knew exactly what he was doing. He pumped into her again and again, making her take him, owning her body. She muffled her cries of pleasure against the pillow, murmuring mindless words of love and lust in her native tongue.

He reached between their bodies and touched her sex again, making her body wind up like a spring. When he finally sent her over the edge with a flick of his thumb, she bit his shoulder fiercely. He pumped into her again and again. Finally, he wrenched himself from her and spent his seed on her belly with a savage groan.

CHAPTER THIRTY-NINE

Cade woke in the middle of the night. He rolled over to stare at the gorgeous woman lying next to him. Had he told her she was beautiful? She was incomparable. Trying not to wake her, he pulled her gently into his arms, cuddling her against his side. She sighed and snuggled into him, one arm draped across his middle. That got him hard again.

Damn. He wanted her again. He'd expected that. He wouldn't have seduced her if he'd thought he'd bore of her quickly. It wasn't as if he could escape her on a ship in the middle of the ocean. Yes, he'd known he'd want Danielle again and again, but he hadn't expected to want her so fiercely, so constantly.

He traced his fingertip along the veins on the back of her delicate hand. Her hand was lovely, petite. He gently turned it over and . . . calloused? She had unmistakable calluses on her palms, the pads of her fingers, between her fingers. The same calluses he had from pulling lines and running sails for years. She was telling the truth about her time on a ship.

These were the hands of a sailor. He'd know them anywhere. She'd truly worked on a ship? For years? Just like he had. Incomprehensible, but apparently true. Why would a beautiful young woman choose to work on a ship? What had forced her to it? "What are your secrets?" he whispered to her sleeping form.

How could he ever let this affair end? The thought surprised him. He'd never, *never* had such a thought before. He'd always been the one to end his liaisons with a woman, always been the one to get bored soon, first. Always been the one to walk away. Danielle had left him a note once. She was clearly willing to walk away. That was a new experience for him. Then last night, before they'd made love, she'd gone and given him a speech he well recognized. He'd given it himself countless times. It was the speech about how them spending the night together didn't mean anything, that they had made no promises to one another. No commitments. The most insane thing was that he hadn't even wanted to give that speech this time. The one he could practically recite in his sleep. No, he'd just been ravenous for her, wanted to touch her, kiss her, hold her, have her. He'd been willing to agree to anything to give her pleasure. And now, now he only wanted to pull her closer.

He turned her hand over again and stroked her arm. He'd intended to turn her over to Grim in San Sebastian. Now? Now he didn't know what the future held. He'd be interested to hear Grimaldi's excuse for his actions, but whatever the general was up to, Cade and Danielle would be in each other's company for at least two more days. They might as well enjoy themselves.

Danielle pretended to sleep, but she felt Cade stroking her arm, tracing the calluses on her hand. She heard him whisper, "What are your secrets?" For the first time, she was actually tempted to tell someone. He was holding her, actually *holding* her. That had been a surprise, to wake up in his arms with him stroking her and whispering in her hair. She'd been shocked—paralyzed really—and she hadn't known what to say. Should she pull out of his arms, push him away? Hadn't he heard her when she'd told him their physical relationship didn't mean anything? Did she need to repeat herself? Remind him? Only it felt so good to have his hand stroking her skin, his arm cradling her. She moved her hand, pretending to still be sleeping. She touched his flat abdomen, allowing her fingertips to glance over the muscled planes. She might just get used to this. He'd rubbed the tips of her fingers. Was he horrified by the evidence of her hard work? He might be a pirate but what did he think of her being one? She was thinking too much, wasn't she? She must stop that. At least while she was in bed with a ridiculously handsome man. She let her hand stray a bit lower. She might as well enjoy herself. As long as they were careful.

She was glad her head was on his shoulder so he couldn't see her face. A grin cracked the corner of her lips. Her hand moved even lower before he caught it and lowered it even farther to curl around his stiff member. She squeezed it.

"I have an idea," he said into her hair.

She laughed against his shoulder. "I can guess what it is."

"Do you want to take a bath with me?"

CHAPTER FORTY

It was tricky getting Martin and a few of the deckhands to bring heated water in buckets from the galley to fill the brass tub in the captain's cabin. To avoid scrutiny, Danielle gathered her clothing and hid in the wardrobe.

"Cross isn't feeling well." Cade's voice boomed as the crew filed into the cabin. "I expect he's somewhere hanging over the side of the ship casting up the contents of his stomach while I had to bother you poor lads to prepare my bath. Damn cabin boy might not last the rest of the journey. I might toss the useless baggage overboard."

A few minutes later, Cade whispered into the wardrobe, "Martin's gone. He left a towel and a bar of soap. But wait a moment. I'm counting to fifty to ensure he hasn't forgotten anything. Don't want to be surprised by him coming back."

Danielle couldn't help but squirm inside the wardrobe. She wanted to jump out, wrap her arms around Cade's neck, and have her way with him. The count to fifty seemed interminable. Finally, Cade knocked three times on the side of the wardrobe.

Danielle pushed open the door with her bare foot and climbed out, naked and smiling.

"You're going to sack me for my incompetence before we reach San Sebastian, are you?" she huffed in a mock-angry tone.

"*Cross* might be sacked for incompetence," Cade clarified, "but you, my lady, are welcome to stay as long as you like."

She approached the tub, ignoring those words. He didn't mean them. He wouldn't allow a woman to stay as long as she liked. She was a novelty at the moment and unlike her stolen moments with Robert, Cade happened to be a captain and have a private cabin to himself. So they might enjoy themselves a bit longer. But she mustn't ever forget that this was still only temporary. Amusing, but temporary.

"Only one towel?" she asked, staring into the steaming water.

"We'll have to share." He came up behind her and traced the outline of her neck with his finger. She tilted her head to the side to provide him with better access. He swept her hair aside, bent down, and kissed the top of her shoulder. She closed her eyes and he pulled her back against him. His erection was rigid against her back. He'd already pulled off his breeches sometime after Martin quit the room.

Cade's mouth trailed over her neck, her shoulder. His hands moved up past her belly to cup both breasts. He twisted the nipples lightly and a zing shot between her legs. The man knew where and how to touch her. She had chosen wisely for her second lover.

"Bath time?" he whispered against her ear.

"Mmm hmm."

He scooped her into his arms, cradling her, and slowly lowered her into the tall tub. She sighed as the steamy water slid over her skin.

He handed her the waxy bar of soap and she dunked it, then rubbed it in both hands, creating a plethora of bubbles along the steamy surface. She breathed in the lavender scent and relaxed back into the deep, heated bath. "Did you have this tub specially designed for two people?"

"Yes."

She blinked. She'd been jesting because the tub was so large, but it stood to reason.

"Then why aren't you in here with me?" She gave him a sultry look.

"With pleasure." He climbed in without a hint of embarrassment at his total nudity. She took her time watching his perfect body move. He slid in across from her, then pulled her atop him. They were both facing the overhead. He stroked her shoulders, her neck, her breasts. He worked both nipples with his thumbs and forefingers until she was mindless with wanting him again. She squirmed against him. The soap bobbed along the surface of the water, forgotten. "I want you," she whispered, this time in English.

"In due time," he whispered, her breasts cupped in

his large hands. One of his hands moved down between her legs and he found the nub between her thighs once again.

She nearly arced out of the water. His one hand continued to tug and torment her nipple, the other rubbed that spot of pleasure. Her hand clenched his upper leg beneath hers. Her thighs fell open on either side of his legs and he pushed out his knees to widen them. She moaned. He kept up his gentle assault on that perfect spot in her cleft until she clenched her jaw. "Remember, you can't scream," he whispered in her ear, teasing her unmercifully.

It was a fight to keep her mouth closed. When she finally came, Danielle closed her eyes, arched off him nearly out of the water, and moaned loud and long. Her body was still deliciously shivering when he flipped her over as if she weighed no more than a doll, positioned himself with one hand, and let her drop onto him.

The long slide of him inside her made her moan again. She'd never imagined anything like this before. The steamy water and the soap bubbles, their wet skin sliding against each other, and now this. Cade's wide hands moved down to her hips and he guided her movements. He pulled her up, to slide up his length, then pushed her down, showing her exactly how he wanted her to move. He braced his hands on the sides of the deep tub and let her take over. His face was a mask of pure ecstasy.

The cords in his neck went tight. "God, Danielle, you feel so good," he murmured. His eyes weren't closed. On the contrary, they remained quite open, watching her breasts bounce as she slid up and down him. Watching the look on her face as she took him fully into her body. Watching her set a rhythm she enjoyed.

The second time she came, it was underwater and Cade held her while she muffled her screams against his shoulder. He pumped into her again and again and again until he clenched his jaw and pulled out, spending his seed in the water and groaning.

He held her against him, panting, his heart pounding madly until his breathing was right again. Then he cradled her in his arms, stepped out of the tub, set her on the edge of the bed, and used the towel to dry her off before drying himself. He pulled back the covers and laid her down. Then he climbed in next to her, pulled the covers over both of them, and clasped her against his chest.

Danielle lay there, not daring to breathe for what felt like hours, but was likely only mere minutes. She'd expected him to ask if she wanted to sleep in the bed with him. That would only be polite. But carry her over, dry her off, and cuddle up to her? It was nearly beyond belief. Was this the same Cade Cavendish whom she'd met in London? The same man who had gorgeous women chasing him on Bond Street and, according to Lady Daphne, lying naked in what they thought was his bed after hunting him down?

She continued to hold her breath for fear that this figment of her imagination would disappear. Then another disconcerting thing happened. He began to run his fingers through her hair, combing it. He leaned down to her bare neck and breathed in deeply. "I'll never tire of the scent of lavender."

He'd never tire of—

She didn't have time to even finish that thought before he said, "Can I ask you some things?"

The question made her stomach churn but she promised herself to answer honestly. "Of course." Things were different now, regardless of whether she wanted them to be. It was both a frightening and a comforting thought.

"Are you really French?" he asked.

She laughed at that. "*Oui*. Half French. As I told you."

"Is your mother really sick?"

Her nostrils flared. "I would never lie about that. She's quite sick. Grimaldi's promised to pay me enough to allow me my cottage by the sea after this mission."

"That sounds like Grimaldi. Blackmail and holding things above other people's heads."

She turned to lie on her back. Cade's arm was still wrapped over her waist. "He knows how to get what he wants. He's helped me immeasurably. I cannot fault him."

"How has he helped you?" Cade asked.

"He saved my mother's life." She shook her head, not wanting to continue this part of the conversation. "That was a long time ago."

"What did he do?"

She should have expected he'd want to know more. Could she face these memories while she was so raw and emotional from his lovemaking? She would try. "My father was murdered when I was young. My mother was sent to gaol for the crime."

Cade took a breath to speak.

"She didn't do it," Danielle hurried to add. "But the French were prejudiced against her. She was tried and convicted with little evidence. She was shipped back to England, traded for some French prisoner. I expect her family had a hand in that."

"Where were you?"

"I was left alone."

"What didn't your mother's family take you in?"

"My mother had never told them about me. All I knew was that I had to get to England. To save my mother."

"And you met Grim?"

"He found me on a smuggler's ship and offered me a job."

"He tends to show up at opportune times, doesn't he?"

"I know he did for me." She snuggled farther into the bed. "I agreed to work for him in exchange for his helping my mother. He knew I'd be loyal because I'm half English and the French had ruined my family. By the time my mother was released from prison, she'd contracted consumption."

Cade searched her face. "I'm sorry, Danielle."

She shook her head to dispel the tears stinging her eyes. "Can I ask you something?"

"Of course."

"Why is your ship named *The Elenor*?" She winced, prepared to hear him say it was a woman he'd once loved.

"My mother's name," he said quietly, nudging her shoulder with the tip of his nose.

"Was it?" she answered in awe.

He nodded again and kissed her shoulder. She tried to ignore the flicker of lust that shot through her. How could she want him again already?

She moved quickly to another question. "Were Daphne and Rafe already married before their wedding last month?"

His bark of laughter filled the room. "Who told you that?"

"Mary mentioned it."

Cade pushed himself up on one elbow against the pillows. "I'm not certain. I wasn't there when they made their infamous trip to France."

"France?"

"Rafe and Daphne performed a mission together. With Grim actually."

"They did?" Danielle blinked rapidly. "You must tell me all about it."

Cade kissed her neck. "I'm certain they'll tell you all the details someday. It was swashbuckling and romantic. They fell in love in France. Only the *ton* doesn't know they were together. That part is a secret. Whether they were already married, well, it wouldn't be a surprise if Mary knows more than I do about my own brother."

Danielle glanced away. More tears stung her eyes. Daphne and Rafe wouldn't tell her the story one day. Cade was wrong about that. She would never see them again and if she did, they'd be angry over her duplicity.

"It sounds quite romantic," she murmured.

Perhaps sensing her sadness, he changed the subject.

"So, you're chasing Baptiste to get the money to take your mother to the sea?"

She shook her head slowly, tracing her finger against the soft sheet. "It's more complicated than that. I have my own grudge against Lafayette Baptiste."

"You do?" He raised up on an elbow and searched her face. "So do I."

CHAPTER FORTY-ONE

Danielle diligently attempted to end her affair with Cade. She reminded him they would probably be working together. She reiterated Grimaldi's strict rule about fraternization between agents. She even tried to argue that she didn't think Lady Daphne would approve.

None of it proved effective. Cade simply pulled her close and kissed her neck and once that started, it wasn't much of a leap to be splendidly naked in bed with the man. There were times when Cade went above deck to see to his duties, of course, but whenever he returned to the cabin, it wasn't long before he'd coaxed her into bed, forcing her to scream his name so he could muffle it with his hand.

It was going to end badly. Her heart would be broken and he would leave and she'd never see him again. But while she was in his arms, in his bed, it felt as if she'd been brushed by heaven. She couldn't make herself stop. Even worse, she didn't want to.

Three days later, Cade snuggled her against him after having just made exhaustive love to her. Her body felt limp and delicious. It also felt sensitive and tingly. And satisfied. Stroking her arm he said, "McCummins tells me we'll be pulling into port tonight."

She shot up to her elbow, pulling up the sheet to cover her naked breasts. "So soon?"

"Yes."

She turned her head and a lock of dark hair fell across her shoulder. "This is it then."

"What?"

"The end of our affair."

"How do you know that?" He tried to pull her close and kiss her neck, but she scooted away.

"We shouldn't get attached," she said.

"I'm already attached." He advanced on her.

A thrill shot through her, but that was the kind of thing all rakes said. Probably just before they walked out the door and you never saw them again.

"I know how these things work," she informed him.

"These things?" He shook his head. "What are you talking about?"

"Love affairs. You might recall, ahem, I was no virgin."

"Neither was I. What does that have to do with us?"

"I don't want you to feel guilty when you . . . when this ends." She cleared her throat. "I don't want to feel guilty, either."

"Why does guilt have to enter into it?" He pulled her close, his hand dropping between her legs, reaching for the spot he knew she would respond to. She moved her hips away.

"Grimaldi will explain his plans and either you'll agree or you won't, and either way, after it's over you'll go your own way and I'll go mine and . . ."

"Do we have to discuss that right now? I only have a few more hours in bed with you. Can't we just . . . have fun?"

"I think it's best if we cut it off now."

"We made love not half an hour ago."

"Yes, and it was enjoyable."

"Enjoyable? I nearly smothered you with a pillow to keep you from screaming my name. Twice. I have scratch marks down my back that make me look like I've been mauled by a she-tiger. I—"

She'd never been so glad she wasn't a blusher. "As I said, it was enjoyable. But I think it's time to be reasonable."

"Reasonable?" He groaned. "That's Grimaldi talking, not you."

"It's all been quite a lark, as the English say." She slid out of the bed and gathered her clothing. "But it can't happen again."

Cade grabbed the clock on the table next to the bed and flung it against the far wall where it smashed into a hundred pieces.

That night, *The Elenor* crept into port at San Sebastian in Spain. They purposefully dropped anchor on the far side of the wide harbor to ensure they would be out of sight of *The French Secret*, which had arrived earlier in the day. According to O'Conner, the plan was for the

French ship to remain here for two nights. Meanwhile, Danielle and Cade waited for Grimaldi to arrive on whatever ship he'd commandeered to follow them.

Cade had been out of sorts ever since Danielle had summarily announced the end of their affair. Why couldn't she just enjoy the moment and whatever this thing was that they had together? When Grim arrived, whatever he had to say, Cade was not in an understanding mood to hear it.

"I'm off to drink with Danny and Sean," he announced after all the ship's business had been seen to for the night.

"In town?" Danielle asked nonchalantly. She'd tucked her hair back up in the damned ridiculous cap and was acting as if they hadn't spent the last three nights and part of the days tangled naked in each other's arms.

"Have fun." She turned back to the book she'd been reading. Wolsey? She chose a book about bloody Wolsey over him? By God, he would find a better time in town with Danny and Sean. The Irishmen loved to frequent taverns and brothels while they were in port. Tonight he'd join them.

Four hours later, Cade found himself propped up against a stone wall outside a Spanish brothel. Danny had come out with a buxom woman on his arm and was fondling her in the alley. Sean had come out so foxed he couldn't stand up straight. He slid down the wall and sat next to Cade.

Cade had downed something in the vicinity of four bottles of Spanish wine and was half passed out, leaning against the side of the establishment. He had not

gone into the brothel. Even if he'd been sober enough
to have a cockstand, he'd known the minute he left the
ship he couldn't touch another woman.

Being with Danielle these last few days had been . . .
well, damn it, he didn't know what it had been but he
hadn't been ready for it to end. That much he knew. He
wanted her still. Even now. He couldn't erase her from
his mind.

He should have stayed sober tonight. Should have remained on the ship. Should have made the plan to meet
Grim. But the dismissive way Danielle had treated him
had made him want her to think he would find comfort
in another woman's arms.

He pushed himself upright and tried to whistle for
Danny, but the noise that emerged from him lips was
more of a sad blowing sound.

"McCummmmmmins!" he finally called.

Sean stumbled to his feet. "We leavin', Cap'n?"

"Aye. We've got to get back to the ship." He tried to
focus but his eyes were blurry. "Daannny!" he called
again.

"Hold yer horses. I'm comin'," came a muffled voice
from the alley. "Give me a minute, ye blighters."

Sean started laughing while Cade opened his mouth
to call his first mate yet again. A sharp blow to the head
stopped him. He fell to the ground, his vision even worse
than the drink had made it.

He rubbed a hand over his eyes. Had he imagined
the painful crack to his skull? He glanced over to see
Sean fiercely struggling against two large men. Cade
looked up. His hand reflexively went to the back of
his breeches where he always carried a knife. It was

gone. He scrambled to his feet, his fists cocked and ready to fight. Two other huge men grabbed him from behind and held his arms behind his back. He'd barely got a blow in on one of them before he was tackled to the ground.

Lafayette Baptiste stepped out of the shadows, a club in his hand. He thumped it against his gloved palm. "Well, well, well. If it isn't Captain Rafferty Cavendish. Followed me from London, I see. I had zee chance to kill you once when I ordered Donald Swift to be killed. I won't make zee same mistake again."

CHAPTER FORTY-TWO

"What are we going to do?" Danielle hated how frantic her voice sounded. General Grimaldi stood across the table from her in Cade's cabin, his fists braced atop the panel. "We've got to save him."

Danny and Sean had returned from their excursion and informed both Danielle and Grimaldi—who'd come into port early and boarded *The Elenor*—that Cade had been captured. Apparently, Baptiste had mistaken him for Rafe. The Frenchman must have allowed Danny and Sean to go free so they could repeat the tale.

Mon dieu. Why wasn't Grimaldi saying anything? She'd tear this ship apart splinter by splinter before she'd allow him to turn it around and leave without Cade. Why did the spymaster have to be so *maudit* stoic? She stared into Grimaldi's dark eyes, almost willing him to disagree with her so she could have someone to fight, right here, right now. She felt so impotent, unable to save the man she loved.

The thought nearly brought her to her knees, but yes, she *did* love him. It took losing him for her to realize that, but she loved him and she was going to save him. She couldn't bear the thought of him being hurt or worse by Baptiste.

Danielle clenched her fist. It took all her strength to keep from striking the man in front of her. "Damn you, General. Why didn't you tell me Cade was on our side?"

Grimaldi scrubbed a hand against his light beard. "We couldn't risk it. We were watching you. We knew you'd grown . . . close to him. We couldn't take the chance of you backing out if you knew he was the captain of *The Elenor* before you came aboard."

Her eyes went wide. "*You* were watching *me*? Wasn't the whole point that I was watching him?"

Grimaldi nodded. "Yes, but—Bloody hell, Cross, we're spies. We're watching everyone."

She rolled her eyes at that.

"Once we realized you might have"—Grimaldi cleared his throat—"feelings for Cavendish, we feared it might compromise the entire bloody mission."

She didn't flinch at the improper language. She'd long ago become accustomed to that and worse in her line of work. It was the other part of what he'd said that had her hand itching to slap him again. "Feelings! What made you think I had *feelings* for him?"

Grimaldi's arched brow smacked of skepticism. "Don't you?"

She glanced away. "I've been stuck with him on a

ship for days. He had me acting as his cabin boy. Not a cook's assistant. I—"

"We saw you kiss him in London."

Danielle snapped her mouth shut. *Maudit*. She contemplated that for a moment. *Maudit. Maudit*. Had that kiss revealed so much? But wait. . . . "Which time?" she blurted before cursing herself for her stupidity.

Grimaldi's brow remained arched. "I rest my case."

Danielle glared at the general. "What were you planning to do once I'd seen him on the ship if I wanted to leave?"

"We ensured you were underway before you were taken to see him."

"How in the devil's name did you manage—?"

"Suffice it to say we had full confidence that you weren't foolish enough to jump overboard."

She sucked in air through her nostrils, still itching to slap the general. "You could at least have warned me."

"We'd just learned that night that Cavendish was on our side. He was leaving to come after Baptiste, too."

"You could have at least—"

Grimaldi held up a hand. "Do you want to continue arguing with me or make a plan to save him?"

Danielle let out her breath. The general was right. They were wasting time. "Have any ideas?"

Grimaldi cracked a rare smile. "Of course I do."

"I should have known." She crossed her arms over her chest and tapped her boot against the wooden floor. "What's the plan?"

The door opened behind her and in walked none other than Lord Rafe Cavendish.

CHAPTER FORTY-THREE

"Cavendish," Grimaldi said. "Are you ready to make them see a ghost?"

"Why didn't you tell me Rafe was here?" Danielle asked after she sufficiently recovered from her shock.

"You know I never show all my cards at once." Grimaldi's reply was a bit too smug for Danielle's taste.

"That's an understatement," she murmured.

"Mademoiselle LaCrosse, a pleasure to see you again." Rafe bowed to her.

"It's just Cross out here, my lord," she replied, returning his smile.

"Likewise, it's just Rafe for me out here."

"Very well." She'd never been so happy to see someone. She had no idea what Grimaldi had planned, but Rafe Cavendish helping could only be a good thing. Her mind spun with possibilities. "Is your lady wife here, too?"

"No. Daphne was still tending to the ball when I left. She decided to forgo this particular adventure."

"Probably best," Danielle agreed.

Grimaldi rubbed his chin. "Especially given that I'm going to have to beat the hell out of you to make you look like Cade no doubt does."

Danielle winced. They all knew the unpleasant task was necessary. Danny and Sean had told them Cade had been beaten bloody by his captors even before he'd been hauled away. There was little chance he wouldn't have been beaten more since. If they needed to convince Baptiste that Cade was Rafe or vice versa, they would have to look alike in every way.

"Please," Danielle said to Rafe. "We must save him."

Rafe's face was a mask of stone. "I haven't always been my brother's biggest supporter, but I'll be damned before I lose him this way. I lost Donald Swift. I've no intention of losing anyone else in my family."

Grimaldi pulled out a rough drawing of Lafayette's ship from his coat pocket and pinned it to the table. "Here's what we need to do."

Rafe crossed his arms over his chest and leveled a glare at the general. "First. I must ask something. Something I couldn't bring myself to ask on the journey here. But now I must know."

Grimaldi nodded his assent. "Yes?"

"They say Cade's the Black Fox. Is it true?"

"No," Grimaldi answered simply.

"He's not," Danielle agreed.

"Are you certain?" Rafe asked. "How can you be?"

"I'm certain." Danielle's voice rang out loud and sure. She raised her chin to meet the viscount's gaze. "I'm certain because *I* am the Black Fox."

CHAPTER FORTY-FOUR

Cade moved a bit to the right. Pain shot through his middle. He winced. At least one of his ribs was cracked. No doubt about it. The bloody Frenchmen had beaten him half to death. If he hadn't been so foxed, no doubt he would be dead right now. Though if he hadn't been so foxed, he wouldn't have been caught off-guard. Damn it all to hell. Instead, he was locked in a cell in the hold of Baptiste's ship.

He was exactly where he deserved to be after his bout of stupidity last night. What in the hell had he been thinking? Leaving the ship. Getting so drunk. He should have at least stayed and spoken to Grimaldi. He'd been angry, hurt because Danielle wanted to end their affair. And jealous. Jealous of a bloody book about Wolsey. He was an idiot.

Of course Baptiste had suspected he'd been followed. Years of hunting him had taught Cade that the man was no fool. Now Cade knew Baptiste was to thank for his being jumped outside of the theater in London. He'd said as much as he'd beaten Cade trying to get him to admit that he, or rather Rafe, was the Black Fox. The Frenchman wanted revenge for his stolen map and foiled plan.

Cade hadn't said a word. He'd allow the man to murder him before he would betray his brother. Cade had long suspected Rafe might be the Black Fox. His interest in the case, his constant questions. It made sense somehow. Cade would go to his death pretending to be his brother if it came to that. He wondered if Baptiste even knew Rafe had a twin.

Had Baptiste been under the impression that Rafe had been after him all these years? When Cade met Grim in Spain two years ago, the general had mistaken him for his brother who was being tortured by the French. After Cade had explained himself, Grimaldi had offered him a proposition. Work with him to save Rafe, and Grim would ensure the black marks were erased from Cade's past, including his criminal record. Grim would even deliver a convenient set of letters of marque making all of Cade's and his crew's ventures on the high seas perfectly legal. There had been no choice, really.

Cade had allowed the general to assume he was doing it for the personal benefits, but the real reason, the only reason, was to scrub his blackened conscience clean. He'd let his brother down once. He would not do it again. So Cade had traveled with Grimaldi to France, but by the time they arrived, Donald Swift had been killed and

Rafe had escaped. Still, true to his word, Grimaldi had done what he'd promised. Cade's criminal record had been destroyed and his letters of marque had been delivered.

But Cade didn't leave France. He remained to find out why his brother had been taken in the first place. He'd learned that Russians were involved and there was smuggling and secrets traded for money. After pulling away layers and layers of lies and deceit, Cade had discovered the French sailor and politician, Lafayette Baptiste, had ordered Rafe's torture and Donald's murder. The Frenchman was a thief, a scoundrel, and a killer who had done many wrongs to many people.

It was only recently that Cade had discovered Baptiste's latest plot to bring Napoleon back from St. Helena. The Frenchman's first step was to work with London turncoats who planned to help Baptiste and his men get past St. Helena's guards. Those scoundrels were somewhere on the ship in which he was currently imprisoned. He'd like to rip each one of them limb from limb.

Cade had never intended to return to London until he learned Baptiste would be there. While posing as the gadabout black sheep of a brother, Cade began to suspect Rafe was the Black Fox. The Black Fox kept getting in his way, got everywhere before Cade did, even stole the map and foiled Baptiste's plans at every turn. For months Cade called in every favor. Met with every contact. Still he hadn't been able to track down the elusive Black Fox.

He'd tried to find out what British Intelligence knew

about the operative from Tomlinson. He purchased the stolen map from Moreau. From O'Conner he'd learned when *The French Secret* would be leaving for St. Helena and where it would be stopping along the way. Cade's intention was to hunt down Baptiste, expose him as traitor to his country, and depending on how angry he was that day, either kill him or turn him over to law enforcement.

Then Danielle had stepped into Cade's life and everything had been turned upside down. He should have guessed Grim was also after Baptiste. Cade had just never counted on the fact that Grim had placed a spy . . . a beautiful female French spy, to watch him in his brother's home. He could almost laugh about it if his ribs didn't hurt so much. He had to give it to Grimaldi. Cade had never suspected Danielle. Despite all that, he still wanted her with an intensity that frightened him.

Where was Danielle now? The Frenchmen had let Danny and Sean go. The two men would have hurried back to *The Elenor* and informed Grimaldi and Danielle (or Cross) of what had happened. There was likely a plot hatching this very minute. Whether they would bust him out of gaol or leave him to rot, he wasn't certain.

He didn't deserve their help. Especially Danielle's. She wasn't like the other women he'd known. She was beautiful and passionate and kind and caring. She was also a spy. Albeit an English one. Not a French one. He'd never met anyone who could fool him so thoroughly. And she'd been so passionate in bed. He wanted her again. He knew he'd keep on wanting her. Forever. She was like an incomparable diamond. He'd never forget her.

He winced again. Yes, damn it. His rib was broken.

CHAPTER FORTY-FIVE

Danielle stayed in the cabin explaining the plan to Danny and Sean, who'd been shocked to learn that Cross the cabin boy was a woman. Meanwhile, Grimaldi and Rafe went to the quarterdeck where Grimaldi had apparently proceeded to beat the hell out of poor Rafe. Danielle had winced when she'd seen him. She was nothing but glad that Daphne wasn't here to witness her husband's bleeding and bruises. The man must love his brother indeed to take such a beating.

After that unpleasant task was through, Danielle, Rafe, and Grimaldi had dressed all in black. Along with a small band of men trailing them, they silently made their way across the Spanish docks hiding in the shadows. They stole one by one toward *The French Secret*.

"It's every man for himself," Grimaldi whispered. "Wait until the watch turns his back. You'll have about thirty seconds to get onto the ship before he turns again."

The watch stood on the foredeck. He carried a sword strapped to his back and a pistol in his hand.

First Grimaldi, then Rafe stole aboard the ship, perfectly counting the man's time. It was Danielle's turn next. She kept to the shadows, her breath roaring in her ears, her heart pounding. She waited for the watch to turn his back for a third time, then bounded across the gangplank. Once safely on deck, she pressed her back to the foremast.

Rafe and Grimaldi nodded to her. Both were hidden in the shadows against the bulwark. Sean and Danny and the other men would come if needed. For now, they remained hidden among the crates on the dock.

Rafe's task was to fool the guards if they were to discover their prisoner had escaped. Grimaldi's task was to wait with Rafe on the main deck and come when and if he was needed. Danielle's task was to find Cade. She knew the ship. She'd been on it before.

She stole across the quarterdeck and past the mainmast, making her way toward the hold. She crept down the ladder on soft-soled boots, descending into the dark, dank hold. She stole past the crew's quarters, pressing her back to the wood. Snores filled the air. A door slammed open down the corridor and she pressed her back to the wall, hard, her breathing coming in fitful spurts.

"I'm just goin' ta take a leak, ya blighters," she heard an Englishman's voice call. Soon the man was in the corridor coming toward her. She slipped behind another open door and held her breath. The man passed her, continuing up the ladder to the deck and Danielle expelled her breath, trying to calm the pounding of her heart.

She continued down the corridor, pausing to listen outside the door of the room the man had left. From the sounds of it, a card game was in full play. Bottles clinked and much raucous laughter erupted from the room. There was no help for her. She would have to pass by and hope she wasn't seen. She peered inside, her eye barely showing at the side of the door. Thankfully, the two other men in the room were not facing the door. She waited until they broke out into more laughter at some jest one of them had made and she flew across the space. Not waiting to hear if she'd been seen, she continued her flight to the end of the corridor and down yet another ladder to the bottom of the hold.

A single guard lay sleeping outside the small locked cell. She took another deep breath. Was that where Cade was being held? For all she knew, Baptiste had more than one prisoner aboard. "Cade," she called in a loud whisper. The guard stirred in his sleep.

"Danielle?" Cade's hoarse voice replied in a similarly loud whisper.

Danielle pressed her hand to her chest. She'd found him. *Merci dieu*. She eyed the guard. This time, he stirred more and his eyes fluttered open. She didn't have time to waste. He blinked and rubbed his eyes. Then he stood and turned to her. There was no help for it. She would have to fight him to save Cade. She whipped her knife out of the back of her breeches and tossed it at the man's skull, handle first. It hit exactly where she'd meant it to, squarely on the spot on the side of his head. He grunted and crumpled to the ground, unconscious. Cade's surprised, bruised face appeared behind the grate in the door.

"Grim?" he called. "Are you there?"

She stepped out of the shadows, retrieving her knife. "I'm alone." She pulled off her black cap to reveal her face.

"Danielle, where's Grim? You could be hurt. You must get out of here."

She shook her head. "You still don't believe I'm a spy, do you? Shut up while I do my job." She pulled a pin from her hair and knelt in front of the lock. Now that he couldn't see her face, she took a deep breath and shuddered. She didn't want to contemplate the bruises she'd glimpsed in the dim light from the one lantern hanging from the bulkhead.

Cade's fingers gripped the bars of his cell. His knuckles were white. "To the left," he instructed. "Push it up and over."

Danielle rolled her eyes. "You're not in charge now. I know what I'm doing."

She fiddled with the lock for a few more seconds before it gave way and the door swung open. Cade stepped out of the cramped space, pulled her against him, and kissed her. "Let's go!"

"For the record, it was to the right," she announced smugly, trying not to let the horror she felt at the sight of his bloodied face show on hers. It felt so good to be held in his arms again.

"Where's Grim?" he asked.

"With your brother."

Cade paused. "Rafe's here?"

"It's a long story. Follow me." They hurried away from the cell toward the stairs. "And by the way," she said as they went. "I'm the Black Fox."

"What?" Cade's voice was completely shocked.

"I'll explain later."

They raced up the first ladder, Danielle leading the way. They flew past the door where the men still sat playing cards. Just before they scaled the stairs near the captain's cabin they heard footsteps running above them. "It could be Rafe and Grim," Cade whispered.

"Or it could be the crew," Danielle whispered back. "In here," she ordered. In a flash, she had the captain's door open and pulled Cade after her. She shut the door noiselessly and they pressed their backs against the shadowed bulkhead on either side of the door.

Footsteps sounded on the ladder, then the door to the captain's cabin was flung open.

Danielle held her breath. It was Baptiste. He stopped two paces into the room, his breathing heavy. He smelled like wine and old sweat. He surveyed the room. He held a pistol in his hand. If Danielle had been alone with him, she would have attacked right then, but she couldn't risk Cade being hurt. What if the captain fired a round before she was able to subdue him? If they were lucky, beyond lucky, Baptiste would back out of the room and continue his search of the ship. One endless moment passed. Two.

Danielle closed her eyes.

"I hear you breathing," Baptiste said just before he whirled around and trained the pistol on the door.

They were not lucky.

Cade stepped out of the shadows, his hands raised. "Don't shoot."

"You are not alone." Baptiste's eyes darted back and forth. "I know zis. Who else is—"

This time Danielle stepped out of the shadows, her hands raised above her head.

"Damn it, Danielle," Cade muttered under his breath.

Danielle kept her eyes trained on Baptiste and his pistol but her words were for Cade. "You don't think I'm going to allow you to get shot alone, do you?"

The barrel of Baptiste's gun swiveled back and forth between them and the Frenchman backed up a few paces into the cabin to secure his position, holding both of them at bay. "Danielle?" he asked. "Danielle who?" His eyes narrowed.

"Why don't you put the gun down so we can formally introduce ourselves?" Cade asked, the hint of a smile on his cracked lips. "Perhaps ring for tea."

Baptiste's lip curled in a sneer. "So funny, Captain Cavendish. It will be a pity to kill you."

"I'm certain you'll find a way to live with it," Cade replied, still grinning.

Baptiste cocked the pistol. Danielle braced herself, ready to jump in front of the bullet to save Cade. More footsteps sounded on the stairs outside the cabin and Danielle and Cade turned in time to see Rafe and Grimaldi fly into the room. Grimaldi held a pistol, too. He quickly trained it on Baptiste. Baptiste's eyes narrowed and he glanced between the brothers, clearly confused. "There are two of you?"

"Seeing double?" Rafe smirked.

"Put zee gun down," Baptiste ordered Grimaldi.

Grimaldi's eyes were hard pieces of coal. "Why should I?"

"Because you have more friends here for me to kill." Baptiste sneered.

Grimaldi's lips twisted. "You only have one bullet. I'll kill you as soon as you fire. I'm willing to bet my life on the fact that I'm a much better shot than you are."

Another sneer from Baptiste. "Your own life, perhaps. But which one of your friends here would be worth it for you to lose?" He waved the gun at all of them.

Grimaldi cursed. His finger gripped the trigger.

"Don't do it, Grim. He's bluffing," Rafe growled under his breath.

"Am I? Captain Cavendish, or whatever your name is, do you want to be zee one to find out for certain if I am?"

"Shoot me, you son of a bitch," Cade ground out.

"No!" Danielle yelled. She stepped toward Baptiste. "You can only get out of here safely if you take one of us with you. Take me."

"I don't want *you*," Baptiste scoffed. "I want zee man who started all of zis. I want *le Renard Noir*. Now which one of you two bastards is it?" Baptiste waved the gun at the twins. "Admit it and I will let zee rest of you go."

Cade and Rafe exchanged uneasy looks.

"Come now, brothers," Baptiste taunted. "Which one of you will betray zee other to save himself?"

"If you want the Black Fox," Danielle ground out, "then you're going to have to kill *me*." She ran for the window and vaulted onto it.

"No!" Cade made a move to follow her but Baptiste's gun brought him up short.

"Danielle, don't!" Cade shouted.

Danielle remained perched on the edge of the window. Baptiste had barely spared her a glance.

"Let her go," the Frenchman said. "We don't need her."

"You couldn't be more wrong, you bastard," Danielle said from the window. "For I *am* the Black Fox."

"Don't jump," Cade called to Danielle. "You can't swim."

Baptiste swiveled around, a look of equal parts confusion and horror on his face. "*Quelle?*"

Danielle glared at the Frenchman. "The night I stole your map you said to me, 'I want to see the face of the *man* who would steal my secrets.' Do you remember? Well, here is the face of the *woman* who did it. Take a good look."

Danielle turned her gaze to Cade. "I'm sorry," she murmured. Then she vaulted from the window.

"No!" Cade shouted. "Danielle, I love you!"

A splash was his only answer as Baptiste went racing for the window.

CHAPTER FORTY-SIX

Baptiste fired a shot out the porthole at Danielle before Grim and Rafe tackled him. They knocked him onto the floor and wrested the pistol away from him. Cade leaped over the fray to try to jump out the window after Danielle. It was no use. He was too large to fit through. He was only able to get his head and one shoulder out, enough to look down and see a shadowy spot growing in the water. It was too dark to tell for certain, but cold nausea gripped him. No doubt it was blood. He clenched his fist and pounded it against the side of the hull, screaming her name. But there was no sign of Danielle.

"No!" he cried in anguish as he turned and ran back through the captain's cabin, up the ladder, and across the quarterdeck toward the aft where Danielle had jumped. He was vaguely aware of Rafe behind him calling him to stop, but Cade was mindless. He ran past Baptiste's crew who were sword-fighting Danny and Sean and the other men from his crew. Cade ripped off his leather vest, tossed it to the deck, and vaulted off the side of the ship and into the harbor. He landed with a splash, cutting his knee on a waterlogged piece of debris. An unholy pain ripped through his right leg but he didn't stop. He sprang to the surface, gasped for air, and turned frantically in all directions. "Danielle!" he cried. "Danielle! Where are you?" It was too dark to see much. He lifted his hand from the water. Blood covered it. It was not his own. "Danielle!" he called again, but silence was his only answer.

Two hours later, Cade lay in his grand bed back on *The Elenor* with a broken leg. Sean had set the break by forcing Cade to down a half bottle of whiskey and stuffing a rag in his mouth. The leg was still broken, Cade was not foxed, and the whiskey bottle sat on the table between him and Rafe.

"How does it feel?" Rafe asked, nodding toward Cade's leg as he leaned forward and braced his elbows on his thighs. He was sitting in a chair next to Cade's bed.

"Hurts like Hades," Cade muttered.

Rafe scrubbed the back of his arm across his forehead. "You shouldn't have jumped overboard."

Cade crossed his arms over his chest and glared at his brother. "Don't *ever* say that to me again. Now, please tell me Baptiste is dead. Or at least beaten within an inch of his godforsaken life."

Rafe shook his head. "After Danielle jumped and we overpowered Baptiste, Grim took him to the hold while I chased after you. Baptiste was caught so off guard learning he'd let the Black Fox slip through his fingers, he didn't put up much of a fight. The rest of your crew subdued Baptiste's men."

Cade groaned and leaned his head back on the pillow. "So, he's not dead."

"No. But along with the English turncoats aboard *The French Secret,* he will be coming back with us to England to answer to justice. Grimaldi's packed them all off to his ship."

Cade's fist gripped the covers. He nearly ripped them. Danielle was gone. They hadn't even found her body.

"Don't worry, Cade," Rafe continued. "Baptiste will be tried for Danielle's murder as well. He won't see the outside of a prison for the rest of his life."

"It won't bring her back," Cade whispered in a rough voice. He struggled to keep his face straight. His leg hurt like bloody hell but his heart hurt worse and his leg would heal someday. He deserved this. The one time he'd actually fallen in love with a woman and she was ripped away from him. He could admit it now that she was gone. He loved her.

"I'm damned sorry." Rafe hung his head and studied his boots.

"You shouldn't be. You risked your life," Cade replied, his mouth dry. "For mine."

"Of course I did. You're my brother."

Was it Cade's imagination or had Rafe's voice gone up a bit on that last word? As if it had been difficult to say. Rafe cleared his throat. "You would have done the same for me."

"I'm no hero," Cade ground out. He should have

downed the entire bottle of whiskey. Unlike the pain in his leg, this pain was too much.

"You could have fooled me," Rafe replied.

Cade narrowed his eyes on his brother, questioning.

"Grimaldi told me," Rafe said. "You've been working with him since you learned I was captured in France."

Cade nearly growled. "He had no right to tell you that, but it's not because—"

"Yes, it is," Rafe said. "It's because of me. I know it. Grimaldi confirmed my suspicions. You've been working against Baptiste ever since, to avenge me."

Cade clenched his jaw and glanced away. "Those bastards nearly killed you."

Rafe shook his head. "I don't understand why you didn't tell me when you came to London. Why did you let me go on thinking you were hardly more than a petty criminal? I'd no idea you were a privateer, working for the War Office."

Cade's jaw clenched again. "Would it have made a difference how you felt about me after all these years?"

"Of course it would have, I—"

Cade looked at his brother, allowing the years of hurt and misunderstandings to shine in his eyes. "That's why I didn't tell you."

Rafe scrubbed a hand through his hair and sat up to face him. "Damn it, Cade. Why do you always have to be so contrary? Why can't you ever let anyone be proud of you?"

Cade shrugged. "Perhaps for the same reason you've always done things to make people proud."

Rafe cursed under his breath. "Which is what reason?"

"Because it's what's expected of us. Rafe and Cade, the good son and the bad one, the white sheep and the black, the hero and the ne'er-do-well."

"Stop it!" Rafe shouted. He jumped to his feet and pounded his fist against the table, making the whiskey bottle jump.

"Why? You don't want to hear the truth?" Cade let his head fall back against the pillows. He'd saw off his damn leg to escape this room right now.

"It's not the truth," Rafe argued. "It's nonsense. It's—"

"Mother told me it was true," Cade said softly, staring down at the sheets that rested over his legs. They were only a green blur.

Rafe shook his head. "No."

"It's true. I heard her. One day she asked me, 'Why can't you be more like Rafe?'"

"What did you say?" Rafe's lips formed a tight white line across his face.

"I said, 'Why can't *you* be more like Rafe and stand up to Father?'"

"No." Rafe pressed the back of his wrist to his mouth as if he might throw up.

"Yes," Cade replied. His brother had to finally hear the truth. "That was the day I left. I had nothing more to say to her."

Cade scratched savagely at his bandaged head, welcoming the physical pain.

"You left me, too, you know," Rafe said. "You didn't even say good-bye."

Cade pulled the whiskey bottle from the tabletop, pulled off the stopper, and took a healthy swig. If he was going to continue this conversation, he needed more to drink. "I asked Mother to say good-bye to you for me."

Rafe hung his head. His words were low, angry. "She didn't."

"Why doesn't that surprise me?"

Rafe lifted his head to look at his brother. "She thought you were coming back. She used to ask me to leave a candle lit for you. We kept it lit for years."

"I had no intention of returning *ever*," Cade admitted, taking another swig. He'd need another bottle before this conversation was through.

"I didn't blame you. I never blamed you for leaving," Rafe said, his words holding an edge.

"I did." Those were two of the hardest words he'd ever spoken. The hardest and the most truthful.

"Why?" Rafe pressed his knuckles against his forehead. "I know how miserable you were there."

Cade took a third swig and winced when he wiped his hand against the back of his raw mouth. "I've hated myself every day since."

Rafe held out his hand for the whiskey. "You shouldn't have. You did what was right . . . for yourself."

Cade handed him the bottle. The dark liquid sloshed as he delivered it to his brother. "You stayed. You were the hero."

"I stayed," Rafe ground out, taking a long swig. "I stayed like a martyr. I did what I thought I had to and so did you."

"I suppose that makes some sort of sense." Cade

sighed, his hands falling uselessly to his lap. "Thank you."

Rafe nodded and took another long drink. "Promise me something."

Cade didn't look at him. "What?"

Rafe's voice was solid, sure. "Promise me that you'll never again forget that you're my brother, that you're not alone, and that you have family."

Cade nodded once. "I'll never forget." He waited for Rafe to hand him the bottle and took a final swig. "Danielle told me her fondest wish when she was a child was to have a sister. I suppose if I've been given a brother—and such a handsome devil at that"—he cracked a grin—"that I shouldn't take my time with him for granted."

Rafe grinned, too. "I promise the same." He took a deep breath. "I'm damn sorry about Dani—"

"Don't," Cade warned.

Rafe merely nodded.

Feeling warm inside from something other than the whiskey, Cade reached out to shake his brother's hand. Rafe leaned down to the bed and pulled Cade into an embrace. Cade clapped him on the back. Both men were choked up when, seconds later, Rafe left go and stepped away.

"Now," Cade said. "Let's see about getting back home."

CHAPTER FORTY-SEVEN
London, September 1817

"You're positively morose, Cade. You've got to cheer up." Rafe leaned back against a cushion as the coach jolted over a pothole on the way to the docks.

Cade scowled, crossed his arms over his chest, and glared out the window. "I'm a pirate without a ship. How do you expect me to be?"

Rafe rolled his eyes. "You're *not* a pirate, sir, and you're *not* without a ship. Your ship just happens to be in Portugal at the moment."

"Without me," Cade grumbled.

"Danny and Sean are more than capable of sailing it, sir, and you *had* to stay here because you broke your leg."

"Danny and Sean are no doubt passed out drunk in a Portuguese brothel and please don't remind me about my leg. I can't remember the last time I've been so bloody miserable, not since I was a boy."

"I'd venture to guess the reason you're miserable has little to do with your leg, sir."

"Don't say it," Cade ground out. Danielle had been gone for six long weeks and Cade missed her desperately. He was still struggling with the fact that she'd been the Black Fox. "And if you call me sir once more, I may well beat you to death with my cane." He waved the weapon about menacingly.

Rafe just laughed. "You'll have to catch me first, and I happen to know I can outrun you at present."

The coach came to a halt at the docks, right next to where a beautiful single-masted cutter was moored. Now that his leg was mostly healed, Cade wanted to get back out to sea, away from here, away from memories of Danielle. Memories would haunt him aboard, too, but it was worse in Rafe's house. The library. The foyer. Even his bedchamber where she'd wrapped his hand and teased him about his boots.

"She's a beauty," Rafe whispered, nodding at the cutter. "Remember, you promised to let me go out with you on her maiden voyage."

Cade was barely listening. All he could do was stare at the beautiful ship. They'd started work on her when he'd first come to town and she was finally ready. He'd christened her two days ago. *The Danielle*. Of course doing so would remind him of her, too, but it seemed fitting.

Cade pushed himself out of the coach and stood admiring the vessel. Rafe hopped down beside him. A shadow peeled away from the side of a nearby warehouse. A man strolled over to them, his hands in his pockets. Impeccably dressed and stoic as usual. Mark Grimaldi.

"Well, well, well. If it isn't two of my favorite employees," Grimaldi said.

Cade turned to look at the general and curled his lip. "What are you doing here, Grim?"

"Is that any way for you to greet your employer?" Grimaldi asked.

"*Former* employer," Rafe clarified.

"And possible *future* employer," Grimaldi replied.

"I knew you wanted something," Cade said. "You never find us to inquire about our health. My leg is mostly healed now, by the by."

Grimaldi tilted his head to the side. "Glad to hear it."

"I bet you are," Cade scoffed.

Grimaldi shrugged. "You are two of my best. Is it my fault if I need your help?"

"Spit it out, Grim. What do you need us to do?" Rafe tipped up the brim of his hat.

A wide smile spread across Grimaldi's face. "At the moment, I merely need you to board your ship and meet my other two best agents."

Cade's throat closed. He clutched his cane so tightly his knuckles turned white. Two months ago, Danielle would have been one of Grim's other best agents.

Cade led the way across the gangplank, anger making his strides long and aggressive, despite the lingering pain in his leg. "Why in the hell you've helped yourself to my ship, Grim, I'll never know," he tossed back over his shoulder as he walked.

Rafe and Grimaldi followed him. The three made their way across the main deck and down the steps to the captain's cabin.

Just as Cade pushed open the door, Grimaldi said,

"My apologies. I thought perhaps the woman for whom the ship was named would be welcome on it."

Cade stopped. All the air in the room had been sucked away. Standing across the cabin, directly in front of him was Danielle. She wore a bright blue day dress that matched her gorgeous eyes, her hair was pulled back in a chignon, and she had a look of supreme uncertainty on her face.

Daphne was there, too, standing in the corner, but Cade barely noticed her.

"What . . . ? What are you doing here?" he breathed, staring at Danielle.

Danielle moved around the table and came to him, a wide smile on her face. "Good afternoon, gentlemen." She threaded her arms through both Cade's and Rafe's. "In the last year I must have participated in half a dozen missions, but the one with you two was by far my favorite."

Cade continued to stare at her as if she wasn't real. She was touching him, actually touching him. He could smell her familiar orchid perfume, but still he couldn't believe it. He glanced at his brother. Rafe looked nothing other than thoroughly amused and simultaneously surprised.

"What are you doing here?" Cade asked, searching Danielle's heartbreakingly lovely face. She looked as if she'd gained a bit of weight since he'd last seen her. It agreed with her. "You died."

Danielle looked up at him through her dark lashes. "I didn't die."

"But you can't swim," Cade breathed.

"I never said I couldn't swim. I said I *didn't* swim. I told you. I've been on ships since I was thirteen."

"But there was so much blood."

"Bastard got a good clean shot right through my shoulder," Danielle replied. "Hurt like hell but it's healed nicely."

A storm cloud gathered on Cade's face. "Why didn't you come back?"

"I had no choice." She gave Grimaldi an accusing stare. "Care to explain, General?"

"My orders," Grimaldi replied. "She couldn't tell you she was alive. Until today."

Cade turned toward Grimaldi and lunged at him across the table. The man must have been expecting it because he stepped back quickly while Rafe held Cade at bay.

"What the hell is wrong with you?" Cade shouted through clenched teeth.

Grimaldi had the grace to look away, his mouth twisted in regret. "I had to do it. We couldn't risk Baptiste finding out she was alive."

Cade wanted to wrap his cane around Grim's neck. "Baptiste is in prison, you ass."

"Yes, but he had spies everywhere," Grimaldi replied. "We couldn't risk Danielle getting actually hurt."

That shut Cade up. For a moment. "You're a sadistic bastard, you know that, Grim?"

"All in the name of His Majesty," Grimaldi replied, bowing. "We came to tell you the truth as soon as we could."

"I swear I didn't know about this," Rafe hastened to add.

"On the contrary. I wasn't about to make your brother keep such a secret," Grimaldi said.

"Is she safe now?" Cade demanded, studying Danielle's face. He still couldn't believe this was real. That she was truly here, standing in front of him.

He turned to look at Daphne, whose pretty gray eyes were swimming with tears. "Believe it, Cade. It's true. I only found out today myself."

Some of Cade's anger dissolved when he saw how upset poor Daphne was.

Grimaldi continued. "We've rounded up most of the men who were working with Baptiste. Danielle's been staying with her mother by the sea for the last several weeks."

Her mother? She'd got her wish. Cade turned to Danielle. "How is she? Your mother?"

Danielle's voice was low but sure. "Doing much better. The sea air has worked wonders for her condition and there is a talented doctor near Brighton who has been helping us."

Cade drank in the sight of her as if she were fresh water in the middle of the ocean. "I'm happy to hear it."

Danielle searched Cade's face. "Aren't you happy to see me?"

As if upon agreement, Rafe, Daphne, and Grimaldi all exchanged looks and quickly left the cabin, closing the door behind them.

"I can't believe it's you," Cade whispered once they were alone.

Danielle reached for him. "I'm here, Cade. I'm real."

"I'm still planning to kill Grimaldi," Cade growled.

"Don't be too angry with him. He was only trying to protect me. I seem to recall a certain captain locking me in his cabin for the same reason."

Cade was fighting an internal battle. Was he elated or incensed? It wasn't clear to him any longer. He felt half-mad. "How were you the Black Fox?" he finally asked, focusing on something that might actually make sense if it were explained to him.

Danielle sighed and smoothed her hands down her skirts. "I'd done it for years. To avenge my father's death."

"Your father's death?" What did that have to do with the Black Fox?

"Baptiste killed my father," she murmured.

"He did? Why?"

Danielle raised her chin. "He and my father became political rivals. My father had been spreading the word through his lectures and writings that Baptiste was corrupt."

"You're certain Baptiste killed him?"

"I was standing in the doorway and saw him shoot and kill *Pere*."

Cade clenched his jaw. "Danielle, I'm sorry."

Danielle stared at the table, her eyes unfocused, remembering. " 'This will be our little secret,' he said. And then my mother was arrested for murder. No one believed a small girl's word over such an important politician's, especially not when the accused was English."

"But the Black Fox did other things, struck other places."

Danielle paced away from him. "I had to keep from

seeming as if I was after Baptiste. I never knew the papers would begin following my stories. I never expected to be famous because of it."

Cade shook his head. "If you were the Black Fox, why did Grim allow me to buy the map?"

"I believe that's when he began to suspect you were on our side. Until then he didn't know whether you were one of the turncoats, what with your sudden return to England. He wanted to see what you would do with it."

"I was never a turncoat," Cade ground out.

"Of course you weren't." She returned to his side. "Cade . . ." she finally whispered. "I'm waiting."

His head snapped to the side to face her. "For what?"

"For you to tell me you're happy to see me, that you . . ." Her voice trailed off and she looked away.

He searched her face. "Can I trust you, Danielle?"

"You can trust me, Cade. And I finally realize that I can trust you."

"What do you mean?"

"I heard you. When I jumped from the ship. I heard you say you love me."

A barely perceptible nod was his only answer.

"Did you mean it?" she asked. "Do you still love me?"

He paced away and scrubbed his hand through his hair. "I don't know how to love, Danielle."

She held out a hand toward him. "Neither do I, but I'd like to try . . . with you."

The hint of a smile touched his lips. He turned back to face her. "Are you saying you love me?"

"If you're saying you love me." She stepped toward

him and trailed her fingertip up his chest to tug at his cravat.

He crushed her to him and took her mouth in a fierce kiss. "God, yes. I love you madly and I'm never going to let you go."

"Good," she replied as they tore at each other's clothes. "Because I'm never going to let you go, either."

Cade pushed his fingers into her hair. "You're going to have to make a decent man out of me and marry me."

Her eyes widened. "Marry you? I don't know how to be a wife."

"That's perfect because I've no clue how to be a husband. We'll learn together." His shirt half off and his breeches unbuttoned, he fell to his good knee. "Will you marry me, Danielle LaCrosse?"

She opened her mouth to reply.

"Wait, before you answer, you should know that I've been given this exceedingly annoying title of sir by the prince, and I can't think of anyone else I'd rather share it with. Rafe cannot stop teasing me about it."

Her eyes widened even farther. "If you're a sir and we marry, that would make me . . . a lady?"

"*My* lady." He stood again and pulled her into his arms.

"What will we live off of?"

"Didn't Grimaldi tell you I was an official privateer for many years? Privateering is a lucrative business."

"Is it?"

"Very. I don't intend to stop my work on his majesty's behalf. You should join me on the high seas, mademoiselle."

She opened her mouth to reply when Cade interrupted, "Wait. Your name *is* Danielle LaCrosse, isn't it?"

She laughed. "You have to ask?"

"I wasn't expecting you to be the Black Fox, either."

Danielle nodded. "I suppose you have a point. Yes, my name is truly Danielle LaCrosse."

He spun her around in his arms. "Then, marry me, Mademoiselle LaCrosse, and make me the happiest man on earth."

"What will Rafe and Daphne think of having a maid in the family?"

"They'll be delighted. Daphne will have her hair arranged for life. And you heard Grim. The four of us are his best spies. We can all go on missions together. Who would ever suspect a family of spies?"

"I suppose you have a point." She laughed. "Daphne was extremely forgiving of my deception. She said she'd grown used to such surprises, having fallen in love with a spy herself. She also told me I may come and visit Mary and Mrs. Huckleberry whenever I like. Apparently, Mary and Trevor are close to announcing their own engagement."

"Is that a yes?" Cade asked, bending down and kissing her neck.

"Yes, you ridiculously handsome man. I will marry you, but first, let's study something else."

He continued kissing her neck. "Like what?"

"Like what husbands and wives do in bed."

"I'm all for it." He kissed her ear. "I have something new to show you."

"Really?" She closed her eyes and pressed herself against him, shuddering a little.

"Yes. Do you trust me?" Cade asked.

"Hmm. I'm not sure." She giggled. "General Grimaldi gave me some excellent advice once."

Cade's lips moved to her ear. "Oh, really, what was that?"

She shivered as her gown fell away from her shoulders down to her waist and he bent his head to kiss her bare skin. "He said to never trust a pirate."

Cade lowered her to the bed, flinging off the last of her clothing. "Then it's a good thing I'm not a pirate."

Thank you for reading *Never Trust a Pirate*.
I hope you enjoyed Cade and Danielle's story.
This was such a fun one to write. I adore a
black sheep paired with an unpredictable heroine!

I'd love to keep in touch.

- Visit my website for information about upcoming books, excerpts, and to sign up for my email newsletter: www .ValerieBowmanBooks.com or at www.ValerieBowman Books.com/subscribe.
- Join me on Facebook: http://Facebook.com/Valerie BowmanAuthor.
- Follow me on Twitter at @ValerieGBowman, https://twitter.com/ValerieGBowman.
- Reviews help other readers find books. I appreciate all reviews whether positive or negative. Thank you so much for considering it!

And look for the next novel in the Playful Brides series

The Right Kind of Rogue

Available in November 2017
From St. Martin's Paperbacks

JUN - - 2017